P9-BIX-990

SEP 1 2 2022

Magnolia Library

NO LONGER PROPERTY OF
SEATTLE PUBLIC LIBRARY

AN UNNAMED PRESS BOOK

Copyright © 2022 Naheed Phiroze Patel

All rights reserved, including the right to reproduce this book or portions thereof in any form whatsoever. Permissions inquiries may be directed to info@unnamedpress.com. Published in North America by the Unnamed Press.

www.unnamedpress.com

Unnamed Press, and the colophon, are registered trademarks of Unnamed Media LLC.

ISBN: 978-1-951213-60-2

eISBN: 978-1-951213-61-9

Library of Congress Control Number available upon request.

"Mirror" from *Playlist for the Apocalypse*, W. W. Norton, New York, NY.
© 2021 by Rita Dove. Reprinted by permission of the author.

This book is a work of fiction. Names, characters, places and incidents are wholly fictional or are used fictitiously. Any resemblance to actual events or persons, living or dead, is entirely coincidental.

Designed and Typeset by Jaya Nicely

Cover Photograph by Robert Keane

Manufactured in the United States of America by McNaughton & Gunn.

Distributed by Publishers Group West

First Edition

MIRROR

a novel **MADE OF RAIN**

NAHEED PHIROZE PATEL

The Unnamed Press
Los Angeles, CA

To the memory of my father, Phiroze, who'd find a kind word for any person that needed one

Mirror,
take this
from
me:
my blasted gaze,
sunken
astonishment. Resolve
memory & rebuild; shame'll
dissolve
under powder pressed into
my skin

Mirror,
this take
from
me:
gaze blasted, my
sunken
resolve, astonishment.
Shame'll rebuild & memory
dissolve
into pressed powder under
skin, my

—Rita Dove

MIRROR MADE OF RAIN

PART ONE

PART
ONE

For March it was unseasonably hot. Summer in Kamalpur began in late April, and by May, the earth was an anvil for the sun. Birds fell out of trees; stray dogs sheltered under parked cars. Scooterists and rickshaw-wallahs tied damp cloths over their heads to protect themselves from the Nau Tapa, the nine days of fevered winds.

That night, Sheila Sehgal had pedestal fans placed around her garden, where their lazily moving blades provided a paltry breeze. Rice lights were strewn over the trees; a champa's leaves were painted gold and silver. The glass gazebo at the end of the lawn had its air conditioners on, the dust covers removed from its sofas. Women in georgette saris and men in bush shirts jostled for a place to sit. Light refracted from the gazebo's thick glass walls, and appeared to make their limbs move a fraction slower, as if in an aquarium.

In the weeks leading up to Sheila's Holi eve do—more select than her Diwali open house and more opulent than her New Year's Eve party—her guest list was the favorite topic of conversation in the drawing rooms, verandas, and dining rooms of Kamalpur's wealthy families. Knowing who was *not* invited was as important, to some, as knowing who was. An invitation from Sheila was a stamp of approval; a snub meant that you'd been banished, for that year, to the humdrum backwaters of what passed for fashionable society in town. It was important to find out who was off Sheila's list. This time, the Seths were out: Sheila had caught her husband with Mr. Seth's jiggly wife. The philandering wasn't really the problem—it was that they hadn't been discreet about it. The same went for the Tutejas, who'd neglected a few too many times to call and wish Sheila well on her birthday. The Agarwals were *definitely* in; they'd recently purchased three new cocaine-white Audis and their son was going to marry a carpet-empire heiress. Jeh, my father, joked that if Sheila and her friends were shipwrecked on a desert island, they'd go all *Lord of the Flies* but still maintain a pecking order. Jeh and I arrived at the Sehgals' garden neither too early nor too late, dressed in our finest: he in a white kurta, me in a blue sari. Heavy chandelier earrings stretched out my earlobes. Perfumed sweat pooled between my breasts. While I fought with my ill-fitting sari blouse, Jeh nodded and smiled at acquaintances. Some returned his smile, others did not.

"Remember," Jeh murmured, "we are telling everyone that your mother is home sick."

"Why do we have to lie," I said, adjusting the sari's pallu across my chest.

"We have to," Jeh said. "Just stay out of trouble tonight, okay, Noomi? Please. For my sake."

"Okay," I said. "Oh, here comes Aunty Rhea."

My father's cousin lolloped over like a drunk rabbit. Rhea Puri, with a teardrop mole above her cheekbone, was as glamorous as an old-fashioned movie star and, in many ways, as tragic. Rhea and my mother had shared an airy flat overlooking the Arabian Sea when they were art students in Bombay. Thinking of Jeh, her favorite cousin with a sorry track record in love, Rhea brought Asha home to Kamalpur one summer. Jeh and Asha spent most of July 1978 having disheveled, confused sex in my grandfather's silver-and-blue Fiat on the wooded banks of Rani Lake. I don't think my grandparents ever forgave Rhea for introducing Jeh to Asha. They didn't even attend Rhea's sudden wedding, a year later, to her unwholesomely rich boyfriend, whose family owned resorts in Goa and Alibaug. The boyfriend, now husband, a politician-goonda, was both wealthy and controlling; Rhea needed his permission for everything. She had to run her outfits by him every day. She couldn't have a job. She was allowed to drink alcohol only in his presence. Once, he'd caught Rhea smoking pot she bought off a waiter at the Gymkhana Club. He locked her in their bedroom for days. Rhea was forbidden from going anywhere by herself. A chauffeur/bodyguard brought her, most afternoons, to our house, where she and my mother drank chai, smoked, and bitched up a storm about living in Kamalpur. Jeh said that their friendship was fed off nothing more than a mutual love for self-destruction.

Rhea's high heel dug a divot out from the lawn. She stumbled toward us and stopped from going splat because I pulled her up by the arm. The drink in her hand fell to the ground; its ice cubes gleamed like crystals in the dark grass. Rhea looked from me to Jeh to the glass and back at us again. Dismay Etch A Sketch–ed itself across her forehead.

"Oh, fuck. I had to work so hard to sneak that drink!" Rhea said, looking like a child with a broken toy. "Jeh, please. Get me another one? My husband won't notice you in this huge crowd."

"That's not a good idea," I said, cutting off my father, who'd rather have a tooth pulled than say no to anyone, let alone his glamorous cousin. "We don't want to get you into trouble."

Rhea's hands grabbed the points of her elbows. I couldn't help but stare at her diamond solitaire ring, the size of an almond. She loved to tell the story of that ring, how her husband had slipped it on while she was asleep: "He wanted it to be a surprise." Later, we'd found out it was for surprising her with an STD—he made frequent "business trips" to Thailand.

"Where's Asha?" Rhea asked, scanning the crowd, eyes hooded with boredom.

"Asha couldn't make it tonight. She's... not well," Jeh said. He picked up the fallen glass and handed it to a passing waiter. "We're telling everyone that she's ill with... with food poisoning."

"Oh no, poor thing," Rhea said, with sympathy in her voice. "I hope she feels better."

"She needs to sleep it off," I said with a shrug.

At least that was the hope—that Asha was sleeping off the vodka she'd drank earlier that evening and hadn't dug right back into her stash under the bathroom sink. Two hours earlier, I'd barged into Jeh's bedroom as he was putting on his kurta. His hands bloomed out of its sleeves; his head popped out from its pearl-buttoned collar.

"Mom's hammered. We can't take her with us," I said.

"What are you talking about?" Jeh asked, sliding his feet into his shoes.

"See for yourself," I said, throwing the door open.

We went out into the hall to find Asha standing beside the dining table, her hands clamped on to a high-backed chair. She looked concussed, as if the alcohol had struck her head like a mallet. A stain, like a shadow, staggered over the folds of her sari, a gara that had been passed down in the Wadia family for three generations. It was a wedding present from my grandparents. I was supposed to inherit it one day.

"Why are you two staring at me like that? We're late. Let's... let's go," Asha said. A wilted rose drooped over her ear, pinned where she had made an attempt to sweep her hair back on one side.

Jeh and I didn't move. Asha said, louder this time, "Chalo! I'm ready!" She wheeled her eyes from my face to Jeh's, then lifted the corner of her sari to wipe away kohl smudges. A few shaky steps toward the front door, and her foot twisted in her heels. She cried out. Jeh grabbed her. Gently, he helped her back to the dining chair.

Asha doubled over, rubbing her ankle. I watched her from a corner, rage filling me like a balloon. The rose fell to the floor. Black kajal tears made tiger-streaks on her face.

"I'm not going to stay home, I'm fine," she said. "I'm fine, I'm coming with you."

"You're not leaving this house," I said. "If you take one step toward that door, you'll regret it." I pulled my cell phone out from my purse. "I'll make sure of that."

"You can't threaten me, Noomi," Asha said, chinny and belligerent. "For that I would have to care."

I decided to try another tactic. "What's the point of fighting? Stay home and do whatever you want. No one will stop you. Let Dad and me attend this boring party." I waved the cell phone in the air. "But if I call Lily Mama or Zal Papa, they'll bring up rehab again. You don't want anyone to see you when you're like this. Trust me, Mom."

Usually, Asha thrived on the toxic energy of an ugly fight. It powered her like a Duracell bunny. But at the thought of my grandparents, who lived on the ground floor of our two-story bungalow, barging in, asking all sorts of uncomfortable questions, she shuffled off back into her bedroom. I waited a few minutes, then went inside to check if she'd gone to bed. Jeh lingered at the doorway. Asha lay curled like a question mark in her blouse and petticoat. Her sari, my future sari, lay in a heap on the floor. Black tears dribbled onto the pillow.

"You hate me so much," she said as I pulled the bedclothes over her.

"Ma, no one hates you more than you hate yourself/ sleep. We'll show our faces at the party and come back It'll be lame and boring. You sleep."

I sat with Asha until she blubbered into silence. Then, closiⁿₑ door behind me softly, I left with Jeh.

In the late '90s, Sheila's husband, Pali Sehgal, used to be a small-time government tout. For a bribe, there were rumors that he could get you a contract for cement or small machinery or something like that. The details were, and are, fuzzy. Back then, Pali, Sheila, and their son, Siddharth, used to ride triples on a Bajaj scooter. Hard to imagine now, when you saw the fleet of SUVs parked in their driveway or attended their parties, where the alcohol was imported, the DJ and the caterers flown in from Delhi. There was a rumor that Pali owned factories that produced the most low-grade, adulterated, your-building-will-collapse-in-a-year cement. And rumors that he owed gangsters money. Every year, people predicted Pali's downfall, but the Sehgals' parties only got more lavish, their cars fancier, and their holidays abroad longer.

In Kamalpur, rich people made their money in one of two ways: by mixing one thing in another (sand in concrete, stones in rice, water in milk, kerosene in petrol) or by changing one thing into another (black money into white, agricultural land into commercial, employees' pensions into destination weddings), while the authorities mostly looked the other way. An income tax raid was, in fact, considered a status symbol: if the Income Tax Department people weren't snooping around your business, you weren't making a lot of black money, which meant you were paying your taxes, which meant that you were, as they say, a chutiya. A putz.

In contrast to the Sehgals, my family, the Wadias, were the ultimate putzes. Not only did we pay taxes, but we also never cheated octroi, never hid assets from the company balance sheet, never ate into employees' salaries or bribed government officials. As a consequence, while everyone else's star was on the rise, ours was in slow but steady decline. Our bungalow and its sprawling garden were temple elephants: grand to display but grueling to maintain.

It was universally anticipated that, this year, Sheila Sehgal's parties would be even more extravagant. Sid, her only son, was getting married that December. The Holi eve soirée was to casually (yet ostentatiously) introduce Sheila's new daughter-in-law-to-be in an outfit that cost as much as a midsized car. At the start of the party, Sid and Anushka had been led by their over-smiling families to a sofa under an arch of flowers and sat side by side like a pair of dolls. Sid held up Anushka's hand, and with a sharky grin, he slipped a diamond on to her finger. The crowd broke out into oohs and aahs. Someone did a loud two-fingered whistle. I turned my head toward the sound. I saw Ammu, my best friend from middle school. We hadn't spoken in ten years. A peculiar thing about Kamalpur was that the wealthy families all had their roots tangled up like banyan trees; it took some skill to figure out where one household ended and the other began. Ammu was Sid's cousin on his mom's side. Sid was one of the most popular rich boys in Kamalpur. Everyone knew Sid Sehgal. He went to expensive boarding schools and then college in America. His parents bought him a Mercedes at seventeen. If Sid thought you were pretty, the other boys did as well.

When I saw Sheila Sehgal walking over to us, I grabbed Jeh's hand and then, thinking that I must look stupid, let it go.

"Jeh, so glad you're here," Sheila said, tilting her head to one side like a cockatoo. "I wasn't sure you'd be able to make it—sorry that the invite was so last minute." Sheila had on a sari the color of old ivory, trimmed with soft white feathers that shivered gracefully with every movement. Around her neck were six strands of uncut diamonds. Her smoky eyes flitted from Jeh to me. "And, Noomi, long time no see." A pause. A little frown. "Where's Asha?"

Jeh shifted his weight from one foot to the other. His lips gathered in a small, nervous moue.

"Asha's not feeling well. She's at home. She sends her best." He smiled wanly.

Sheila Sehgal's eyebrows shot up into her luxurious hair. She raked and fluffed her layers with talon-like red nails. "Oh! I'm sad to hear that. I was looking forward to seeing her," she said, sounding not at all sad. "Achcha, you must get yourself a drink. The bartenders are from Russia, or Ukraine, or someplace like that." She waved a hand toward the bar. "I don't know where my Sidoo finds these people, to be honest. But they make the most amazing cocktails."

After Sheila sent Jeh off to the bar with a smile, she turned her attention to me. "Noomi, where have you been hiding? Haven't seen you at any of the usual parties. Of course"—Sheila gestured at the crowd—"I've been so busy organizing Sid and Anushka's engagement."

"I've been around, Aunty. Not going out much these days," I said, not wanting to tell her that I hadn't been asked to any of the usual parties. "You look very pretty."

"Bespoke Raaj Lulla," Sheila said, preening. "A gift from Anushka's parents. I hate his off-the-rack stuff, but this I adore. Did you know they've got him to do the flowers?"

"The... flowers?" I said stupidly. "Raaj Lulla does flowers?"

"Not for everyone," Sheila said with a wink. "Anushka's parents have a very close relationship with Raaj. He's done all her outfits." She scanned my sari. "That's a pretty color. Turn around so that I can see the whole thing."

I turned. My sari was blue chamois silk with a silver sequin border. I'd worn a shimmery blouse and high heels to match. My blouse chafed painfully at the armholes. I'd gotten it stitched weeks ago but forgot to try it on to see if it fit. And then it was too late to get it altered. The hooks fought to stay buttoned across my chest; the front had gaps that I'd covered with my sari's pallu, praying it would stay in place for the rest of the night.

"Ah, lovely. I admire how you wear just anything, no need for designer brands," Sheila said.

"Thank you." I smiled, pulling at my pallu. One could detest Sheila yet crave her approval like a dog panting after treats.

"Darling, you're twenty-three! I'll tell you the same thing I tell Anushka: at your age, you should look your best. All. The. Time," Sheila said. "Anushka works out for one two hours in the gym every day. I said to her, 'After marriage, please take my son along with you!'" She cackled, amused at her own joke.

"That's nice," I said.

"Go congratulate them," Sheila said, shooing me away. "They're around here somewhere," she added, searching the growing crowd on the lawn. "Oh, the chief minister and his wife just walked in. Excuse me, I have to go say hello."

The only reason we'd been invited to the Sehgals' was because Sheila always respected the old Kamalpur hierarchies. My grandmother Lily Mama came from old, aristocratic money. A ferocious beauty in her day, she still had enough power in her gaze to raise you up or send you tumbling. When I was four years old, a nursery teacher used to pinch the inside of my thighs if I didn't "sit like a lady." Lily Mama discovered the bruises one afternoon while I was playing with a doll in her lap, shouting at it to sit like a lady. The next morning, she marched into the school office, wearing battle pearls, purse under her arm, to roar at the principal. The teacher was fired. After Jeh, I loved her the most.

I wandered around until I saw Lily Mama on a sofa placed under a twisty banyan tree. She was one of those women whose girth enhanced their magnificence, like Aretha Franklin. I put a hand on her silken shoulder. Absentmindedly, she covered my hand with hers. On her forefinger was a huge ruby mounted on a cage of pearls. I sat down next to her with a little puff of air.

"Hello, pudding," Lily Mama said.

"Hello," I said, kissing Lily Mama's cheek. She smelled like flowers baked into a loaf of bread.

"Jeh went to get me a drink," Lily Mama said. "But your mother wasn't with him. Where is she?"

I blew out another puff of air. "Mama was too drunk to come," I said, leaning on a cushion.

Lily Mama's smile evaporated. "She'd quit drinking if she loved you," she said. "A mother has no business being a lush."

"Papa drinks too," I said. "They should both quit, na?"

Lily Mama didn't answer. Her gaze had snagged on my badly fitting sari blouse. She grimaced. "You didn't try this on beforehand, did you. I can see your bra through the gaps. Really, Noomi."

"Forget it. No one will notice," I said, covering the blouse with my sari.

"Give it to me tomorrow. I'll send it to Dashrath Tailor."

"Why don't you tell Daddy to quit?"

"Jeh is a grown man, he can decide for himself."

I let out a groan. "Lily Mama, you are an MCP."

"A what?"

"Male chauvinist pig." I smiled. "Technically you're a female chauvinist pig."

Lily Mama looked down the nose that she'd inherited from my ship-building, Anglophile, colonial-apologist Parsi ancestors. My father's family passed down money, noses, and fair skin; a predilection for rage and alcohol was the only inheritance from my mother's side.

"Don't be rude!" Lily Mama said, thumping my head.

"I didn't mean it like that!" I grinned, clinging to her. "I'm sorry!"

"Come on, get away," Lily Mama said, prying me off. "You're ruining my sari. Horrible child."

"Hug me back," I said, clinging tighter. "I'm sorry."

"What a fancy party," said my grandfather, arriving just then with a plate of food, sitting down next to us, and shaking his leg. "Bet they've spent a fortune. Didn't your mother come? She's missing out on this khao suey. I asked the chef—he said the lobster cost two thousand rupees per kilogram."

"She's drunk again," Lily Mama said to him.

"Tch, tch, tch. What a shame. My son deserves better. I hope you'll turn out a finer woman than your mother," Zal Papa said, fixing his eyes on me, waggling a piece of lobster on his fork. "But perhaps not."

Zal Papa had been fond of his nightly double pegs of whisky until a stroke in his fifties left one side of his face looking like Droopy's. Now all he had to entertain himself was a habit of poking his nose where it didn't belong. Even his friends looked a bit wary when he sidled up to them, half his face stretched in a grin.

When Zal Papa moved to Kamalpur from Bombay to set up his business, my father, the younger of his two sons, was a toddler. Zal Papa bought an acre of land on Banyan Street opposite Nirmala Girls' Hostel, whose gray walls were busy with lewd graffiti and I LOVE YOU signs. As Jeh and his brother, Cyrus, got older, went to college, found love, and got married, our bungalow grew alongside them, sprouting new wings and verandas. Eventually, Zal Papa built each of his sons a home on the same plot of land. So that they'd have a good income to support their wives and kids, Zal Papa augmented his vast home goods empire and gave each son a business. Zal Papa had given our family everything; for that we had to be continually grateful. And if we weren't, he'd be sure to remind us.

My mother told me that when I was four or five years old, my father brought home a friendly white-and-black cat he'd found sitting on a postbox outside his office. I have no memory of this; before Jeh could bring me the warm, soft cat curled up in his arms, Zal Papa had ordered him to take it away. "No cats in this house, ever," he'd said. Cats were bad luck, like living on a cul-de-sac or traveling on a moonless night. My father gave the cat to a neighbor.

Jeh was his father's favorite—he craved Zal Papa's approval much more than his elder brother did. One of the rare times my father ever defied Zal Papa was when he chose to marry my mother. As in the case of the cat, Zal Papa made it plain that he'd prefer it if Jeh would put Asha back wherever he found her. Zal Papa prided himself on his good instincts when it came to character. "Character is destiny," he'd told me once. "I never wanted your parents to marry. But at least we got you out of it." I thought of myself as some sort of consolation prize.

As it turned out, Zal Papa's instincts were correct. My parents never had a happy marriage. Then Asha lost her second baby late in the third trimester and, with that, her mental health. There were moms who put love notes in their children's lunch boxes, and there was Asha, who'd once picked me up from school five hours late, who sent me to birthday parties wearing torn underwear. Jeh's reaction to Asha's rapid decline was to retreat further and further into his books and passive, absentminded denial. I was raised part-time by two women: a loving ayah, and Lily Mama, who would take me downstairs to her bed when I was sick, put Vicks VapoRub on my neck, and tie a handkerchief around it to ease my frequent coughs and colds.

Sometimes, as kids, my cousin Adil and I would sleep in our grandparents' bed, between them. After they'd managed to get us to stop wiggling around and fighting about who was hogging the blanket, Zal Papa would put down his Jeffrey Archer, switch off his bedside lamp, extend his hand to Lily Mama, and say, "Haath aapo." *Give me your hand.* Their arms would form an arch over our sleepy bodies, as a slowly whirling fan dusted our heads with a soft breeze.

I'd always read to Adil before we fell asleep: Enid Blyton's stories of English children, foolhardy but always well dressed, with shiny shoes and not-torn underwear, with neat side parts and pink fingernails. Their mothers were good eggs, the fathers charmingly neglectful. I was determined to live in England when I grew up, where I would eat buttered scones and crumpets every day. I carried a Famous Five book with me everywhere I went, stuffed in a teddy bear backpack my parents bought in London. I'd read in the park, at school, at the dinner table.

I'd even tried to read by the light of orange streetlamps as they sprinted past the car window, on the way to the Gymkhana Club for Saturday tombola. In the front seat, my mother pulled out a water bottle from her handbag. Holding it between her knees, she lit a cigarette, blowing tusks of smoke from her nostrils. She unscrewed the top and took a swig before passing it to Jeh, who said something that I couldn't get over the roar of a passing water tanker. It was funny, whatever he said; my mother tossed back her head, letting out a beautiful, brassy laugh. She hadn't laughed like that in weeks.

"Ma, look what I'm wearing," I said, putting down my book, smiling from the dark of the back seat. I had on a dress with a bib of frills that my mother had purchased on one of her foreign trips, with money smuggled in a talcum powder tin. I didn't like the clothes she brought me: tight, outlandish Western outfits that, in our town, invited *looks*. Asha would complain to anyone in earshot how I never wore all the expensive clothes she'd bought. I wore the dress, hoping that she'd be pleased.

Balancing the bottle on her thigh with one hand, Asha turned around to look at me. The car went over a speed bump, and the drink splashed all over her sandals. The car began to smell like the cotton swabs nurses dab on your skin before a shot.

"Oh, fucking shit," Asha said, jerking her head back to the front, shaking her leg like it'd caught fire. I groaned. I was eight years old and knew about hangovers. I was in for a few extra slaps tomorrow.

Saturday tombola was the most exciting thing in town, and Asha, Jeh, and I found our seats at a checkered-cloth table on the club lawn. A few men stopped by to talk with Jeh, but no women stopped by to talk with Asha. Standing fans coaxed the sluggish air. Kids roved about in bands.

"That was rude," Asha said, as the man who had been speaking with Jeh walked off.

"What was rude?" Jeh asked, waving for a waiter in a black bow tie to come over.

"He didn't even say hello to me," she said, taking her cigarettes out of her purse.

I squirmed on the plastic seat, scratching out numbers without enthusiasm, while my parents sat in silence, drinking sweating glasses of beer and eating peanuts. Earlier in the evening I'd seen Adil, sitting under his parents' table, playing with kids from school. I went over and asked if I could play with them. They refused and stuck out their tongues. Empty beer bottles multiplied like rabbits under my parents' table, and mosquito coils burned in the grass. In the still and airless night, the smoke rose straight up like white puppet strings. After she'd finished her cigarettes, Asha lit the leftover matches and flicked them at the coils. I stared, mesmerized by the small, tumbling flames.

Asha leaned over and gave my thigh a vicious pinch. I screamed.

"When will you learn to sit properly?" Asha said. "You want to show the entire lawn your underwear?"

"I'm sorry, Mama," I said, crying, looking around for Jeh, who'd left us to get a whisky. This was Asha's gift: to keep the world odd and puzzling, to make me feel guilty of crimes I hadn't committed, to mangle reality until it was bled of truth.

"Asha, what the hell are you doing?" Jeh said, coming back. "Why is she crying?"

"Just teaching her how to sit," Asha said, her face like a storm cloud as she began raking through the ashtray with her forefinger, spilling ash on the table.

"You're completely sozzled," Jeh said. He placed his hands protectively on my shoulders.

Asha found a half-finished cigarette and, lighting it, replied, "Yeah? So are you."

"Asha," Jeh hissed, and I saw two dozen necks craning toward us. "You see any other women, other mothers, drinking or smoking? People don't let their kids play with Noomi because of you, because of your reputation."

"What about you?" Asha shot back. "What're you doing to help her, huh? Jack shit, that's what." She crossed her arms and blew smoke rings. "Fucking hypocrite."

Jeh and Asha hissed and spat insults at each other, their faces twisting into rageful masks, neither caring if people stared. When I couldn't take it anymore, I made an excuse to get away.

"I'm going to the bathroom," I said. "I need to pee."

The stall door did not shut all the way. I pushed it closed as far as it would go, then crouched over the smelly squat toilet and peed. I hoped my parents were done fighting. While I was dragging up my underwear, Adil pushed open the stall door. He and his friends stared, mouths open like baby chicks. I'd wanted to grab their heads and knock them together, but shock glued my feet to the ground. My face felt like a hot skillet. I screamed. They scattered, giggling, guffawing. I pulled up my underwear, tears pricking at my eyes.

The bathroom's oval mirror was clouded with fingerprints and was cracked in the bottom right corner. I pried at it until a chip the size of a guitar pick came off. I ran my thumb along its edge. Blood bloomed from a small cut. I put my thumb in my mouth; it tasted like a one-rupee coin. *Maybe I'll cut Adil with this,* I thought, slipping the mirror piece in my pocket. I turned on the tap and watched my blood swirl into the drain.

Outside, tombola was over, and people had begun to leave. Adil and his friends were nowhere to be seen. I'd have to wait until tomorrow for my revenge. Jeh came walking up from the lawn, helping

Asha how you'd help an injured athlete off the field. She was humming to herself, softly.

"Let's go, Piglet," Jeh said as he came to where I stood. "Mama isn't well."

"Actually," I said, looking at my grandfather. "I plan on getting nice and fucked up tonight."

"Noomi! Your language!" Lily Mama said, crinkling up her nose. "Apologize at once."

"But Zal Papa said…"

"At once, Noomi."

"I'm sorry."

Lily Mama felt my forehead with the back of her hand; her touch was cool, soothing.

"Are you ill or something?" she asked.

"I'm fine," I said, moving my head away.

"Why are you so rude?" She lifted one of my earrings in her palm. "Oh, those are pretty." She frowned. "They look expensive. Real or fake?"

"Fake," I said.

"Not bad," Lily Mama said. "Could've fooled me."

Jeh came up to us, holding a drink garnished with a flower. He kissed his mother's cheek. "Mama, I had them make you a daiquiri," he said. "I hope that's okay?"

"Thank you, darling," Lily Mama said.

For a moment, I admired their twin Mona Lisa smiles. More family members began to collect around us. Adil strolled across the Sehgals' lawn with his mother—all bright eyes and tall hair and broad shoulders. Aunties loved him. Adil responded to them all politely, while his mother smiled like a pope. Several years ago, Adil was a pudgy teenager headed off to engineering college in America, his suitcase filled with hair gel and vast supplies of Haldiram's snacks. Oftentimes when he got drunk and lonely, Adil would call us late at night and talk for hours. He got a job at a multi-national, but after several months of emotional phone calls from our grandfather, who wanted all his children under his roof, Adil moved back into our family home.

"Ah, here he is," Zal Papa said. "My boy. Look at these women eyeing you like a bar of chocolate." He grabbed Adil's hand. "How many shots have they forced you to have, huh?"

"None so far," Adil said, smiling. "Mom and I just got here."

"Come on," Zal Papa said. "At your age, I'd drink all my friends under the table."

I snorted. "Even your double standards have double standards, Zal Papa."

"Sarcasm is anger's ugly cousin, cousin," Adil wagged a finger at me. "I'm happy to see you, though. Didn't think you'd be invited." He unclasped his mother's hand from his elbow and gave me a hug.

"Why wouldn't I be?" I snapped.

"They must've spent a fortune on this thing," Adil said with a low whistle. "And to think, this is just the engagement party. The wedding'll be sick!"

He rubbed his palms. My face must have given away something. All of a sudden, Adil wanted to look everywhere but at it.

"Sorry," he said.

"It's fine."

"I mean, how long does it take to get over someone?"

"Well, I—"

"Never mind that," Binny, Adil's mother, interrupted. "I noticed Asha isn't here. What's the story?"

"Well," Jeh began, "we planned to tell everyone that she's ill. Food poisoning, or something like that."

"You mean *you* planned," I said.

"I ran into her at the market this afternoon," Binny said, shaking her head. "She tried to hide this big shopping bag that she was carrying with two hands, but I could hear the clink of bottles." She gave a little sniff. "Who buys alcohol in the middle of the day like that?"

"You didn't actually see any bottles," I said, frowning. "The clinking could've been anything."

"Oh, come on, Noomi," Binny said. "Let's not kid ourselves."

When she was in high school, Binny had won a Princess Diana contest and chopped off her hair in Di's signature bob. "Streamlined working princess" was the aesthetic she'd chased ever since. Back in the '70s, when coeducation was taboo, there used to be a prestigious all-girls convent school that all the ambitious mothers in Kamalpur sent their daughters to, hoping that a convent education full of English poetry, choir, and crochet lessons would land them a good match. Asha and Binny attended it a few years apart. Years later, when Jeh's mother expressed her desire to find a suitable wife for Jeh's awkward older brother, Asha, struggling to win favor with in-laws who didn't like her, introduced them to the pretty, polite junior who'd kept in touch with her: Binny. This backfired quite spectacularly a few years later, when there was a falling out about a ring or some other bit of Wadia jewelry that was supposed to be for Binny but ended up going to Asha. Binny's superpower was that if she had her knife out for you, soon all her friends did too.

"Well, I'm off to the bar," Adil said.

"Cool, I'll come with you," I said, getting up.

"You'll do no such thing!" Zal Papa said.

"Why not?" I cried out. Fool that I was, I expected my family to treat me like an adult. At least a faint hope remained that they'd let me order a drink without basting me in lectures.

"This family doesn't need another scandal. You're like your mother when it comes to alcohol, Noomi. I think it's time you and your father come have another chat with me," Zal Papa said. "It takes years to build a reputation and only seconds to destroy it." This sentence was punctuated by a smug little nod from Aunt Binny. "I'm not about to see mine torn down because my son can't control his wife."

"She's not his pet!" I yelled. "You expect her to roll over, play dead, put out a paw to shake."

"Noomi, that's enough," Jeh muttered. Turning to Adil, he said, "I'll need another whisky, or three, to survive this evening."

"No problem, Uncle." Adil smiled. "I'll get you one."

"Oh, Adil, can you get me something to drink as well?" Binny trilled.

"Of course, Mama. What would you like?" Adil said. I expected him to bow like the Air India maharaja.

"Oh, I don't know. I'm such a lightweight," Binny simpered. "Some Bristol Cream, perhaps, or Baileys with ice?"

"I'll have a vodka tonic," I said, grinning. "With lots of ice."

"I don't think that's a good idea, Noomi," Jeh said.

"Why?"

"Because," Binny hissed, "as Zal Papa says, you handle alcohol like your mother."

"This is none of your business, Aunty."

"Noomi," Lily Mama said, "I've warned you not to talk to your elders like that."

When I was little, on the nights my parents stayed up fighting and screaming at each other, I'd creep downstairs into Lily Mama's bedroom. In the day, I'd follow her around like a puppy, holding the end of her sari. I loved her, but Lily Mama could be a real bitch sometimes. I looked over at Jeh, hoping he'd say something in my defense. But Jeh didn't say a word.

"Apologize to Binny," Lily Mama scolded. "Come on, do it. Don't spoil everyone's mood."

"Why do I need to apologize?" I said, wrapping the end of my pallu around my wrist.

"You'll do it because your grandmother said so," Zal Papa said.

Zal Papa's words hovered in the air like a bird of prey.

"I'm sorry," I said to Binny.

The DJ began playing again; the bass traveled up through the soles of my feet as I walked away.

An unspoken rule in Kamalpur was that well-bred women did not order their own drinks at the bar. They had to wait until a man fetched them one. I avoided my father's frowning stare and made my way into the press of shouting men surrounding the bartenders. There, I bumped into Ammu, waiting on a drink, and looked away quickly. I felt a hand on my shoulder and turned. Ammu stood with her drink in hand, a smile filling up her eyes. She was one of those childhood friends whom you don't quite remember ever having met—they'd just always been in your life. In the years since we'd last spoken, Ammu had moved abroad and returned only recently to start an NGO. This Ammu seemed different from the quiet, intense, over-protected teenager who'd left home. This older but even lovelier

Ammu had a gold purse hanging by a strap from her bare shoulder. Her skin looked soft and plush like velvet; her long black hair reached to the middle of her back. She had huge eyes that she liked to make even larger with smudgy kohl.

Ammu seemed to be suggesting that we sneak off for a smoke.

"*You've* got cigarettes? You?" I said.

"Argh, yes," Ammu said, widening her eyes.

"When did you even start smoking?"

"There's a lot you don't know about me, obviously." Ammu smiled, raising her scimitar-shaped eyebrows. "I mean, we haven't been in touch for... I don't know how long."

"We were thirteen," I said with a lopsided smile that I hoped was coolly ironic.

"Oh," said Ammu. A shadow glided across her face. "But," she continued, brightening, "that's why we need to get wasted and catch up. Come on, I know somewhere no one will bother us."

Holding our drinks away from our saris, we pressed up against the white stucco wall and skirted the dance floor, where paunchy uncles holding glasses on their heads and aunties eager to show off their Madhuri Dixit moves were gyrating to loud Bollywood music. No one noticed us. We walked down the driveway to sneak behind the multicolored food shamianas, with their tempting, steaming pans of khao suey and Rajasthani dal and a pasta station manned by a bored-looking boy in a crooked chef's hat.

Behind the shamianas was an ill lit courtyard as utilitarian and ugly as the front of the bungalow, with its sparkling garden, was lovely and impractical. I sat on the cement edge of a covered well, wondering how this part of the evening would turn out. Ammu took out a cigarette from her gold purse. The little wax match she lit burned so fast, she had to drop it or risk singeing her fingertips. She took a few puffs and offered it to me. I smiled. We could make each other out by the light coming from a chauffeur's quarters. Framed by the doorway was a toddler asleep on a charpoy, her mouth open, her hands curled into earthen cups. Probably the child of one of the Sehgals' army of domestic staff. Her parents were likely busy help-ing out at the party. The kid slept under a thin sheet. She didn't seem bothered by the mosquitoes alighting to feed on her arms. Surely, I thought, Sheila could afford a mosquito net or two.

I was six years old the first time I held a baby. It was a rainy, noisy afternoon. I recall dancing barefoot across the smooth tiles of my parents' living room. A radio played film songs. It was the '80s, so my hair must have been in a side ponytail, swaying rhythmically to the sound of Lata Mangeshkar's chaste yet sex-kitten-like voice. Over the song, I could hear my mother screaming. Apparently, our high-caste, vegetarian cook (the one we had before my beloved ayah, Shanta Bai, arrived) had refused another delivery from our butcher.

"In this house we eat meat!" I heard my mother scream from the kitchen.

The doorbell rang. Then it rang again. I turned off the radio, still sashaying to the music in my head. I pulled the heavy front door open with all my might to find... no one. I was about to let it swing shut, when a small gurgling noise made me look in the direction of my feet. An infant, naked except for a black thread tied around his swollen belly, lay on a dirty cloth, cycling his legs.

"Ma! There's another one today!" I yelled into the house.

"Oh, lovely timing," came my mother's reply. "Bring it inside."

My mother had rented out the ground floor of Nirmala Girls Hostel, the one with obscene graffitied walls opposite our bungalow, to set up an orphanage. Soon, it gained the depressing distinction of the lowest infant death rate of any orphanage in Kamalpur. People began abandoning babies at our doorstep. At one point, it got so bad that Lily Mama stationed a chowkidar at each entrance, with instructions not to let anyone holding a baby through the gates. One night, a fight broke out when a business associate of Jeh's, whom he'd invited over for dinner, started shouting threats and obscenities from where he stood outside our front gate. They would not let his wife, holding his infant son, enter.

I lifted the baby up the way I'd seen my mother do, supporting his head, like a lotus on a stem. The rain had receded to a drizzle. I felt it on the back of my neck. The child's gaunt face was a skull painted the color of flesh. He weighed as much as a bundle of twigs. He opened his lips and turned, hoping to find a breast. Disappointed, he let out a wail. I carried him back into the kitchen.

"Look, Mama," I said. "So tiny!"

I waited for Asha to notice me. I wanted her to say that I was holding the baby the right way, that I was a clever, responsible girl. The orphan children called her "Asha Mai." They'd gather around her like chicks around a hen, chirping, "Asha Mai! Look at this picture I made!" "Asha Mai! Look how tall I am now!" My mother, in her cotton kurta and oversized sunglasses, would smile and say, "Very good, Mira. Well done, Govind. I'm so proud of you," as she ushered them all back inside. Asha would encourage the children to do crafts and make jewelry out of Popsicle sticks and discarded ribbons. She'd wear their creations to parties, and when someone asked—which they always did—she'd chuckle and say, "Oh, this? One of my orphanage kids made it for me. I promised her I would wear it." She always called them "my kids" or "my orphanage bachchas," while I was "the brat," "the little nuisance"—spoken with a what-can-you-do smile.

How jealous I was of them.

"You crazy woman!" Apparently, my mother was too busy squabbling with the cook to pay me attention. "People who eat meat are not rakshasas!"

The cook threw down her frilly, turmeric-stained apron, shouting that Asha calling *her* crazy was the limit. She quit. I took the news with glee. I hated her weak dals and sickly bhindi fry. There'd be no dinner ready when Jeh came home tonight. He'd find my mother in a snit and take us out to the Gymkhana Club, where he'd order a whisky for himself and a vodka for my mom while I sipped Thums Up through the gap between my front teeth.

"Here. Please, Mama," I said, and pushed the baby into her arms. "I think he's wet himself."

My mother took the infant to the window and held him up in the watery light. Turning his pointy little body this way and that, she inspected him. "Hmm, malnourished. Probably dysentery," she said. She pulled off his rough cloth diaper and gave him back to me. "Hold

him a little while longer. I still need to sort this stupid woman out."
She turned around to face the sulky frowning cook.

"But, Ma!" I protested as the naked baby was thrust back into my
arms. My mother resumed fighting with the cook, barring her from
leaving by standing in the doorway. I watched them argue and felt
something warm and foul drip from my hands. The baby, freed of his
diaper, had pooped a mess. Vomit pushed up against the back of my
throat.

"Those are pretty earrings," Ammu said.

"Thanks," I said. "They're my mom's, actually."

"How's Asha Aunty?" Ammu asked. "I don't see her around
tonight."

"She's... not feeling well," I said, making quotations marks in the
air.

"Oh," Ammu said, "I'm sorry."

"Don't be," I said.

"Nothing serious, I hope?" Ammu prodded further.

"The truth? She was too drunk to leave the house," I said. "She
drinks all day these days. She's anxious, depressed, et cetera. Nothing
new."

"Poor Asha Aunty. She used to be such fun when I came over to
your house as a kid," Ammu said. "Remember that time we wanted
to turn your balcony into a garden, so we carried buckets of mud
through your living room?" She blew a plume of smoke and laughed.

"It was a disaster," I said, recalling that day. "Mud all over the
floors and on the curtains."

"But your mom wasn't even angry!" Ammu smiled. "She yelled
for the gardener to come upstairs, and he helped us make a little thing
with bricks for the mud and some seeds. My mom would've had a
meltdown." She held her tongue between her teeth.

"You had to catch her on a good day," I conceded, grinning.

On days that Asha's demons took a holiday, she transformed into
the kind of mother one reads about in Enid Blyton's stories. She taught
me how to play Scrabble. She would read to me for hours. We'd go to

the fish market and she'd make the pomfrets move their mouths and pretend to sing. She had the most beautiful voice, like a crystal glass struck with a spoon. But her anger always returned. One mother sang me to sleep; the other woke me up with her screams. How frightening a parent's anger is for a child, like God hating you. After Asha hit me, her gold bangles clinking to keep time, I'd run crying to a mirror to see if I'd changed, if the beating had registered and I was more like the children she loved—the ones in her orphanage.

"Have you ever thought about getting help?" Ammu asked. "Or like, taking her someplace she could dry out for a few weeks?"

"She won't." I stared at my feet. My high heels glittered in the dark. "She doesn't trust anyone. Not even us. Perhaps Dad and I should get help. My mother certainly thinks so, since she seems to blame us for all her problems."

"What does she blame you for?" Ammu frowned.

"I don't know," I said, taking a large sip of my drink. "Once, when I was really young, she and my dad had this massive fight. And I think it was because I... I pushed her. I mean, I was eight and lost my temper. I was pretty evil, as a child."

"You're not evil," Ammu said, putting a hand, cool and dry, on my shoulder. "I know it's been hard for your family. Everyone knows."

"Oh, and my mom can't stop complaining about the fact that..." I paused, tilting my glass up to finish my drink. "...my dad hasn't touched her, you know, in fifteen years."

Ammu shook her head. "These aren't your problems."

"You know what? Forget about it," I said, annoyed at myself for spilling my guts. "Let's just get drunk and dance." The last time I'd been vulnerable with her, Ammu had stopped speaking to me for a decade.

"Have you ever thought of moving out?"

"Where would I go?" I said blearily. "And what would I do?"

"What do you want to do?"

"It's not what I want to do as much as who I want to be," I confessed against my better judgment. "Someone who isn't automatically written off."

"You could move somewhere new," Ammu offered. "A fresh start.."

She smiled, took back the cigarette, and stood holding it up and away from her sari, which shimmered like ripples in dark water. There was a flash at her wrist. She was wearing a bracelet. A bracelet I'd given her, many years ago. A gold circlet ending in two lion heads that I'd discovered in my mother's jewelry box. I took the cigarette from between her fingers, then slipped a nail under the gold band.

"I can't believe you've kept this all these years," I said. "I thought you hated me."

"I was an idiot," Ammu said. "I blamed you for things—things that weren't your fault."

"Why haven't you reached out?" I slurred. *Reeshed out.*

"I was afraid," Ammu said, shaking off my hand. "I'm sorry."

"Afraid? Of what?" I said, studying the lines notched into her forehead.

"Afraid of looking you in the eye."

"Why?"

"Because," Ammu's gaze zigzagged from her feet to my face. "I finally understood what my brother had done to you."

I'd given Ammu the bracelet in her bedroom before we were to attend a party for her older brother's law school graduation. In those days, I spent most of my evenings at Ammu's old family mansion across from the sandstone high court building. I adored that house. In my thirteen-year-old mind, it looked like an ancient wedding cake. The monsoon rains had battered its plaster-corniced façade for years. Repairs and whitewashing had little impact: the octogenarian house had stayed, stubbornly, in aristocratic decay, walls thrumming with the patter of small creatures. Ants trudged into lightning-shaped cracks near the ground; through the walls a vine pushed out its green limbs; googly-eyed lizards and furry bats hid in the nooks; brown mice scurried along the floor, into doorways that swallowed the sunlight.

The inside was no better. Although the Atales had pots and pots of money, their furniture looked like the sort used in government guesthouses: ugly, functional. The tables were topped with indestructible plywood. The curtains were synthetic and slippery. There was a large, ungainly hall on the ground floor, and the bedrooms on the first floor opened to each other like train carriages. Any notion of private space remained theoretical. There was a musty smell to the bed linen.

When I arrived, Ammu had been fighting with her mother over a top she wanted to wear. It was one of those sheer, confectionary-shaded pieces that Ammu preferred, chiffon with a collar bow. The argument was about whether the top was see-through: Ammu was firmly on the side of it wasn't, her mother insisted that it was.

"Aai, please?" Ammu said, fidgeting with the collar in front of a full-length mirror. "Look how modest the neck is!"

"Amrita," her mother said, pinching the bow like she wanted it to squeal. "This blouse is *transparent*. We've invited your father's colleagues to the party. Do you want the entire legal fraternity of Kamalpur to know what color bra you're wearing? Think of Baba! How humiliated he would feel."

"But, Aai," Ammu said. She was close enough to the mirror to almost kiss her reflection. "You can only see it if you look *very* carefully. Like they would literally have to be *this* close to see it."

"I think it looks really good," I said.

Ammu's mother, who didn't like me much, threw me a look. "That's exactly what men do, they look *carefully*," she said to Ammu. She took a shimmery anarkali out from the closet. "This is much better. Very nice and elegant. And modest. Wear this."

"Why do I have to dress like a forty-year-old lawyer while Noomi gets to wear jeans and a cute top?"

"Aunty, Ammu looks pretty in that blouse," I said.

"Noomi, please stay out of it," Ammu's mother warned.

Ammu snatched the anarkali from her mother's hand, stomped to the bathroom, and slammed the door. She came out a few minutes later, a scowl smeared over her pretty features. I took her hand and slipped the bracelet on to her wrist. Ammu traced the lion heads with her finger and her face relaxed into a smile.

"That's cool," she said. "Where did you get it?"

"It's a secret," I said .

"And why are you giving it to me?"

"Because it's pretty and I want you to have it," I said, giving her hand a squeeze.

Standing outside the Atales' drawing room, we could hear talk and laughter, clinking glasses, plates, and bangles, all muffled by the hum of an air cooler. I opened the door, and a damp breeze blew wisps of hair away from my face and encircled my wrists. Ammu's mother called her name, and she disappeared into that roomful of starched saris and pomaded comb-overs. Then I heard music. Simon and Garfunkel's "Mrs. Robinson." My father loved that song. The music brought me to the other side of the hall. At the foot of an Akai music system sat the guest of honor, sifting through a bunch of LPs. He had on a white shirt with the sleeves rolled up, which I thought was the most stylish thing ever. There was even something stylish about the lines of his cheekbones. The muscle that twitched in Ammu's jaw when she was thinking twitched in his. When their mother ruffled Arjun's hair on the way to the kitchen, he bent his head sideways like a little boy.

"Pass me that one, please," Arjun said, pointing to an album that lay by my feet.

I knelt and picked up *Led Zeppelin III*. "My dad loves this one," I said.

Arjun took the vinyl from me without looking. "Hmm?" he said. "Who?"

"Dada?" Ammu seemed to materialize out of nowhere. I slid away from Arjun. "You know Noomi, right? Jeh Uncle's daughter."

"Oh, hey, nice to see you again, Noomi. I'm a big fan of Jeh's." Arjun looked as if it were a pleasant surprise that a person came attached to the hand holding out the LP. "Wow," he said, and smiled, his lips shaped like an archer's bow. "You've grown up! I see your dad's eyes."

"You do?" This was the best compliment anyone could give me: that I resembled my father. "I don't have his 'stache, though, ha-ha."

"We have all these albums thanks to Jeh," Arjun said, waving a cover around so hard that the record popped out of its sleeve. "He used to order them for Baba from abroad and then bully him into listening to them, night and day, until, eventually, Baba became a fan too."

At that moment, Ammu and Arjun's father walked past the stereo system with a colleague. Baba was a tall, imperious-looking man with hair like gray steel wool. In the high court, where less successful lawyers flapped about like crows, he stood out for his Buddha-like calm. Rumors abounded that he'd be tapped to become a judge soon.

"Mr. Kaptan, this is my son, Arjun," Baba said to his partner. "He has just graduated from the National Law School in New Delhi, and now he spends all his time telling me how I should run my firm."

"Hello, young man." Mr. Kaptan, well into his eighties, was the sort of person who looked like he called anyone under sixty "young man." "I hear that you will be joining our chambers very soon. That's most wonderful."

"No, Uncle, I'm starting a free legal aid clinic," Arjun replied.

"A what?"

"See what I mean?" Baba rolled his eyes.

"Arjun, can't you put on Asha Bhonsle or something like that?" Ammu's mother said, walking past with a tray that she handed off to a server. "This music is giving Mrs. Rai a terrible headache."

"This will take care of Mrs. Rai's headache," Arjun grinned, placing a record on the turntable.

"Immigrant Song" blasted from the speakers. There were loud gasps. Mrs. Rai dropped her samosa. Another lady, frail and elderly, clutched her sari pallu and let out a frightened squeak: "What is this unearthly sound? Is it a demon?"

"We're out of... uh... ice cream," Ammu's mother said, and punched the stereo's off button. "Why don't you go to the store?" She pulled Arjun off the floor. "Take Ammu and Noomi with you for company."

The night was quiet but for the sound of crickets and the crunching of our shoes on the driveway gravel. Ammu's father's car glowed silver in the moonlight, under a creeper of sweet-smelling night jasmine. Jauntily, Arjun held open the car door, first for Ammu and then for me. The inside smelled like leather and Arjun's cologne, which I realized was a bit too strong.

"All set?" Arjun rolled down the window and lit a cigarette.

"Dada!" Ammu gasped. "What if Baba and Aai find out?"

"Shh, we won't tell them," Arjun said. "Wanna try?"

"No!"

"I'll try," I said, stretching out my hand.

Arjun turned sideways and looked at me from the corner of his eye. "I wasn't serious, Noomi," he snorted. "Girls from good families don't smoke. Your dad would kill me."

"They'll be able to smell it," Ammu said with a prudish frown, waving a hand in front of her nose.

"Why do you think they invented cologne?" Arjun said, blowing a smoke ring. He took out a small travel-sized spray from his pocket and misted the air over his head. Then he pushed a tape into the deck. Some more Simon and Garfunkel. *Parsley, Sage, Rosemary and Thyme.*

We stopped at a red light. A young woman holding a baby in a cloth sling knocked on Arjun's window. Showing him the child's dirty, matted head, she begged for money, making a cup with her hand. Arjun rolled down the window and gave her a few rupees. She touched the coins to her forehead in thanks and moved off. The light changed and we drove on. Arjun's jaw muscle twitched. He made a sudden U-turn. Ammu braced herself by holding on to the dashboard, while I slid from one end of the back seat to the other.

"Dada, what are you doing?" Ammu said. "The ice-cream store is that way."

"We're going to make a quick detour," he said. "I want you guys to see what I've been working on."

Something slid out from under the front seat and bumped my foot. It was a cricket bat.

"Why is this in the car?" I asked, picking it up by the handle.

"Oh, that's for security. In case anyone ever tries anything funny with you girls." He parked the car in a thin lane. "Come on, it's over here," he said, grabbing the bat.

"Wait, this is Baba's old chambers," Ammu said, squinting up at a building outlined by darkness. We looked at each other, clueless as to why we were standing outside a dilapidated office. "What are we doing here?"

"Come in and I'll show you," Arjun said, fiddling with a rusty padlock. He used his shoulder to push open the door and was swallowed by the dark. Soon, a tube light flickered on, and then another. The office, littered with leaves and broken light bulbs, smelled like mold and rodent droppings. In the middle of it stood a dusty, old, demented-looking metal Godrej desk with a swivel chair that, miraculously, still swiveled. Arjun sat down and went round and round. I began to feel dizzy.

"Um, Dada, won't Aai be wondering where we are?" Ammu kicked at a box on the floor. Unwise. A lizard leaped out of it. Ammu and I jumped up onto the table, screaming. Arjun leaned back in the swivel chair and linked his hands behind his head.

"Relax, you're with me," he said with a wink.

I brought my knees to my chin. Arjun suddenly leaned forward, opened a drawer, and took out what looked like a blueprint of an open-floor office.

"Look, this is what I have planned for this place."

I traced the white lines with my finger. "That's cool," I said, and looked up at him with a smile. Arjun stared at me in a way that made my heart work like I'd been running in a race. I hopped from the desk and dusted off the seat of my jeans.

"I'm not going to spend my whole life copy-pasting my father's success," Arjun said, folding the plans. "I want to help people—people like that woman on the street."

"Dada, please, let's go home." Ammu slipped from the desk too and pulled her brother up by his arm.

In the car, I kicked off my shoes and lay down on the back seat, my feet outside the window. I lifted my T-shirt a little, to feel the seat's cool, soft leather against my skin. Ammu leaned against Arjun's shoulder. He pressed his cheek to her head. Jealousy pinched my heart.

No one talked on the ride home. I could tell that Ammu was dreaming by the way she stared out the car window, like the trees along the road were whispering to her. When we got back, the party was over and everyone had gone home. Ammu's mother asked why we all looked like we'd been crawling around inside a dusty cupboard. Arjun told her about our little detour. Aunty rolled her eyes.

The office had been filthy. Ammu said she needed to shower before bed. I sat on the cool, hard marble floor in the bedroom. I thought about Ammu's see-through blouse, which lay on her chair like a fainted princess. I thought about the old lady's face when Arjun played "Immigrant Song." I thought about how Arjun had stared at me, and I began to feel nervous, like I'd done something wrong, but I wasn't sure what. Perhaps it was best to go home. I slipped my scrunchie off my wrist and tied up my hair, then went to Ammu's closet (Ammu often borrowed my clothes because her mother bought her only frumpy kurtas and stuff). I balled up a T-shirt and tossed it onto the bed, along with a pair of jeans that I'd been laboriously slashing with a pair of scissors.

"Hello, hello." Arjun, like his sister, could also appear out of nowhere, like a cat.. "What have we here?"

"I'm leaving," I said, pushing the clothes into a bag.

"What's the rush? I thought you were going to spend the night." Arjun yanked my scrunchie off from my ponytail, making my hair tumble over my face. "In fact, I was hoping you would."

"I changed my mind," I said, trying to grab the hair tie from him. "Give that back, Arjun!"

"Try and take it, pocket rocket," Arjun said, dangling it in front of my face.

I dug my nails into his arm.

"Ouch," Arjun said. He swung me around by the elbow and smacked my bottom. "Bad kitty."

"Ow," I said.

Arjun still had the scrunchie. I stood on the bed to grab it from his outstretched hands, and was taken by surprise when he scythed a foot under my legs, causing me to fall backward. He pinned me down. His fingers tap danced down my ribs. It tickled. It hurt. Breathless, I pleaded with him to stop.

We heard Ammu turn off the shower. Arjun stood up and ran his fingers through his hair. He sat down on Ammu's chair, on top of her precious blouse. His eyes walked slowly over my body as his mask of playful irony slipped, showing something raw and greedy underneath. He looked away at the sound of the door bolt. When he turned back, his face was normal again. Ammu stepped out of the bathroom wearing cotton pajamas. She rubbed her head with a towel.

"Dada, what are you doing here now?" she said. Arjun gave a playful growl, flung his sister over his shoulder, shouted, "Khamosh!" and galloped out the bedroom door. Ammu squealed and hit him with her little fists, her long black hair swinging wildly down Arjun's shirt.

It became the summer of Watching Arjun Do Stuff. At the Gymkhana Club, Ammu and I would look on as he and his friends jumped about in bulgy white shorts, playing badminton, swearing coolly in English. We'd lurk in the shallow end of the pool while they took turns dunking each other and belly flopping from the noisy diving board. We'd watch Arjun drink beer and chain-smoke cigarettes on the club lawn, fussing with his hair as he called to the waiters to bring more tandoori chicken, more beer, his feet up on another chair. No one ever told him to put them down. At home, we'd admire him as he argued nimbly, like a fencer, with his father,

Baba, who wanted him to join his law practice instead of frittering away his time doing "social service" at his new legal aid clinic.

"I don't care about money," Arjun said, taking a book from the library shelf and flipping through it.

"Because you've always had money," Baba said, puffing on his pipe.

I sat, unobserved, on a leather chair, the seat of which stuck to my bare thighs. The library smelled of tobacco, books, wood polish, and well-oiled leather. It was Baba's pride: the only room in the house that got a fresh coat of paint every single year.

"My money," Baba added, infuriatingly.

"I happen to think what I do is important, Baba," Arjun said.

"Your mother wants you to get married soon, but how will you be able to support a wife?"

"Actually, I hope for it to be the other way around," Arjun said. Then he winked at me—me!—and my cheeks burned. A ballet dancer spun in my chest. Had Baba noticed? Did that really happen, or did I imagine it?

"I'll join your practice, Baba," Ammu piped up from behind his chair, putting her arms around her father's neck. I rolled my eyes. "I can't wait to argue in court with you."

"You?" Baba turned to look at her over his bifocals, wrinkles lining his forehead like a musical staff.

Arjun snorted—he'd heard enough. He slid the book back into its place on the shelf and loped out of the library through a side door that opened onto the driveway. Ammu's mother called her from somewhere inside the house. Obediently, Ammu went off to find her.

After a few minutes of pretending to look for a book, I followed Arjun outside. He was in the driver's seat of his dad's Mercedes, listening to music, one hand behind his head. Cigarette smoke floated like strands of hair around his face. He saw me looking in, threw the cigarette out the window, and opened the passenger door.

"Come on, let's go for a drive," he said, starting the car.

I wiped my damp palms on my cotton skirt and got in. "What about Ammu?"

"I don't want to be around anyone else right now. Only you."

I wanted to touch his hair, his face. The muscle in his jaw began to twitch violently. I managed to pat him, collegially, on the shoulder. Arjun leaned over and gave me a kiss on the forehead. It was a kiss that left sparks on my skin; it made me feel precious, delicate, like a porcelain doll. I noticed a gold "om" symbol on a thick chain under his unbuttoned shirt collar.

"Let's go," he said, shifting the gear.

He took me back to his office, which was now completely made over. It had a new desk and chairs, a new floor, a smart new coat of paint; the white tube lights had been replaced with expensive lamps. Legal clinic fees did not pay for all these renovations, Baba had. Arjun switched one light on and unlocked his filing cabinet. He sat down at his desk. I attempted to drag over a chair.

"That chair won't fit on my side of the desk," Arjun said. He patted the wooden tabletop. "Up."

I sat on his desk, bunching my skirt between my legs. Arjun pulled open a drawer and took out a brown file. From inside it, a picture fell out. An old man who looked like his head had never known a soft pillow, his mind never had the peace of being his own master.

"That's a senior abuse case I filed for dad's old clerk," Arjun said, pointing at the photo. "He's retired. His sons tried to throw him out of the house. I got a magistrate to evict them. I plan to cite his case in my application."

"Application?" I asked, putting the file aside. "What are you applying for?"

"A master's degree in the UK," Arjun said. Slowly, as if afraid, he slid his hand over my bare knee. I examined his face. It had that greedy expression again. I smiled and put my hand on top of his. Feeling shy and uncertain of how to proceed, I patted it. Pat, pat.

"Is it okay if I kiss you?" Arjun whispered.

"Yes." My heart was a madman slamming against the walls. I closed my eyes and leaned forward. My eyes flew open when Arjun thrust his tongue in my mouth. His hands crept under my skirt.

"Is this okay? Are you okay? Are you sure?" he asked, not really waiting for an answer.

A sharp pain made stars appear behind my eyes. That Arjun wanted me felt like I had a superpower. The idea that I, someone just out of middle school, could make a man beg, could make crazy with desire someone who was so much older, so much smarter than me—was thrilling. Yes, yes. Every time he asked, I said yes. Because I didn't know I could say no. Because I was thirteen and he was my first love. And he seemed so excited. I was okay, either way. Because he'd winked at me when he said the word "wife." He'd kissed my forehead. I'd let him do anything he wanted in exchange for more of that.

I learned how to become invisible. A ghost. When, on the pretense of dropping me home, Arjun drove me to his office for sex, I learned to duck down at traffic lights. I hid in corners of the house while Arjun put his hands down my shirt. I learned to stop myself from squealing when he pulled me into empty rooms. He got bolder. We were nearly caught once by his mother, wanting to know if Arjun needed the driver or could she let him go? "No, Aai," Arjun said, as I, small and half naked, hid under a cotton blanket, my lumpen shape obvious to anyone with a pair of eyes. But his mother had selective blindness: a common affliction among women with sons.

One rainy afternoon, Arjun brought me over because the house was going to be empty. Ammu and her mother were out on errands. The staff, taking advantage of the lull in housework, had gathered in the kitchen for chai and gossip. Heavy clouds had turned the sun into a milky pearl. It fooled you into thinking it was late evening. I walked down the upstairs corridor, listening to rain so heavy that it sounded like deer running on the roof. As we passed by Ammu's door, Arjun yanked me inside by my arm. I managed to stifle my scream.

Arjun lifted me off the floor, hooking my legs around his waist. Then he tumbled me onto the bed. I giggled to hide my terror.

"What are we doing in Ammu's room?" I whispered. "What if someone comes in?"

"Shh," Arjun said, locking the door. "Ammu and Aai won't be home for another hour at least."

"It's so gloomy and cold today," I said, hugging a pillow to my chest. "Let's just snuggle for a bit."

"Shh, now," Arjun said, taking a leg in each hand. He flipped me on my belly and began to pull down my pants. That's when we heard the bathroom bolt slide open with a sickening shot. Ammu stepped out. She dropped the hairbrush she'd been using to untangle her wet hair. Arjun leaped off me, and I scrambled up against the headboard, covering my body with Ammu's sheets. Ammu looked afraid, as if we were ghosts. She kicked the hairbrush away from her feet. It slid across the floor without a sound.

Arjun stood up and walked out of the room, head down, hands in his pockets.

I got up off the bed, my legs all wobbly and unsure, like a newborn lamb's.

"Get out," Ammu said flatly.

I stared at her, blinking. When I didn't move, she crossed her arms and walked past me out the door. At the window, a crack of lightning broke the world in half. Rain poured down from the ashen sky. Crying, I searched the house for Ammu, only to find her when I stepped out on the driveway, pacing up and down the gravel, her arms hugging her small body. I said her name. Then I shouted it. I caught up with her, grabbed her shoulder, and turned her to face me.

Ammu looked at my hand on her shoulder as if it were a splatter of bird shit.

"I'm sorry you found out like this," I said, wedging my hands in my armpits. The rain slipped inside my T-shirt and trickled down my back. "We were going to tell you."

"We?" Ammu said with a look that was both incredulous and cruel. "Who do you think you are? My sister-in-law?" She pushed me aside and began to walk back to the house.

I grabbed her hand. "Maybe one day? He loves me. Look, he gave me this." I showed her the "om" necklace.

Ammu shook her hand free so hard it made me flinch. "That's definitely fake," she spat. "He doesn't need to waste expensive things on you. You're cheap."

For months afterward, I'd call Ammu and she'd hang up. Everything that happened was my fault. Poor noble, kind, legal-aid-clinic-running Arjun. I had tempted him, corrupted him. My life was forever altered, while his didn't change a hair. His work thrived, and he was accepted to a prestigious master's program. Deprived of Ammu's friendship in school, I became more of an outcast. I ate my lunch on the steps outside the chemistry lab, which farted acrid gas through its open doors. Eventually, Ammu stopped hating me. If she crossed me in the hallways, she'd say hi, but we'd never talk for more than a few minutes.

M y happy memories with Ammu had withered like a dying tree, leaf by leaf, until nothing but air filled its branches. Luckily I was too drunk to wallow much longer in the past.

"Why are men... ?" I said, squinting in the dim courtyard light at present-day Ammu's face. "Sid once told me he'd only marry a virgin." I threw my hands up. "Is this Anushka a virgin? If you know, you have to tell me."

"The men in my family," Ammu said, avoiding my eyes, studying the dozing child on the charpoy instead, "they've learned to appraise a woman like a house or a car."

"How's your brother ?" I asked, looking at her sideways.

Ammu shifted uncomfortably. "He's doing great. He's getting married next year. She's Indian but born in England. They met at Oxford."

"That's nice," I said, feeling lousy.

"Noomi," Ammu said. She held my gaze for a second and then looked away. "I know what he did to you was bad. I see now that it was... You couldn't consent. You were a kid."

It pained her to say the words out loud. "It's okay," I said. "We were both young and stupid."

"I feel guilty about how I treated you after. I was brought up in a certain way by my mother"—she paused and gave me a soft, pleading look—"and I didn't know any better. Can you forgive me?"

"It's okay," I repeated with a smile. "We can be friends again, right?"

"Your kajal is all smudged," Ammu said. "It's giving you raccoon eyes."

"Oh no," I said, and rubbed a finger under my lower lid.

"No, stop," Ammu said, "you're making it worse. Here." She snapped open her gold purse and handed me a compact mirror. "Just lick your thumb and swipe it outward under your eye."

"Ew," I said, looking at the mirror. I tried Ammu's trick.

"That's better," Ammu said, smiling.

"You didn't say anything," I said.

"What?"

"When I asked if we can be friends again." I stared at her. "You didn't answer."

Ammu brought her fingertips together, like a lawyer. "You see," she began, "I still love my brother. It's hard for me to reconcile what he did to you with how he's been to me." She took a puff of the cigarette. "I think that's why I've been avoiding you. I'm a coward, I guess."

"So... we can't be friends again?"

"I want to," Ammu said. "But I don't know how it would work. I hurt you. I don't know how you could even want me in your life after that." A strain of loud Punjabi music floated in from the party. Ammu looked back in the direction of the garden. "I mean, I'll always be here for you, and if you ever need any kind of help with your mom..."

For a moment, I wished that the well I was sitting on wasn't covered so that I could jump into it. These sorts of thoughts often popped into my head, thoughts of ghosting existence. I wanted one of those black spots you saw in *Looney Tunes* that you could toss on the ground, and it would become a hole you could escape into. But then, wouldn't it be as good to get really, *really* wasted? I'd better get back to the bar.

"I get it," I said, standing up. "I'm too messy to be friends with. Here, catch."

I tossed the compact at Ammu. It missed her and smashed into the wall. She twisted her head in alarm.

"Fuck," I said. "Sorry."

"That's seven years' bad luck," Ammu said. Mirror shards lay scattered like stars at her feet.

"Listen, my buzz is starting to wear off. Let's head back."

I was about to walk off when the baby on the charpoy inside the chauffeur's quarters stirred, sat up, and let out a wail.

"Isn't that child too young to be left alone?" I asked, rubbing my eyes, smudging my kajal again.

The room was smaller than it appeared from the outside. It was lit by a single bare tube light. In a corner, on top of a rusty metal suitcase, was a little shrine with pictures of gods and goddesses, all resplendent in gold and jewels like the guests at Sheila Sehgal's party. The room had been recently cleaned, and a faint smell of phenyl lingered in the air. I sat down at the edge of the charpoy, which made a few complaining creaks under my weight. The child was blubbering softly, sucking on the end of her bedsheet.

I looked around the room for something to distract her. Ammu stood quietly in the doorway, looking on. I indicated that it was okay if she wanted to return to the party. My chandelier earrings swung forward as I leaned toward the child. A sound escaped from her tiny lips. She stared in wonder.

"You like these, baby?" I asked with a smile. I took off an earring and twirled it in front of her. The tube light caught it. Thousands of stars danced across the limewashed walls of the small room. The girl smiled and held out her hand, and I dropped the earring into it.

"It could be fun to have one of these one day," I said to Ammu, who smiled.

We heard the screen door of the kitchen across the courtyard fly open. A moment later, a woman ran into the room, glaring at me in a confused way, and picked up the girl. When she saw what was in her child's hand, she snatched it. Ignoring her daughter's screams of protest at losing such a sparkly toy, she gave the earring back to me, spouting apologies.

"That's okay," I said. "I gave it to her. She can keep it." I pushed her hand away gently. "It's fake."

"No, no," the woman said. "Please, I don't want to be accused of stealing."

"We should head back to the party," Ammu murmured, crushing the cigarette pack in her fist.

"Thanks for talking to me," I said as we walked away from the wailing child and her mother in the little room. On an impulse, I wrapped my arms around Ammu's shoulders. She'd always been so slight—all angles and points. It was like hugging a bird. She smelled like sandalwood and roses—the simple smell of the house temple. It gave me goose bumps, as if I'd heard a beautiful piece of music. I wondered what it would feel like to kiss her, to feel the shape of her small, neat breasts in my hands. I didn't want to fuck her. I wanted to *be* her. I wanted to crack open her mouth and climb inside her body. Instead, I broke away and ran off toward the booming music.

The door of the gazebo flew open, and a young man ran past to vomit into a hibiscus bush. "Bitch!" Sid's booming laugh seemed to bounce between the gazebo's glass walls. "Lightweight pussy ass bitch."

Sid and his friends were tossing back tequila shots. They stood about in groups, smoking, talking. The women sat on the sofas, feet propped up on the coffee table, toes painted in shades of pink and pearl. In the center of this shimmering group was Sid's fiancée, sitting on a jeweled pouf, a champagne flute in one hand and a tiny, glittery purse in the other. Her outfit was identical to her future mom-in-law's, but in pink. She looked like the sort who'd wear pink well into her fifties. Her brief blouse showed off a belly button studded with a diamond. She reminded me of Dinshaw's strawberry ice cream: pink, sweet, and very cold. Or a heroine from a Yash Chopra film. But when she laughed at a joke, a vein popped out on her forehead, like secretly, she was plotting your murder.

A waiter came in with silver tumblers full of iced milk mixed with saffron and rose petals and laced with bhang, that essential Holi narcotic: the slim finger that undoes prudish corsets for a day. When it was officially Holi, at midnight, Sheila would have a man with a dholak start playing. Tomorrow, her staff would clear away the remains of the party and put out vats of colored powder. There would be plates piled with bhajiyas and mithai. There would be more bhang. Tonight's fine guests would return in their oldest, shabbiest clothes. They would smear each other's bodies with pink and orange color. Laughing, men would touch women in ways that could get them arrested on any other day of the year. "Bura na mano, Holi hai!"

I took a tumbler of bhang and drank it down. Nothing happened. Ammu had joined the circle around Anushka and picked up the thread of conversation. I didn't feel like introducing myself, knowing I'd get *that look* once Anushka had placed me: that look, a mix of condescension and contempt, a look that meant: *Ah, yes. You're that Noomi.*

Standing outside the knot of women, I got tired of waiting for the bhang to kick in. A server passed by with tequila. I drank a shot and became desperate for another cigarette. I glanced at Ammu, getting all pally with Anushka. Couldn't blame her—she and Sid were cousins, after all. Ammu was out of cigarettes anyway. I'd have to ask someone else. I scanned the group and spotted Sid at its edge. He was in a kurta with loose salwar trousers, and I had to admit, he looked marvelous.

Sid was engrossed in his phone, as if his own engagement party bored him. I sidled up and nudged his shoulder. He looked up but didn't smile or say hello. I grinned.

"Congrats, yaar!" I said, full of fake heartiness. "What an amazing party."

"Thanks," Sid said. "Have you met Nushki yet?" He nodded in the direction of his fiancée.

"Oh, she's probably met so many people," I said. "I'll say hello later. At the wedding, maybe?"

"The wedding's in Goa," Sid said. "Mama's booked two hundred rooms on Calangute Beach."

"Wow."

"It'll be a mad scene," he said, making it sound like a chore.

"Awesome. Cool. Achcha, listen, do you have a smoke?"

Sid patted his pockets. "Looks like I'm out."

"Oh, okay," I said, a bit disappointed. "Never mind."

"I have a pack in my room," he said, looking at me.

"Ooh, if you're going inside, can I come with you?" I asked, placing a hand on his arm.

"Why?" Sid shot a reassuring grin at Anushka, who'd begun to stare at us. She smiled back, not looking reassured at all. The vein on her forehead throbbed like a hungry python. "Why can't you smoke out here like the rest of us?"

"I'd prefer to smoke in your bedroom so there's no chance anyone might see."

"For fuck's sake, who cares?" Sid said, appalled.

"Well, my dad would be pissed if he caught me. 'Girls from good families don't smoke,' after all," I said, scratching quotation marks in the air with a stage whisper.

"You don't count, though. No one wants to, like, marry you," Sid said. "Okay, fine. Come on."

Our progress toward Sid's house was slowed by guests constantly stopping Sid to congratulate him, their faces cracked in ecstatic smiles. Sid had a way of receiving praise that I had to admire, like it was only natural, like every day was his birthday. I lingered in Sid's shadow. Waiters with trays full of canapés and drinks nudged past me. I took a glass of wine. The dance floor blared Bollywood wedding hits.

Sheila Sehgal materialized from the crowd like a figure pulled out of clay. She grabbed Sid's arm and whispered. Sid didn't seem to resist as his mother steered him toward a prominent local politician and his wife. "This is my son, Siddharth," she said. Sid dived to touch the couple's feet, his expression morphing smoothly from arrogance to subservience.

"Thank you, Uncle, Aunty, for coming tonight," Sid said, straightening up.

"Of course, of course," said the politician, slapping Sid on the back. "Your father and I go back many years." He nodded. "And congratulations on your MBA. Harvard, was it?"

"Wharton, sir."

"You know, we could use more smart young men like you in our party."

"Maharashtra has never had a leader like you, sir," Sid said. "I've promised Papa that Anushka and I would help him with his business."

"And is that Anushka?" the wife asked, smiling when she noticed me lurking between an outcropping of sofas. "Hello!"

"Oh no," Sheila said, whipping around. "That's... a family friend." She gave me a pained smile. "Noomi, what are you doing there all by yourself?"

"Just... taking a break," I said, sipping my wine. "Please, carry on."

"I'm sorry Sheila ji, but we must be going," the politician said. "I have an early flight."

"We are so happy that you came tonight." Sheila joined her hands in a namaste.

"Sir, you look so familiar," I said. "Were you the one who called South Indians Africans? Because of their darker skin color? During one of your tevelized... televished... one of your speeches on TV."

"Are you a journalist?" the politician asked. He looked around as if expecting an ambush.

"Don't mind her, ji. She's had too much to drink," Sheila said, then turned to her son. "Siddharth, go find Noomi some coffee."

Grabbing my hand, Sid flicked his head toward the house. "Come on."

I saw Sid for the first time when he drove up in his big white car to pick Ammu up one day in ninth grade. He pushed his Ray-Bans onto his head and waved to her from the driver's side. Ammu's friends, envious, had whispered, "Is that your boyfriend?" Ammu had wrinkled her nose and said, "Eww! That's my cousin Sid. Our moms are sisters." Sitting a few feet away on the school parapet, flagrantly ignored by Ammu and her new friends, I hooked my ankle on the metal railing. My legs were the only part of my body I didn't hate. I was careful to show as much leg as I could without coming off as vulgar. Sid didn't notice. He and Ammu drove off in his white car with black-tinted windows. Then Sid began to cruise by school at dismissal. I realized that he had, in fact, noticed. He was seventeen, while I was fourteen, and very stupid.

One night, my parents were out. The phone rang. Sid's voice was like sand warmed by the sun.

"I love you," he said.

"What?"

"I love you."

I laughed. "Okay. Thanks. I'm hanging up."

"Meet me tomorrow after school," Sid said. "I'll take you for a drive in my car."

I thought about how Ammu looked at me nowadays, with a mix of pity and irritation.

"Okay," I said. "I'll wait for you by the bus stop. Don't be late."

"I won't," Sid said. "Bye, baby."

After months of sneaking around after school to make out half naked in the back seat of his car, Sid said he wanted to bring me home. It was the end of exams. That day, as usual, I pretended to wait for the school bus and then hid as it harrumphed away in the hot afternoon sun. A little way from the bus stop, a street vendor splashed a fistful of water over his bright mangoes. My stomach rumbled. To kill time while I waited for Sid, I bought six slices sprinkled with salt and chili powder and wrapped in a banana leaf. I gave the man a ten-rupee note, and he dropped two shiny rupee coins into my palm. Out of habit, I went over and gave the coins to an old woman who begged by the bus stand. She'd been begging for years, but nobody knew who she was. Her thin sari was a cobweb draped over her collarbones. Her gray hair had been tied into two long, dirty plaits. Madness had shaken all the words out of the woman's head like coconuts from a tree, leaving one phrase, which she repeated over and over: "Dey." *Give.*

"Dey," the old woman said as the coins fell in her lap, and spat on the ground. Her foamy gob raised a small puff of dust. The woman sat leaning against a wall decorated with tiles of gods and a sign that said NO SPITTING OR URINATION. At the other end, a man in a polyester shirt urinated noisily. He finished, gave himself a shake, a squeeze, and zipped up with a bob. Then he sauntered over.

"Nice mangoes," he said, leering down my shirt with a paan-stained grin.

Fear rose in me like a scream—fear that boils over when you realize you've once again stupidly, thoughtlessly, put your body in harm's way. Women feel this fear more than men. I glanced at the mango seller, hoping he'd do something before the man put his hand down my shirt, or worse.

The mango seller seemed hesitant to get involved, murmuring, "Leave her alone."

The man said, "Teri biwi hai kya, behenchod?" *Is she your wife or something, sister-fucker?*

The mango seller came from behind his cart with his fruit knife, holding his dhoti. He looked at me as if to say, *Why didn't you get on the fucking bus?* Fear, it seems, can be catching—like a common cold. The two men and I stood in an isosceles triangle. I stared at the knife the mango seller had gripped in his hand, feeling guilty for making them fight. There was no way to go back to the school for help. I'd have to answer angry questions of why I wasn't on the bus in the first place. Not knowing what else to do, I was about to scream, when Sid's car drove up in a cloud of ocher dirt. The men dispersed like alley cats. When Sid opened the car door to let me in, loud music blasted out, startling a flock of sparrows sitting on the bus stand's tin roof. I got in hurriedly. Sid made a fast U-turn that I think was illegal. He was seventeen and didn't have a license, but he didn't worry much about following traffic rules. The cops were in his father's pocket.

"Had a good day?" Sid asked, trailing a finger down the length of my arm.

"You're late," I said, breathless. "Where were you?"

"Why? What happened?" He frowned.

"Nothing," I said. "Waiting at the bus stop gets a bit boring, that's all." Something in his voice warned me not to say anything. Rule number one of being a girl: we were like medicine bottles. If our seals were broken, we had to be returned. It was important to appear untampered with at all times.

Sid pinched my chin. "Let me know if someone's ever giving you trouble, and I'll kick his face in. Now forget about the bus stop."

"Okay," I said. I pulled down the visor mirror to see how I looked. "Ugh, my skin looks so blotchy."

I took out a small tube of concealer from my backpack and patted some under my eyes with the tip of one finger. I was about to put on a bit of mascara, when Sid yanked the wand from my hand, rolled down his window, and threw it out.

"Why'd you do that?" I asked.

"I've told you a hundred times," Sid said, "I hate it when you use makeup. It looks cheap."

"That mascara wasn't cheap," I said with a frown.

"Forget it. I'll buy you some new clothes or something, okay? Now, how was school today?" Sid asked.

"Uneventful." I shrugged. "I suck at exams. I know the answers, but a clock turns me into an idiot. Luckily, Krish totally let me cheat off his answers. He scribbled them on his eraser and dropped it on the floor near my foot." I laughed. "Micro–cheat sheets. I have no idea how he learned that."

"Who the fuck is Krish?"

"You know Krish," I said with a smile. "He's my study partner. The boy with the huge Adam's apple."

"Oh, that skinny nerd." Sid rolled his eyes. "Listen, I want you to ask them to pair you with a girl."

"But Krish is gay," I said.

"How do you know he's gay?"

"He told me!"

"He's just trying to get close to you." Sid shook his head. "I know how these horny bastards think."

"He is *gay*," I said. "And you're going to make me fail ninth grade, because you're always so jealous."

"Protective," Sid corrected me, pushing his Ray-Bans to the top of his head, where his gelled, spiky hair held them in place. "My dad said..." He looked at me. His eyes, light brown with flecks of green, and his fair skin marked him as high caste, a drop of ancestral wrong-side-of-the-blanket Portuguese merchant blood running in his veins. "He said"—and here Sid made his voice raspy like his father's—"'No point stressing yourself out with studies when you're going to inherit my huge business. I've worked hard all *my life* so that my son can enjoy his life.'"

"How lucky." I pouted and crossed my arms. "Wish my dad was that rich."

"Don't worry, baby. You'll marry a rich guy one day." Sid smiled.

I smiled back: *Whatever could you mean? Please elaborate.*

"Are you excited to meet my mom?" Sid asked.

"I wonder how she convinced my parents to let me come over during midterms," I said.

"Oh please," Sid scoffed. "No one says no to Sheila Sehgal ever. Everyone is too terrified of her."

"Should *I* be terrified of her?"

"She asked," Sid said, and his voice took on a cautious edge, "if you were like your mother at all." He looked at me. "What do you think about that question?" He took my hand.

"It's fair, I guess," I said with a nod. A pebble formed in my throat. If my life were a garden, my mother would be the vines, strangling everything.

Sid's house was the largest on the street. In the corner of the lawn opposite the gazebo, with its sweet-smelling mango, frangipani, and chikoo trees, was a fountain with a lotus pond. Every day, Sheila picked out a single lotus to set at the feet of the gods in the house temple. The living room, which we entered through a short hallway, had a floor-to-ceiling mirror, gilded and clouded to look antique. There was more gold on the armchairs and the sofas, upholstered in muted shades of gray and white velvet. In the corner, by the gold bar, was a floor lamp made of white ostrich feathers.

Sid led me up a flight of marble stairs to a family room, where we found his mother curled up on a white sofa, watching television. Sheila was perfectly coiffed, and her off-white trousers had sharp press lines down the front. The thick-framed glasses perched on the tip of her nose were Burberry, as was the stole wrapped around her shoulders. Issey Miyake perfume hung in the air like an aria.

In contrast to her thoroughly modern appearance, the show Sheila seem engrossed in was a popular Hindi soap opera full of horribly sexist stereotypes: the dutiful wife, the vamp in red lipstick, the girl-friend in a miniskirt, the book nerd in a salwar kurta and glasses. The women spent all their time scheming for the attention of the men. The men seemed happily oblivious.

Sid, crossing the room in two steps, practically leaped into his mother's arms.

"My Sidoo," Sheila said, squeezing his face. "Where have you been all day?"

Sid looked up at me, smiled, and said, "Mama, this is Noomi."

"Ah," Sheila said pleasantly enough. "Noomi. Welcome."

"Thank you, Sheila Aunty," I said with a smile. "It's so wonderful to meet you. Sid talks about you all the time." Something in Sheila's gaze told me that I was hunching. But straightening up drew attention to my breasts, my least favorite body part. I'd given everything a rank. My legs were number one, breasts were number ten. My nose was a solid three and a half. I clutched my backpack to my chest.

"Sid hasn't told me much about you at all," Sheila said. "Now I can find out for myself."

"Of course, Aunty," I said, and giggled stupidly. "Feel free to ask me anything."

"Oh, I will, don't worry. I don't need your permission."

Sheila smiled and pressed a button on the table. Within minutes, a brown-uniformed man appeared at the door.

"Ramu, we're coming downstairs for lunch," Sheila ordered, not looking at Ramu but at the television screen.

"Ji, madamji," Ramu said, and bowed out of the room.

"Come on, children," Sheila said. The soap opera's credits began to roll as she pressed the off button. "Oh"—she pointed to my backpack, which I was hugging like a teddy bear—"leave that here."

The dining room had white-and-blue porcelain vases and white silk screens painted with cranes. The napkin on my lap was white, as were the orchids tumbling out of a white marble urn. Sheila's love of white seemed intentional. She could keep the white untouched by the besmirching sweat and dust that plagued the city's poor laborers and stained the armpits of middle-class office-goers.

"So," Sheila said, as Ramu laid out dishes, "tell me something interesting about yourself."

"Well," I said, making folds in the napkin on my lap, "I like to read. I write poetry sometimes."

Sheila groaned. "I said interesting. All this poetry-showetry flies above my head."

"Noomi is a really good singer, Mom," Sid said, and winked. "Ask her to sing something for you."

"What? No! He's joking. That's not true, Aunty," I said. "I'm a terrible singer."

There was a glint in Sheila's eyes, like a knife catching the light. "Let's hear you sing."

"Come on, Noomi," Sid said with a grin.

"No, please," I said. "When I start singing, dogs howl." My face began to feel warm.

"Sing." Sheila's voice took on a flinty quality, but her expression remained pleasant.

I sang an old Bollywood song, wincing as my voice cracked like an adolescent boy's. I glanced at Sheila and Sid. Their twin expressions of amusement made me want to weep. Still, I swallowed my anger and kept singing, screwing my eyes shut so that I wouldn't leak tears.

Then, in the middle of my song, I heard Sheila yell, "Ramu, you bloody idiot!"

My eyes flapped open. Ramu's face hovered above me, blanched in confusion. Down one of Sheila's white trouser legs ran a long smear. By her foot was the errant spoon that must have escaped when Ramu was serving her a very maroon curry.

"Do you know how much these pants cost?" Sheila screamed again. "They're worth more than what I pay you in a whole year." She threw her napkin at his chest. "I should take it out of your salary."

Ramu clasped his hands over his midriff. He bent at the waist, his head lowered and tilted to one side. "Madamji, I'm so sorry," he begged. "Please, I will clean it up." He dipped a napkin in a glass of water and approached her.

"Don't you dare," Sheila yelled in accented Hindi. "I'll fire you on the spot."

Sid's eyes met mine. He gave a sideways glance at his mother and mouthed, "Do something."

"Sheila Aunty," I said, rising from my chair. "Lily Mama has a stain remover formula that gets rid of absolutely everything. Give me your pants. I'll send them back in perfect condition."

Sheila seemed to mull this over, arms folded. "I want them back tomorrow."

"Yes, of course," I said, gesturing to Ramu to back off with the wet napkin. "Tomorrow."

"Say thank you," Sheila said to Ramu. "She's saved your job."

"Thank you, Babyji," Ramu said.

Giving him a curt nod, I followed Sheila out the door.

"You did so well," Sid said a few minutes later. On the pretext of retrieving my backpack from upstairs, we'd snuck into his bedroom. "My mom likes you—I can tell. That's no easy feat."

"She wasn't impressed by my singing," I said with a frown. "Or my love of poetry."

A delicious smell emanated from Sid's body. Every time he moved, scent molecules dispersed, and I got another whiff.

"I didn't mean to sound snooty or superior or anything."

"I love girls who read," Sid said.

"Really?"

"Sure," he said. A look drifted across his face. "Well-read girls have great imaginations... it makes them wild in bed."

He pushed me up against a tennis poster. I slipped away from him. "All my work in impressing your mother will go to waste."

"You're right," Sid said. He took my backpack from the foot of his bed and swung it on his shoulder. "I'll save it for the car." He held my hand and we cantered down the stairs like a pair of colts.

An hour later, Sid parked in our usual spot on the far edge of Rani Lake. It began to drizzle. Circles appeared and disappeared on the water's still surface.

"Do you know," I said, distracted as Sid began unbuttoning my shirt, "that my nani, my mother's mother, had a peculiar word for 'lake.' She used to call it a 'chashma.' That means 'mirror,' doesn't it?"

"Um," Sid said, clearly not interested in talking. "I think it means 'spectacles.'" He undid a few more buttons.

"No, that's in Hindi," I persisted, brushing his hand away gently. "I think in Urdu it means 'looking glass.' Isn't that pretty? A lake is a mirror made of rain."

I stared out at the glittering water. My mother didn't talk much about her parents—they'd died when I was a baby. She did, one time, say that she had trouble sleeping because, as a child, she had to sleep with her fingers in her ears to block out the sound of her father whipping her mother with the metal part of his suspenders. Even now, any sudden, loud noise could make her jump out of a chair.

"No, babe," Sid said. "'Chashma' means 'spectacles.' 'Aina' means 'mirror,' okay? Now stop talking, please."

A policeman strolled by, twirling his lathi. Sid, cool as a melon, gave him a nod. The policeman tapped a finger to his black topi and sauntered off.

"Relax, my dad is friends with the police commissioner," Sid said, when I gave him a look. "They all know my car. But still, it doesn't hurt to hand out a little bribe once in a while."

"Really? Who else do you come here with?"

"Just you, sweetheart," Sid said, putting my hand to his crotch. "Just you."

Sid put his hands behind my head and pushed me down. I open-ed my mouth and put my lips around his penis. Sid moaned like he was having a sex dream. I suggested that maybe we should do it? Sid bolted upright, opened his glove compartment, and pulled out a condom. He tore the wrapper with his teeth and rolled it on while holding the tip. "That's so no air gets trapped," he explained knowledgeably.

We shifted to the back seat. I remembered to cry out in surprise as he entered me. I could see from the look on his face that it made Sid feel very manly. We found a rhythm. I began, to my actual surprise, to enjoy it. It dawned on me that the sex I'd had with Arjun was not very good, despite him being very beautiful. His face popped, uninvited, into my head. Before I realized what I was doing, I'd whispered his name—right in Sid's ear.

"What?" Sid said, realizing that the name I'd whispered wasn't his.

"Nothing," I said, pulling him back on top of me. "Keep going."

"You said Arjun." Sid raised his voice. "Who the fuck is Arjun?"

"Ammu's brother?" I bit my tongue. I should have lied.

"My cousin Arjun?" Sid screeched. "Arjun? You fucked him? My fucking cousin?"

"No," I said, getting up, "you don't understand." With a blind hand, I fished out my underwear from between the gaps in the seat. I did up my buttons. "It was a stupid one-way crush."

"Why did you say his name like that?" Sid twisted my arm behind my back. "Tell me."

"Ow, Sid," I cried. "You're hurting me."

"Tell me the fucking truth."

"Okay, okay! We had sex, but he wasn't my boyfriend," I burst out. "Please, I'm sorry."

A hand slammed down on the window. I yelped and threw myself, still half naked, to the car floor. Sid dove back into the driver's seat. He pulled his T-shirt over his head, zipped his fly, fixed his hair, and got out. I heard him talk in rapid-fire Marathi with the policeman, whose hand stayed resting on the car window. After a few minutes, he got back in.

"Keep your head down," he snarled. "It's some new guy. I've given him a few hundred rupees, but he wants more."

By the time we got to my house, I'd cried so much my eyes began to hurt. I'd ruined it.

"I'm sorry, I'm sorry," I blubbered, my body wedging the car door open.

"Shut the fuck up," Sid said. He pushed me away. I stumbled backward a few steps. "You told me about Arjun to hurt me. You're a whore like your mother."

He slammed the door shut.

S id slammed his bedroom door, cutting off the faraway noise of the party. I turned with a little start. "Shush!" I said. "What will people think if they knew we were in here?"

Feelings, it turns out, are harder to get rid of than a turmeric stain on a white kurta. While Sid and I never did get back together, some part of me had always remained infatuated with him. We'd continued to hook up every few months—in Sid's case mainly because sleeping with most Kamalpur women without a commitment could get you taken out by their menfolk, and in my case, sleeping with an ex-boyfriend was one way to keep my "number" low.

"What'll they think? They'll think that you"—Sid grinned—"are a slut. I'm the golden boy, remember?"

Sid's bedroom was unrecognizable from the last time I'd been there. But it smelled the same. His bed still had white sheets and a snowy comforter. Above it hung framed photo collages: Sid with his parents somewhere in Europe, Sid making a toast at an American wedding, Sid in New York City with his arms around his Burberry-shawl-clad mother. Happy memories like cash in the bank. In the corner opposite the bed was a flat-screen TV with video game remotes scattered at its base. On the bedside table was an ashtray filled with cigarette butts—the only disorderly object in the room.

Sid rolled open a bedside drawer and took out a fresh pack of cigarettes. The wrapping crackled as he crushed it in his hand and tossed it into a wastebasket. He pulled out a long, slim white tube, tapped the filter on the face of his watch, and handed it to me with a lighter.

"Thanks," I said. I lit the cigarette and took a drag.

"You still can't keep your mouth shut." Sid grinned, moving closer.

"It pissed you off? Wasn't that politician fellow, like, your dad's low-level tout back in the nineties? I remember seeing him running around with a whisky bottle at these types of parties."

"Yeah, well," Sid said, "now he *is* the government. He can block our construction projects."

"Sorry," I said, ashing the cigarette and taking another long drag. "I guess things change."

"Life is a seesaw." Sid said. He opened the drawer again and took out a baggie of coke this time. He chopped out a line on the glass with his credit card and, hunching over, snorted it. Then he looked at me and smiled. I wondered if Sid's fiancée was looking for him. Although I hoped no one saw us go into the bedroom, I knew hoping was pointless. In the world I was from, there was always someone to see you when you least wanted to be seen.

"How's life?" Sid said, brushing my cheek. "I don't know anything about your life. So mysterious."

"And I know everything about your life," I said.

"So does everyone else," Sid smiled. "My life's an open book."

If I were perfectly honest, tonight felt like a humiliation. Which was ridiculous. Sid and I broke up many years ago. But he was engaged, while I remained pathologically single. "What's Anushka like?" I asked, hoping I didn't sound like I cared. Suddenly, I wanted to get out of this room, leave this party, get away from Kamalpur, from everyone, forever.

"She's lovely," Sid said. "Her parents and mine are good friends."

Someone laughed outside the door. We both looked up. I saw the shadow of feet walking away from the gap.

"Why haven't I ever seen you with her?" I asked. "At parties or whatever."

"She's been studying abroad," Sid said with a smile. "NYU. I like smart girls, remember? And also, her parents are super-conservative. That's why she escaped to New York. To have some fun. You've probably seen her house. It's the big white one in Frazer Town with all the security guards."

"Yeah," I said miserably. "I know the house. They must be very rich."

"They are, they are," Sid said, and wiggled his fingers for my cigarette. He glanced down at my hardworking blouse like it was a present he'd like to unwrap. I felt a not unpleasant flutter in my chest.

"What?" I asked.

"You know what," Sid said, smiling.

"What? *At your engagement party?* Are you crazy?"

"Come on. You're excited. Don't deny it," he said. With the flat of his hand, he pushed me down until I lay on the bed. He took the cigarette from between my outstretched fingers and stubbed it in the ashtray.

Halfway into being undressed by Sid, I felt my heart thumping nastily and had to sit back up for air.

Sid propped himself up on a pillow. "What's up?" he asked. "You okay?"

"I feel dizzy," I said, putting a hand to my head. "I think that bhang's finally kicking in." I turned to look at him. "I think we should go back. I'm feeling weird and floaty."

"Float back down," Sid said, pulling me by the wrist. "Just let me finish."

Sid got on top of me. Soon, my sari was bunched up at the waist and my bra lay across my neck. "We should go back," I said, trying to push him off with my legs.

"Listen," Sid said, putting his weight on me. "If Mama finds you in here, you're dead."

"How would she find out?" I said, feeling sick.

"I'm saying," Sid said slowly, as if explaining things to a child, "if my mom finds out we were fucking at my engagement to Anushka, *her best friend's daughter*, forget about being invited to the wedding, you will be on her blacklist till the day you die. Okay? So, let's finish. Then you go out first, and no one will find out what you did."

I let myself go limp. The floaty feeling got stronger. I felt myself waft up to the ceiling and stand there, upside down. I watched upside-down Sid's perfect buttocks bobbing over my body. Sid wore two rings on his right hand on the advice of the family astrologer: a yellow sapphire for success and a pearl for his temper. Their coldness left lines of goose bumps on my skin, like a plane's contrails in the sky. When he'd pushed me down, they'd bit against my rib cage.

"My god, you're so dry," Sid panted. He put his head between my legs, then thrust two fingers into me, pulled them out, and pushed them into my mouth. "Here, taste yourself," he said.

I floated back down after what seemed like hours, and he was still at it. Waiting for him to finish, I saw a sunset sitting on top of a cloud.

It turned out to be the bedside lamp. The cloud was Sid's fluffy duvet. I turned my face toward the orange sun and pretended I'd slipped between it and the white cloud. I wasn't there. I was flying.

The dholak player stood in the center of a crowd in the marble driveway, his massive drum, like the cocoon of a giant insect, hanging from his shoulders by a broad leather strap. He wore an orange kurta and dhoti, and there was a long tilak on his forehead, an exclamation point. He whacked the drum with his curved metal rods. Invisible people standing on the rooftop emptied sack after sack of white, red, and orange petals onto the crowd dancing below.

I made a half-hearted attempt to fix myself up. My sari was far more disastrous than before. I was too wasted to care. I wanted to dance, to show them all that I was more alive, more full of beauty, than any of them could ever be. The dholak's music was enthralling, like an animal's wild heartbeat. I took off my heels and ran across the wet lawn to the driveway. I ran into Sheila and Anushka. They stared at me, faces pinched with displeasure, dressed identically in chiffon and feathers, like a pair of angry flamingos. Sheila grabbed my wrist and pulled me aside.

"Who the hell do you think you are, huh?" she said, digging her nails into my skin.

"What?" I said, trying to focus on her face. "Sheila Aunty, let go. I want to dance."

Sheila yanked me so close, I could smell her tequila-warmed breath. "I told Sid to take you into the house and sober you up. When he didn't return to the party, I came inside to find out why. You were in the bedroom and the door was locked." Her lips curled into a belittling snarl. "You think you can do whatever you want? Look at that poor girl." She gestured to Anushka, standing apart from us with tears leaking from her huge eyes. "Can't you care about anyone but yourself, Noomi?"

I tried to yank my hand away. "No," I laughed. "I can't. Now let me go."

"You don't deserve to be here with us," Sheila said. "You are sick. Demented."

"What?"

"What? What?" Sheila mimicked. "Listen to me carefully. I don't care what happens to you, I don't care if you get crushed under someone's heel like a fucking cockroach. But Anushka is like a daughter to me. So, if I see you try to interfere with Sid and her again, I will make sure that your father knows what happened tonight. Do you understand? Do you want him to find out what kind of a bitch you are? Poor man, he's already got so much on his plate with your mother. Do you want to add to that?"

"No," I said, feeling burning insects start to crawl all over my brain. "Please, let me go."

Sheila didn't let go of my hand so much as throw it away in disgust. "Then go."

I nodded. Sheila hugged Anushka. They seemed to meld together into one strange and glamorous bird, all feathers and diamonds and chiffon. Anushka gave her future mother-in-law a look full of love and gratitude. I turned away from them and ran off in the direction of the music. I pulled Ammu to me and began to dance with her inside the storm of rose petals, not caring if the pleats of my sari unraveled or if my pallu shifted to reveal the gaps in my ugly, ill-fitting blouse. I danced barefoot, on the marble floor slick with petals. I bumped into Adil and almost toppled over, laughing.

"Noomi, your dad has been looking for you everywhere," Adil said, pointing at Jeh, who stood on the side of the driveway with a strange look in his eyes. "Are you okay?"

"Daddy! Come dance with me!" I said. I rushed up to Jeh and tried to bring him to the floor.

"I think it's time to go home," Jeh said. He gripped my hand. "You don't look okay."

"No!" I yelled. "I'm fine. Dance with me na, please."

I began to yank him onto the floor. Jeh's face lit up with anger. He jerked his hand away. I lost my balance. I stumbled forward. The marble floor came rushing up to meet my face.

Darkness.

My whole childhood, I'd believed that if Asha just vanished, somehow all our troubles would vanish along with her. When she was late coming home, I hoped it was because her car had crashed into a truck. When she slept, I'd put a finger under her nose, hoping not to feel her breath. I wanted to be released from the prison of my shame. I wanted to not, when I looked in the mirror, see my mother's face.

Somewhere above my head, I heard Jeh shouting, "Noomi! Get up!" I tried to open my eyes, but there was only darkness, the smell of flowers, and the beating of the dholak.

They took me inside the gazebo and laid me out on the beige sofa. I opened my eyes. Faces loomed over me. My father, Sheila Sehgal, and a man I didn't recognize. He flashed a pen light and asked me where I was, what day it was, who the prime minister was. He seemed satisfied with my answers.

Jeh pulled me to my feet and said we'd be leaving.

"Shouldn't you go to the hospital first?" Sheila asked. "My driver can take you."

"Thank you," Jeh said with a little nod. "But I think she just needs to get home."

"What's your opinion, Dr. Kumar?" Sheila turned to the man holding the pen light.

"She looks okay to me," he said. "Had too much to drink. She's taken after her mother, it seems." He gave a malicious little chuckle. "Nothing to worry about except a bad hangover."

Jeh managed a smile. "Thank you, Sheila. Sorry that we ruined the party."

"Oh, nonsense, Jeh," Sheila said, patting his shoulder. "I'm just sorry you couldn't enjoy yourself."

Sheila sounded considerate. No sign of the person who, just a half hour ago, had been threatening me with all kinds of humiliation. Even in my state, I couldn't help but be impressed at how Sheila could tame her rage like a circus lion.

Jeh took me by my arm, trying to look like he was in control of things, as he walked me out the glass door. I stared at my wild-eyed reflection. I looked like a churail, a she-demon.

When we got home, I tore off my sari. Bundling it in my hands, I threw it in a corner. I began to pull out clothes from my closet hangers to dump them into a suitcase. Jeh came in, wearing crumpled pajamas. He looked surprised, as if he had expected to find me asleep. Yet here I was, at 3:00 A.M., full of energy, stuffing clothes into a suitcase.

"What the hell are you doing?" Jeh asked.

"I'm leaving," I said, throwing a toothbrush into the bag.

"Leaving? To go where?"

"Bombay."

"But why? And where will you stay?"

"In a hotel until I can find a sublet or a flat share or something."

"So, this is your very mature reaction to tonight's behavior, huh?" Jeh folded his arms across his chest. "Running away." He made a shooing motion with his hands. "Do you know how embarrassed I was tonight? No, Noomi, look at me. Like it or not, we live in a particular context, and we must live with decorum."

"Do you hear yourself?" I screamed. "You sound like some pearl-clutching housewife from the fifties. You talk about decorum. Where's your decorum, huh? Where's your dignity? You're spineless. You won't stand up to anyone. You let people run us down, taunt us, belittle us. I'm tired of it. Mom is drinking herself sick every day and you won't do a fucking thing about it!"

"What do you expect me to do? Lock her up? Throw her out on the street?" Jeh yelled. Lowering his voice, he added, "Asha is my responsibility. She has no one in the world but me."

"What about me?" I said. "Don't you see what she's done to me? Are you blind or just really stupid? You stayed with her, and you abandoned *me*. Now I'm abandoning you." I went to Jeh by the doorway, pushed him aside, and walked out of the bedroom.

"Where are you going?" Jeh asked, scrambling after me.

"To get another suitcase from your room," I said. "And some whisky."

"Noomi, if you dare drink," Jeh warned, "I will kick you out myself."

"Perfect," I said, running ahead of him.

In Jeh's bedroom—which was not Asha's bedroom—I pulled a dusty suitcase from the top of his closet. I felt about in his sock drawer until I found the bottle of expensive Scotch he hid there. Stupid Jeh, he lived in a house of thieves and didn't lock up his treasures. I uncorked the bottle and took a deep swig. Something moved in the corner of my vision. For a second I thought Asha had woken up. I turned to look; it was only me, reflected in the closet's long mirror.

"Give me that," Jeh said, trying to grab the bottle. Drops spilled on the floor as we tussled back and forth. I gripped its neck and pulled it from between Jeh's sweaty palms. Aiming for the mirror, I threw the bottle, and when it crashed on the glass a spiderweb of cracks appeared. Hundreds of Noomis stared back at me. I swiveled, triumphant. Jeh's hands went up to his face as sobs moved through his body.

It was the first time in my life I'd seen Jeh cry. His grief held no artifice, like a child whose toys had been smashed by someone big and mean. It was the saddest sound I'd ever heard. If I left tonight, that sound would haunt me for the rest of my life.

"Daddy," I said, rubbing the top of his shoulder. "I won't go anywhere. I was just angry."

Jeh mashed away his tears with the heel of his hand. "Don't do this to me. My heart can't take it."

"I'm sorry," I said again. "I love you. I don't know what else to say."

This was Jeh, who'd read to me in funny voices, who'd get up in the middle of the night if I had a stomachache, who'd lift me onto his shoulders in the street if I was too tired to walk. Who—when I felt so anxious that I forgot how to breathe—would open my palm and trace its outline. "When I go up your fingers, you breathe in, okay?" he'd say. "And now, hold your breath." I'd puff out my cheeks. "Now, as I trace down, you breathe out, slowly, slowly." He'd do this as many times as it took me to calm down.

"It's been a long night," Jeh said, covering himself with a blanket. "I'm exhausted."

I lay next to Jeh, watching his side rise and fall. His face became a mask of sleep. I picked up his hand and kissed his knuckles. "I love you," I whispered. "I'm sorry."

The next day, midafternoon, Asha was in her bedroom as usual with Aunty Rhea, lolling on her bed, surrounded by empty glasses, newspapers, ashtrays, handbags, and a stack of unopened letters and bills. Cigarette smoke drifted into the hallway like a lost guest at a wedding.

"Noomi bachche," Rhea said when I walked in. "Come sit with us. Did you just wake up, lazy girl?"

The walls of the bedroom were washed with sunlight. It made the bottles on Asha's drinks trolley sparkle like some sort of city. Asha was propped up with pillows, holding an empty glass on which she tapped her ring, a signal to Rhea to make her another drink. Her face looked tender, like an overripe fruit. From experience, I knew she was at that point where the alcohol made her calm, just before it began to make her angry, and long before it made her sad.

Rhea rose from the bed and strolled over to the trolley. She smiled at me and began to pour whisky into a peg measure. The first three buttons of her silk shirt were undone. A thin gold chain linked with tiny white diamonds lay against her pale skin. To match the mole on her cheek, there was another beautiful one on her collarbone. I cleared my throat. Rhea looked up at me. Alcohol overflowed from the measure. Shaking her hand dry, she beckoned me over, holding up another glass. I glanced over at Asha, who gave a noncommittal shrug.

"What should I drink?" I said, and picked up the bottle of Lagavulin to admire its amber light.

"Nah-ah-ah," Rhea said, taking the whisky from my hand. "Too expensive for you." She poured Old Monk into my glass, followed by Thums Up. "Rum and Coke. Nice and sweet."

It *was* sweet. I drank it down in big, thirsty gulps. The rum lit my brain like a match to a candlewick. I finished it and made myself another, stronger drink. Taking their glasses, Rhea joined Asha on the bed. It wasn't hard to see why Asha drank the way she did, I thought, as I began to fill up with a delicious peace. Who'd want to feel like heartache on legs when you could feel like *this*. Alcohol was a hug, a song, a conversation in a bottle. Like religion, music, art, it eased the symptoms of living in this world as a woman.

I once saw a video online about an experiment called "Rat Park." Scientists had offered rats two choices of water bowls: one regular, one laced with opiates. They noted that the isolated rats went for the drug water, while the ones with wheels and other rats for company chose the water without drugs. They'd concluded that addictive substances activated the same parts of the brain as love.

Why drink? It was something to do. Life was boring and terrifying at the same time.

I had a portable loneliness that I carried with me and plonked down on tables like a heavy purse.

But there really is no need for a *why*. You drank when happy, sad, frightened, bored, angry. It was a part of you, an arm or a leg. If it were gone, the phantom ache would keep you up at night.

I dragged Asha's velvet dressing table pouf over. "What's new, Rhea Aunty?" I asked.

"I was telling your mother about the party," Rhea said, taking a sip of her drink.

I nodded. "Yes?"

"Such a good-looking couple, no?" Rhea said. "Can you imagine how gorgeous their babies will be? Oof." She rolled her eyes. "I heard their parents arranged the match. That always works out for the best, na? First the families should see if they get along."

"I suppose." I said.

Rhea glanced sideways. "Your mother doesn't think so."

I regarded my mother, who blew smoke out of the side of her mouth and flicked ash into her Murano bowl. Smoke spiraled upward from the cigarette between her fingers. "You make them out to be a pair of pedigree poodles, Rhea," she said, "being mated by their families to breed prize-winning puppies."

When Jeh said he wanted to marry Asha, Zal Papa had screamed, "You're marrying a madhouse!" Jeh, who'd done everything (going to a football-mad boarding school to "toughen up"; pursuing "manly" hobbies like hunting and hiking) to please his father, decided, in his mild-mannered way, to defy him. My parents were married. I was born. Six years later, their marriage fell apart: my mother lost their second baby and had to be put on suicide watch. I remember visiting her in the wards. She was as scrawny as a sparrow. A bird mother. She had to be fed and carried to the bathroom. She wanted me close, but I didn't want her to hold me. It scared me, to feel her ribs through her hospital gown.

"Rhea Aunty," I said, "you've never told me the story of how you ended up marrying your husband. I heard that his family hates you. Didn't they"—I tipped my head to one side—"try to disown him?"

Rhea took a sip of her drink and made a face as if it tasted bitter. She looked up at me. I realized that I'd overplayed my hand.

"I saw you," Rhea said, "at the party last night. You were with someone. I think it was..." Rhea put a finger to her chin and looked at the ceiling. "Siddharth Sehgal?" She leaned forward. "Why did he take you inside the house?" She did a shoddy impression of a scandalized saint. "Was it to sober you up? You looked pretty drunk. Is that why you fell flat on your face later, on the dance floor?"

Asha's eyes gleamed like those of a cat who's spotted a mouse tail as it whisks around the corner. "Were you drunk?" she asked. "So drunk that you fell in front of everyone?" She smirked.

My mother and I were always circling each other like cats in an alley. Some days she had the upper hand, some days I did. Today was not my turn. I decided to leave with what little dignity I had left. "Excuse me," I said, getting up from the pouf. "I think the rum and Cokes have given me a stomachache."

As I walked out, I heard Asha and Rhea giggling.

I changed from my pajamas into a plain cotton dress that hung on a hook behind the bathroom door. It smelled like Shanta Bai had aired it out in the sun. I examined my skin in the mirror. I wasn't sure how I felt about mirrors. I loved how they brightened up a room, echoing light from one wall to the other, but my reflection was another matter. If you stare out at water, you discover things you might've missed at first: birds' nests disguised as holes in the bank, mosquitofish that shimmered and squiggled in the shallows, water skaters tap-dancing ripples with their delicate feet. I couldn't look at myself for long. Blue veins ran below my skin like rivulets. My eyes were pink and small.

An ache spread from my temples. I stuck a finger into my throat to vomit, curling over the sink. Black stuff ran into the drain like spiders. I rinsed my mouth; the water tasted sweet after the acid from my stomach.

Hoping for comfort, I wandered into Shanta Bai's room with a bottle of hair oil. Shanta Bai was at her usual spot by the window, on a chair whose stuffing spilled out through the rips. The television flickered on mute in the background. Shanta Bai held a steaming tumbler of tea in one hand, crumbling up stale bread with the other to feed her squirrel, a half-wild pet. Behind her head, out the window, a white bougainvillea bloomed against the blue sky.

The bougainvillea had been planted when I was six. That was the year my mother hired Shanta Bai to be my ayah. Like most village women, Shanta Bai had never attended school. She was married at the age of twelve to a man twenty years her senior. When she turned eighteen, she left him when he began drinking instead of working and took up a room with her brother and his family. Shanta Bai learned English by working in the homes of families like mine. Her husband's name was tattooed on her arm in green ink. She never spoke it out loud.

Here is a great story about Shanta Bai from that time: Standing on her wooden stool, Shanta Bai liked to fret and mutter over whatever she was cooking. She swore at the dal like it was her nemesis, cursed the ladyfingers, and chastened the chicken curry as she stirred it with a long spoon. On this day, I had come to learn how to make chapatis, but had to wait until Shanta Bai was free to teach me. She threw a handful of red chilis on a pan and they hissed and spat in the oil, and a sharp, peppery aroma stabbed the back of my nose. Her pallu was tied away from the flame. Shanta Bai wore her sari the Maharashtrian way—without a petticoat, with the pleats gathered and looped between the legs and tucked in the back. Her buttocks, quite muscular for someone pushing sixty, looked like a pair of mushroom caps.

At that moment, my aunt Binny sauntered in and picked up an apple from the fruit bowl on the counter. She leaned on the granite, but then seemed to think better of it. Dropping the apple back in the bowl, she held out her white chiffon blouse to inspect it for stains. I went over to chat with a helper who was making samosa patties.

Binny folded her arms over her chest. She cleared her throat once, twice, like an actor in a comedy. Shanta Bai turned the stove to simmer and hopped off the stool, wiping her hands on a towel tucked into her sari. She looked as if she wasn't thrilled to have visitors.

Binny expected people to fall all over themselves to please her, especially the help. Her expression switched from benevolent to haughty.

"Shanta," Binny said, "I heard you have a very clever niece?"

Her niece, a girl of fifteen or sixteen, was Shanta Bai's favorite among her brother's three children. Her grumpy face broke into a smile. "Sumati," she said. "Just passed her board exams."

"Wonderful," Binny said. She passed a glass cabinet and was distracted by her reflection. "Adil's ayah quit yesterday. I need an immediate replacement. Sumati can start working for us next week."

"No. That's not possible." Shanta Bai shook her head hard. "She's going to college. My brother is not going to let her work as an ayah. We've saved money for years to send her."

The kitchen seemed to freeze. The girl folding samosas looked petrified; even the oil ceased to spit. Binny gathered herself up to her full, imposing height, almost a head taller than Shanta Bai.

"That money will be wasted," Binny said. "Who's going to give a girl from her background a job? The daughter of a chowkidar? Please. Send her to me. She'll be well paid." Binny turned and started to walk away. "Better than marrying her off," she said as she opened the kitchen door to exit.

"No."

Binny faltered, then turned slowly around. "You should be careful how you speak to me."

Shanta Bai drew up to *her* full height, all bristling four feet eleven inches. If she were a cat, she would've arched her back and hissed. Pointing her wooden spoon at Binny, she said, in English, "Sumati will never work for you, awful woman!"

It was one of those rare occasions that Binny got what was coming to her. The fact that Shanta Bai wasn't fired on the spot only spoke to how great a cook she was. Her dhansak, which she made by first frying the mutton in ghee, garlic, and onions, brought tears to Zal Papa's eyes. Shanta Bai became my hero as well as my ayah.

I sat down at Shanta Bai's feet. "Give me a tel malish, please," I said, handing her the bottle of oil. The floor was cool under my palms. Shanta Bai's fingers massaging my head were warm and strong.

"Always bothering me, Nooma," Shanta Bai complained lovingly. She poured oil into her hands. I heard the slick noise of her palms rubbing together. I closed my eyes and let my thoughts wander far from the room, into other possibilities, into the sort of life where I could have turned to my mother for comfort.

"I've never thanked you," I said.

"For what?"

"For raising me." I reached for her hand and squeezed. "I wouldn't have survived being a child without you."

"You can thank me by going on your internet to find a nice young man to marry," Shanta Bai said, giving my head a light pat. "Should have his own business... and be handsome, like Chunky Panday."

"Shanta Bai," I said, turning my head to meet eyes as dark as two pieces of coal, "has Mom always been this way? Why don't I have any happy memories of her? Did she even want me to begin with?"

Shanta Bai paused to consider my question and then resumed her kneading. "I think it's because of the child who came after you," she said quietly. "The boy."

"Oh," I said, then paused. "Wait, you said child. I thought that it... it was a miscarriage?"

"He was a baby. When you were little, your mother lost a baby," Shanta Bai said. "He lived for a week. His heart was bad, or was it his lungs?" Shanta Bai shook her head. "I don't remember now. They brought me in to look after you. Your mother refused to. Your father took him to be cremated, carried him in his arms. They covered him with a white handkerchief. He looked like a kitten, so small and broken."

"And my mother?"

"She was never right after that. They'd told her—the doctors, your grandparents—that it was her fault. Even a village woman like me knew that it wasn't. But Lily Mama insisted she'd lost the baby because her mind wasn't strong enough to keep him." Shanta Bai braided my hair back into a shining plait. "And that's when the drinking really got bad."

"Why hasn't anyone ever told me?" I asked, squeezing my head. "Why would they hide this?"

"Ask your father," Shanta Bai said, stroking my head. "What's this?" she asked, slipping an oily finger under Arjun's chain, lifting it from my skin. The gold leaf had come off, showing patches of brass. I'd kept the necklace as a reminder of what men were capable of when they knew no one cared what they did to you. I didn't need that reminder anymore.

I took the necklace off, dropped it in Shanta Bai's palm, and closed her fingers around it.

Confronting Asha was always tricky, and confronting her when she was drunk was a terrible idea, but my feet carried me back to her bedroom. How had Asha, and, for that matter, Jeh, managed to keep such a thing—a dead brother—a secret? *What else have they been hiding?* I wondered, pushing open the bedroom door. The smell of booze was so thick, it felt like smashing into a wall. Asha lay propped on pillows, her long skirt bunched between her legs. As I watched, Rhea, who'd been lying next to her, got up and twisted her body. Rhea pulled out her claw clip, and her hair curtained her face from view. Asha was having a hard time keeping her eyes open. She thrashed a limp hand at Rhea's chest, snagging open the remaining few buttons of her shirt.

Rhea brought her face closer and closer to Asha's. She pried open her mouth with her tongue. I wanted to speak, but something had reached down my throat and stolen my voice. My mother screwed her eyes shut and accepted the kiss. It seemed like she neither liked nor hated it. It was just the price for love of any kind.

I retreated from the room and went to find Jeh. I had no right to be angry, perhaps. Like everyone else, I was a hypocrite. But my rage, as it rushed about to fill the corners of my head, didn't care. I walked into Jeh's room to find him in an armchair, reading, a bowl of white mogras by his elbow. He loved the smell. Jeh picked up a white flower, shook off the water, and put it to his nose, while turning the pages of a leather book embossed with gold print.

"Piglet," Jeh said. "What's going on? Come here, sit with me for a minute."

I sat on the arm of his chair, resting my cheek on the top of his head. Jeh read out loud:

But that the dread of something after death,
The undiscovere'd country from whose bourn
No traveller returns, puzzles the will
And makes us rather bear those ills we have
Than fly to others that we know not of?
Thus conscience does make cowards of us all...

"Isn't that lovely?" Jeh asked, sounding awed. "*Thus conscience does make cowards of us all.*"

"It's not very comforting," I said.

"So what?"

"Dad," I said, closing the book in his hands. "Rhea is here again. They are really, really drunk."

Jeh considered this information for a moment. "Let it be," he said, and put his nose back in his book. "Peace at all costs," he added, when I tried to object. "Your mother will only make a ruckus if I interrupt them. Why cause unpleasantness for no reason, hmm?"

"They're bad for each other," I said. "They're both so... angry."

"You know," Jeh said, turning a page, "as a child, Rhea would come along with her older brother to my birthday parties. My aunt always dressed her in these ugly frocks, the kind they made girls wear back then. On my tenth birthday, I got an air gun. Cyrus, Rhea's brother, and I used my mother's crystal vase for target practice. When we hit it, the vase exploded, pieces of crystal flying out in every direction like birds. My father took out his belt and whipped us with it. Right there, in the middle of the party. I remember Rhea laughing. She was four, or maybe five? A small girl with such a big laugh. It embarrasses me till today, when I remember the sound of that laughter."

"I'm going to call her husband," I said, standing up.

"He won't be happy," Jeh said, resting his head on his knuckles.

I went into my bedroom, exhausted and sick, and fell on my bed. The ceiling had leaf-shaped shadows cast by a tree outside my window. They shivered whenever the wind picked up. It reminded me of the puppets Asha used to make with her hands on the nights she was sober enough to tuck me into bed. I had this terrible, aching need. I wanted her to appear in my doorway. I wished Rhea would leave. I picked up my cell phone and left a message for Rhea's husband, then tossed the phone to the floor. It felt hard to breathe. To calm myself, I did what I used to as a child and imagined that my room was floating in space. That outside my door was a vast nothingness.

I woke up with my heart racing. How long had I been asleep? Minutes? Hours? Screams were pouring out of Asha's bedroom. I ran over and stopped at the doorway, shocked to see Rhea on her hands and knees. Small animal sounds escaped from her lips. Standing over her was her husband with Rhea's hair gathered in his fist. He was trying to pull her off the ground with it, like uprooting a carrot. In the opposite corner, next to the toppled, smashed drinks trolley, was Asha, also screaming, held back by Jeh. I crept to my parents' corner, giving Rhea's husband a wide berth. His face was twisted and cruel.

"Bitch," he snarled, "fucking lying bitch." He slammed the heel of his hand into the top of Rhea's head and began to drag her out of the room. Asha broke free of Jeh and rushed after them, screaming that she would call the police. Jeh scrambled after, trying to grab her by the elbow, his face crumpling in shame. We went downstairs to the driveway. Between handling Asha and trying to get Rhea's husband to stop hitting her, Jeh didn't have a chance to call for help. A pulsating red light of guilt swirled in my head. All I'd said on the phone was that Rhea didn't seem well, could her husband please come pick her up.

"Let her go or I will call the police!" Asha threatened. "I will go to the station myself."

Rhea's husband shoved her headfirst into his car. "Call the fucking cops, whore," he said, and spat on the ground. "I don't care."

"Jeh!" Asha shouted at my father. "How can you let him speak to me like this? Do something!"

"You need to calm down, Asha," Jeh said. "All this screaming and shouting. What will my parents think if they heard it?"

Rhea's husband got into the driver's seat. Jeh took Asha by the arm to steer her gently upstairs, but Asha refused to budge. The car screeched down the driveway and out the front gate. The night was silent again. I saw Zal Papa coming up the driveway toward us in brisk, long strides. Half of his stroke-blighted face was furious, while the other side was calm. He moved with such menace for an old man.

"What the hell is going on?" Zal Papa demanded. "Who was that shouting?" He stared at Asha. She hung off Jeh's arms like a bouquet of dead flowers. I edged closer to them.

"Fucking bastard hurt my friend," Asha sobbed. Her knees buckled.

"It's nothing, Dad, really," Jeh said, pulling her up by the arm. "I'll explain tomorrow."

Zal Papa looked from one distraught face to the other and seemed to weigh whether to let it go or not. He decided on not. "I want to see you both in my office," he said, pointing at Jeh and me. Then looking at Asha, he shouted, "I'm not putting up with this bullshit!" Thick cords in his neck stood up.

"Yes, Dad," Jeh said, nodding. "Of course."

I grabbed Asha's other arm. Jeh and I pulled her back up the stairs. Asha's eyelids drooped as Jeh helped her out of her whisky-smelling clothes. Standing in the doorway, I watched as he put a nightdress over her head and pulled out her arms one sleeve at a time. Burying her face into his chest, Asha cried. Jeh stroked her hair and muttered some soft words, staring at the ceiling.

The doctors suggested Antabuse. We hoped if Asha got violently sick when she drank, perhaps she'd stop. Jeh left it to me to give Asha the pill each night and stand watch until she swallowed it. Deprived of the sugar from the booze, Asha, who normally hated sweets, began to crave them: an encouraging sign. There were other encouraging signs as well. No hidden bottles. No vodka smell. No fights. A month passed, then two, and we let out a slow exhale.

But we'd let our guard down too early. Asha figured out that she could hide the Antabuse in her cheek and spit it into the trash once she was alone. I learned this on the night I showed up in Asha's bedroom without warning. I never went to her room later than 10:00 P.M.—that's when she took her pills. The doctors prescribed more pills each time Asha had a breakdown. These pills were supposed to calm her, but they also made her glassy-eyed and half deaf.

A sign that something was off was that Asha had the TV volume so high I had to plug my ears. The AC was on full blast, and Asha was chattering her teeth under a blanket.

"Ma, you're shivering," I said.

"What?" Asha turned her head, but her eyes stayed fixed on the screen. "Stop mumbling." Her bed was littered with cigarette packs, magazines, overflowing ashtrays, used tissues, and the TV remote by her feet. "Always mumbling. Speak clearly."

"Jeez, Ma, it's cool out, you don't need the AC." I shut it off. I picked up the remote and turned down the volume. As the room warmed up, it slowly began to fill with the reek of alcohol.

"Okay," I said, folding my arms. "Where is it?"

"Where's what?" Asha muttered, lighting a cigarette.

"Where's what?" I mimicked rudely, searching for the bottle in all the usual spots. I couldn't find it. No choice but to walk into my father's bedroom and get him out of bed.

"Dad, wake up, I need help with Mom."

"What's wrong now?" Jeh asked, raising his head.

"There's a bottle hidden in her room somewhere and I can't find it. Wake up."

Like a soldier roused for his rounds, Jeh sat up, yawned, and swung his feet to the floor. Pulling at his pajama strings, he ambled to the bathroom. Jeh's pants tended to slide down his hips, making his short legs seem even shorter. A bar of light moved across the bedroom walls as I heard a car drive past the window. It lit up Jeh's face for a moment. People often remarked that there was something Mona Lisa–like about his eyes. In boarding school, a boy had punched him over a stolen fried egg at breakfast. As a result, the tip of Jeh's nose bent slightly to the left.

Jeh took ages in the toilet, the sound of his urination echoing around the bathroom walls. I tapped my foot. His bedroom smelled like sweaty socks. Apparently, no one had bothered to change his sheets in a while. Jeh hadn't noticed. A space cadet, he was.

Finished with the bathroom, Jeh stepped out. I hadn't heard a tap running.

"Did you wash your hands?" I asked.

"Huh?"

I sighed. "After you finished, did you wash your hands?"

"Uh, no." Jeh shook his head, looking sheepish.

"Dad, go wash your hands." I pinched the bridge of my nose. How was this man going to deal with Asha, when he couldn't even remember to wash his fucking hands?

Jeh came out of the bathroom a second time, wiping his wet hands on his pajamas. Together, we went to Asha's bedroom. The smell of alcohol was stronger now. I resumed searching for a bottle, while Asha lit another cigarette. Jeh put on his best stern schoolmaster impression. Asha blew out a few puffs of smoke and placed her lighter next to a glass water jug. Drops of condensation slid down its sides. I snatched up the jug and took a sip. Asha had hidden her booze in plain sight.

"We can't trust you at all, huh, Ma?" I said, taking the jug to the bathroom to dump the alcohol. "Zal Papa was right," I said to Jeh, "this is not something we can fix by ourselves."

"I'm sorry," Asha said unconvincingly. "This is the last time. I promise."

"Sure." I tucked the slippery jug under my arm and rubbed my wet hands down the front of my nightdress. "Sure it is. But just in case it isn't, I refuse to be your Nurse Ratched."

"Oho! Listen to the big bully. This is my house too. Try and make me leave," Asha said, her ears pulled back. "What're you going to do? Throw me out? This is my fucking house!"

"Noomi's right," Jeh said to Asha. "We are in way over our heads."

"Either she leaves..." I couldn't finish the sentence, so I shoved the jug in his hands and walked out.

"Suit yourself," Asha said. I heard her lighter click, then smelled a fresh cigarette.

"Noomi," Jeh called after me. I didn't answer.

When I was eight years old, I pushed my mother so hard she broke a tooth. It all started with a fight I got into with my cousin Adil. I remember running down the stairs from my parents' apartment and out the back. It was Sunday evening, and I was going to have chai with my grandparents, as Adil and I did every Sunday. I walked along the curved driveway to the veranda overlooking my grandmother's garden. As I walked, I hatched a plan for revenge on Adil for the ladies' room incident at the Gymkhana Club. Jeh never intervened with anyone on my behalf. "Fight your own battles, Piglet."

The front lawn was foamy green, turned over by earthworms that scattered the grass with tiny mud laddus. To our delight, the dogs liked to suck up the worms from the ground like noodles. A mongoose slinked along the boundary wall to its nest, which was below the patch of ground where the gardener buried our pets when they died. Leaning against the wall was a hut that I'd built using trellises stolen from the garden shed and covered with a blue tarpaulin. A bamboo thicket hid it from sight; it was my secret spot. Inside, there was a chatai to lie down on, a few books, a clock, a water bottle, a tube of Odomos mosquito repellent, a packet of chips, and a skull that had once belonged to a dachshund.

On the veranda, Lily Mama gave me my usual cup of tea with ginger biscuits. Zal Papa straightened his newspaper with a crackle and lifted it up to his face. Noiselessly moving my mouth, I tried to read the thin, scratchy captions below the photographs when I was interrupted by the *snick, snick, snick* of a pair of scissors. Adil had snuck in while I was distracted and had been busy snipping off bits of my hair, hidden between the wall and the back of the sofa. I stared at the end of my pigtail in shock. It looked as if a rat had been nibbling on it. My cup clattered to the floor. I shrieked and dragged Adil out by the scruff of his neck. He unfurled on the floor like a rug. I sat astride him, pinning his arms, and snatched the scissors from his right hand.

"I'm going to cut off your pee-pee," I said, pulling off his pajama bottoms.

Adil's penis peeked out coyly from under his T-shirt.

I snipped the scissors and smiled a crazy smile.

Adil screamed in genuine horror.

Lily Mama dragged me off, yelling to her husband that I had gone insane. Adil stumbled, howling, into Zal Papa's lap, pajamas halfway up his little apricot bum. Already exhausted from holding me back, Lily Mama shouted for help.

Ever so gently, Zal Papa slid Adil off his lap as if releasing a hatchling into a pond and stood up. Then, rolling his newspaper into a hard baton, he walked over to me wriggling in Lily Mama's arms and crouched so that we were face-to-face. His grip on my arms was like a pincer. I looked away.

"Look at me," Zal Papa said, holding up the rolled newspaper as if I were a puppy that needed to be housebroken. "If you ever touch Adil again, I will thrash you."

I nodded to show him I'd understood. When he was satisfied that I'd learned my lesson, he let go and I immediately shrieked, "Stupid old goat!" before running away.

I decided to hide in my secret spot. The tarpaulin had kept the hut's interior dry, even though it had rained last night. The rain-steeped earth underneath the chatai filled the hut with petrichor. I lay down and read the book I'd hidden there, *Five Go Down to the Sea*.

My plan was to remain in the hut until everyone frothed at the mouth with worry. I hoped that the loss of his only child would make Jeh stand up, finally, to his father. Zal Papa would have to beg my forgiveness, and in return for it, he would have to demote Adil to the position of least favorite grandchild.

I read until I was too sleepy, and then, placing the book under my head as a pillow, I put my arm over my eyes, listening to the chirps and whirs of the garden.

I woke up not knowing where I was for a moment. I poked my head out of the hut. The sky was pink with orange-gold feathery clouds; sparrows had begun their evening racket. I looked at the time. It had been two hours, and no one had come looking for me. I sat at the hut's entrance, tossing the dachshund skull from one hand to the other. I could see everything from here: my grandmother's veranda, the sun-tinted windows of my parents' flat, a woman with fuzzy outlines hanging bedsheets on the terrace. Whining mosquitos kamikazed down on my bare skin.

The sun set behind the garden wall. Orange streetlights flickered on with a low buzz, and shadows ran across my arms and face. I heard the barking of street dogs. I heard a neighbor's baby crying, high and eerie.

My mind strayed to Shanta Bai's stories of men who stole children who wandered around outside alone. They cut off their legs before sending them to beg, pushing themselves along on carts. "Ratri jhadam pasoon door raha!" she would warn, her eyes big and round. *Steer clear of dark places at night!* Laughing, I would mime tightening a loose screw in my temple to Adil, who would then laugh as well.

But alone in the dark now, I panicked. A madman could be in any one of these trees, ready to put his sticky hands around my neck. A blast from a car horn made me jump, my heart banging loudly. I decided to count to a thousand, hopeful someone would come find me before I finished. I tapped on the dachshund skull to keep count: *tick-tick* one, *tick-tick* two, *tick-tick* three. I got to *tick-tick* one hundred when a shivering-shaking noise in the trees and a *whoop-whoop-whoop* sent icy ants marching down my spine. I jumped to my feet screaming, threw the skull in the direction of the noise, and didn't stop running until I was up the stairs and through my front door.

There was an invitation printed with a golden Ganesh on the telephone table. Jeh and Asha were in their bedroom, getting ready to go out. I went in to tell them not to worry anymore, I had returned. Jeh was on his side of the bed, facing the wall, polishing his shoes with a wood brush. He wore a white silk shirt that showed the outlines of his cotton undershirt. There was a small coin-sized bald patch on the back of his head.

Asha was on the velvet pouf at her makeup table, lining her eyes with a black kajal. Her hair, which used to reach the middle of her back, was swept over one shoulder by a jeweled clip. Her sari was the rich jungle green of a monstera plant. Her oval face was plastered over. With her fine North Indian features and long brown legs, she would've been a beauty, if not for all the acne scars that marred her cheeks from when she was a teenager.

"I ran away from home today," I said, glaring at my mother in the mirror.

Asha threw me a look that was like a middle finger. She twisted her lipstick out of its gold tube to paint her half-open mouth. She smelled of cigarettes, perfume, and minty toothpaste.

"And," I said, turning now to glower at the back of Jeh's head, "I was almost kidnapped... by lunatics!"

"You can stop lying, Noomi," Jeh said, not looking at me. "We know what you did. Why you've been hiding." He gave an awkward little laugh, which meant that he was furious.

"I wasn't really going to do anything," I said. "You always tell me I need to fight my own battles."

"So you threaten to cut off Adil's penis?" Jeh screamed, throwing his shoe brush at the wall. He looked down at his empty hands, surprised at the violence they held. "You're... disturbing. I am so ashamed. He's only a baby. We didn't teach you to behave like a... like a..."

"A maniac," Asha said from the pouf, rubbing her forearms with Pond's cold cream. "A slut."

I am a bad person, so when a little voice asked, *Wouldn't it be nice if Asha died?* I didn't say, *Shut up*. I invited it further into my mind. Offered it a little sofa to sit on, some tea and biscuits.

"A disgrace," Asha continued, smoothing her foundation.

I charged at Asha and knocked her off the pouf. There was a flash of white underwear, black hair scribbled along the sides. The sight of it shocked me. I felt like throwing up.

Jeh turned to find Asha dissolved in a green silk puddle. He rushed over to help her up, but her cream-greasy hands slipped out of his. She landed again on the floor with a thump. Asha cried out in pain. Her mouth was full of blood. It looked like paan juice.

"Get the fuck away from me," she said, slapping his hand.

I made a run for the door, but Asha caught my arm.

"Spoiled brat!" she said, hitting me across the cheek. The pain was a piece of hot metal lodged in my face. Unsatisfied that I didn't cry out, Asha grabbed my shoulders and began shaking me, the way people do to hysterical women in movies.

I went limp like a rag doll, hoping that would stop my mother.

"Arey, arey, Asha!" Jeh said. He pulled me away from her. I hid behind him.

Asha's jeweled clip fell to the floor. Her sari was ruined. Her bedraggled hair covered both sides of her face. She stood to unwrap the sari from her body, turning round and round until it fell to the floor. She stepped out of its green circle. She walked past us to the bathroom, and she locked herself inside.

"Are you okay?" Jeh asked. He brushed the back of his hand against my face. It tickled me in an unpleasant way. I stepped away from him, hunching my shoulders up to my chin.

"I hate Mama," I said.

"Don't say that. Mama is just sad at your behavior. So am I. We expect more from you."

It felt like there was a creature gnawing at the inside of my stomach. I hadn't eaten since biscuits and tea. Pity for myself bloomed like a mushroom in my throat. I gave in and started crying. Jeh picked me up in his arms.

"Daddy, I'm so hungry," I said, sniffling. "Can you get me something to eat?"

Jeh set me down on the bed and blotted my cheeks with his thumb. He stepped out of the room and returned with a ketchup and butter sandwich, my favorite. In bed, we watched *The Jungle Book* on the VCR. Over the voices of Bagheera and Baloo, I heard faint sobbing coming from inside the bathroom.

The year he turned seventy, Zal Papa handed over the day-to-day of his business empire to his sons, loudly and repeatedly proclaiming that he wanted nothing more to do with it. But he kept his old office, and each day, Zal Papa sat inside it, devising new ways to drive everyone crazy. He was prone to fits of dissatisfaction, which he alleviated by treating his sons, Jeh and Cyrus, to lectures on what they should be doing to make the business more profitable. If his sons were avoiding him (which they usually were), he called friends for gossip on his old-fashioned rotary telephone or pored over architectural blueprints to add more follies to our bungalow on Banyan Street. Once, he'd renovated the downstairs master bathroom with a transparent Plexiglas roof to be "closer to nature while answering nature's call"—those were his exact words. For a month, langurs stared down at Lily Mama when she was on the toilet, causing her to hyperventilate whenever she needed to pee. There was also the disastrous vertical garden and the unsightly "tiger" rotunda with an orange-and-black corrugated roof. Another time, he spent a fortune to encase half the front veranda in tempered glass, to create a sunroom. That was actually quite a nice room; I often spent my summer evenings in there, reading.

Jeh and I sat at Zal Papa's desk like students called into the prin-cipal's office. Zal Papa was signing papers, which he handed one by one to his peon, a young man with a birthmark shaped like an island on the side of his nose, who stood by his side. Zal Papa signed with an ink pen. His pens had to be cleaned and refilled every single day.

"Things with Asha are not going well, I see," Zal Papa said, nodding at the peon, who hurried off.

It was midmorning; customers had started to trickle in. Jeh had someone waiting in his office. He crossed his legs and clasped his hands over his knee. His face betrayed nothing, like still water.

"No, no," I said, just to piss my grandfather off. "Things are going great."

Zal Papa's face dissolved into a scowl. "I'll spell it out," he said. "Asha's drinking is not acceptable to this family. Either she gets sober, or she gets out." He pointed to the office door. "Out."

"You've never liked her, Papa. It's no secret. But Asha is..." Jeh said, leaning forward in his chair, hands together on Zal Papa's desk. "We're doing everything to get her better."

Zal Papa took a letter opener out from his drawer and began slashing open envelopes, pulling papers out from between their jagged mouths. His elbows, resting on the desk blotter, put dimples in the brown leather.

"Turning our home into a rehab isn't helping. She needs a professional. Send her to someplace where they know what to do with her," Zal Papa said, more of a command than a suggestion.

"You don't seem to care that she's sick, only that it hurts your precious reputation," I said. "She's been resisting our attempts to get her help. Should we send her to rehab in a tied-up sack?"

"When you've raised a family and created a livelihood for them from nothing, you can flap that big mouth all you want," Zal Papa said. Pointing his letter opener at me but looking at Jeh, he said, "I pity this one's future husband."

Jeh put a hand on my arm, which I took to mean: *Stop, you're not helping.*

"I've been looking into places I can send her, Pa," Jeh said. "Give me time. I can't drag her out of the house to someone waiting with a straitjacket."

Zal Papa looked at Jeh, and his voice softened. "Jeh, my son." Zal Papa put down the letter opener and steepled his hands. "You're a grown man, not a child. You need to take charge. This whole thing with Asha is raising my blood pressure. She must"—Zal Papa put his fist down on the table—"go somewhere to get better."

"Okay, Pa," Jeh said. "I'll make a few calls to find a place that will take her immediately."

"Fine," Zal Papa said. "But she must be gone in a week."

"I promise," Jeh said.

"You're a tin-pot dictator," I said, standing up. "Let go of me, Dad." I pushed Jeh's hand away. I wanted Asha out as much as Zal Papa did. And yet, I was angry. Zal Papa wielded shame against us like a master swordsman.

Zal Papa was an imposing six-foot-one when he stood up. "This business, this house, all built by me. All belongs to *me*. I'll kick out who I choose." He jabbed a finger at my face.

I wanted to sink my teeth into that finger. Jeh hooked my arm and pulled me to the door, murmuring, "No use arguing while he's like this. Let's go."

"Thanks for coming by, son," Zal Papa called after us. "This was a productive talk."

I came home to find Asha in her dressing gown, propped up with pillows on her bed, watching television and smoking. Light brown cigarette butts piled up, like disgusting pasta, in her ashtray. She gave her cigarette a flick; a drift of ash fell on her bedsheet. I stood still for a moment, looking at her. If I crossed my eyes, Asha split into two women: what she'd become, what she could've been. Shanta Bai had oiled her hair and put it in a braid. It made her forehead shiny enough to reflect the lamplight.

"Hi, Mama," I said, approaching the bed.

"Hello," Asha said, in a so-you're-back voice.

"Ready for your pill?"

"Fine." She said.

I popped a pill out of its blister. It sat like a pearl in the center of my palm. I went to the kitchen. I put the pill on a strip of newspaper and crushed it with a pestle. We crushed the Antabuse into a powder now—it was the only way to make sure Asha wouldn't spit it out. Once the pill was a powder, I folded the paper in half and took it back to Asha in the bedroom.

Asha was watching politicians yell on TV. Her eyes glittered like a sunstruck river.

"Okay, open your mouth, please," I said, folding the strip into a funnel.

Obediently, Asha tilted her head and opened her mouth. Her molar had a shiny cap. I funneled the white powder into her mouth, gently tapping the paper to get the last bits. Sadness sat on my shoulder like a heavy bird. It was up to me to break the news about rehab to Asha. Jeh was too afraid of what she might say. Asha was better than any lawyer when she had to come up with reasons to keep drinking. Give her your ear for long enough, and she'd have you going to the liquor store and returning with two bottles of Romanov.

I broke the news to Asha a few days later, at lunch. "You're going to rehab," I blurted out.

Asha raised her head from her plate of mutton curry and rice. She shoveled forkfuls of the food into her mouth as if trying to fill a hole. "Hope you're happy," she said, sucking loudly on her marrow bones.

"It's a nice place," Jeh said. "Lots of, er, Bollywood types go there." He slid a brochure down the table. "I've heard their food is pretty good. They even do Ayurvedic massages."

He looked at me and I gave him a little nod. *Keep talking.*

"It'll be like a little vacation."

In the days preceding her departure, judging by the empty bottles we found and the smell of vomit that permeated her clothes and hair, Asha drank like a camel preparing to go into the desert. The night she left, Jeh ordered a wheelchair to take her to the airport. Asha was too drunk to stand. He'd hired a nurse for the trip—a middle-aged woman with the air of someone practiced in reserving judgment. They helped Asha down the stairs and slid her into the wheelchair. The nurse stopped her from slumping forward. A small mercy that it was late at night. The nurse pushed Asha to the car, and Jeh loaded their suitcases. He needed a backpack for Asha's papers. I gave him mine. The backpack had a bright flower print; it made Jeh look like he was going somewhere fun and tropical, like Goa. Standing at the foot of the stairs, I watched as he and the nurse settled Asha into the back seat. Jeh turned and waved. The smile on his face nearly wrecked me.

The story we gave out if someone asked about Asha's disappearance was that she was getting treatment at an Ayurvedic spa down south. To keep the lie afloat, we organized a welcome home bash for her return, four weeks later. When we mentioned the party, a small smile bloomed on Asha's tired face, like the first green bud after a drought. The shadows under her eyes had lightened. Once we got her settled at home, I went to check on her many nights in a row. No telltale smell. No hidden bottles. We planned for Asha's party with brio. Zal Papa and Lily Mama were so relieved at her improvement, they offered to pay for everything.

A few hours before the guests arrived, Shanta Bai, irritated by me popping in to check on her in the kitchen, threatened to add a whole bird's eye chili to the vindaloo, making it quite deadly, so I ran off to Suzy's Parlor to get my hair done. I regretted my decision when Sheila Sehgal sailed out the parlor's tinkly door just as I was about to step in. I smiled and twisted my body to let her pass. She grabbed my arm and pulled me aside.

"Still gallivanting about," Sheila said with a scorpion smile. "Remember my warning. The wedding is in a few weeks, and I don't want any trouble from you."

"Please let go of my arm," I whispered, not wanting to cry. "I have to get home."

"I heard your mother was back after her 'spa' visit?" Sheila scratched quote marks in the air.

"Yes," I said. "She had a very nice time."

"Oh, spare me." Sheila rolled her eyes. "Poor Jeh," she said, shaking her head. "He must've done something terrible in a past life to deserve the two of you."

My heart pounded nastily in my rib cage. That was Kamalpur for you: disgrace lurked at every corner like a molester. I looked at the floor. "Excuse me," I said, and pushed past Sheila into the parlor.

"Imagine Jeh's face," Sheila called after me, "if he heard about what you did at my party."

Women in silk, tanchoi, crepe de chine, and light chiffon, wearing "casual" jewelry: pearls, solitaires, gold. They weaved, perfumed, into the living room and sat in chatty rosettes on the sofas. The men went to pour themselves drinks and stand around, smoking, gossiping. Everyone was in raptures about Shanta Bai's famous homemade mutton samosas and refreshing mint chutney.

I'd showered with a seashell-shaped soap I kept for special occasions. It smelled like the inside of a rich woman's purse. I chose to wear the demurest outfit I owned: a blush-pink salwar kurta. I walked by the mirror. A glance was all I could stand. I picked and squeezed at a small zit on my forehead until it was inflamed, large, and unnecessarily unsightly. *Shit, now what?* Sticking out my tongue to one side, I tightened my dupatta around my neck.

Parties in Kamalpur reminded me of solar systems: there was usually one or two important personages around whose gravitational pull the rest seemed to orbit. I could tell one old lady in a dove-gray sari was important, as everyone in her rosette had oriented their bodies toward her. I took around a tray of samosas. Strange giggles danced over from the side of the hall. I saw Asha and Rhea on a love seat, heads together, ignoring the rest of the party. Two flutes of champagne with strings of bubbles stood on the table in front of them. They were drunk as parrots, sitting under a gold-leaf painting of gods and goddesses dancing. I'd always hated that painting.

Sitting next to the lady in the gray sari, buttering her up like a piece of toast, was Aunt Binny. "Noomi dear," Binny said, throwing me a bright smile. "Bring the mutton samosas to Mrs. Rao."

The corners of my mouth turned down. I walked over knowing something vaguely unpleasant was about to happen.

"Are those veg or non-veg," the gray woman asked.

"Non-veg," I said.

"No thanks, I'm a pure vegetarian," the gray woman said, putting up her hand with a small smile.

It amused me how vegetarians used "pure" to describe their dietary habits. "I'll find you some paneer ones," I said, and smiled.

Binny, with a vapid giggle, speared a samosa with a toothpick. "Much too oily," she said, rubbing her fingers together. "This is the

Noomi I was telling you about." She gave the woman a look. "Asha's daughter."

Binny's words flew out of her mouth like wasps. I'd walked into her swarm.

"Hello, namaste," I said. Unable to fold my hands, I did a weird little curtsy.

"Ah," the old lady said. "Is that your mother on the sofa?" She pointed with her chin to where Asha and Rhea were cackling about something, champagne flutes in their hands.

"Yes," I said, feeling my cheeks warm to the same pink as my outfit.

"She looks very happy," remarked the old woman. "Preposterously so."

"She's returned from a relaxing spa holiday." I shrugged.

"Is that champagne?" The lady raised her eyebrows. "Lily Wadia allows her bahu to drink?" She lifted a hand to her chest. "Very modern of her. My sons' wives are very old-fashioned. Of course, they're dutiful girls. They would rather stay home with their children on school nights."

An image of two Pomeranians dressed in housewifely finery popped into my mind, raising their heads and whining when they heard their mother-in-law's car turn into the driveway. I let escape a giggle. The rich old woman gave me a frown. Then she stared at my mother. Asha was certainly not a dutiful girl.

Binny gave the old woman a martyr-like smile.

Jeh knocked back a whisky with Ammu's father. He looked relaxed, happy. Baba clapped a hand on Jeh's shoulder. They'd been close friends since college. I caught Jeh's attention. He gave me a smile, which flipped into a frown when I made a drinking motion and pointed my eyes in the direction of Asha and Rhea's sofa. Jeh excused himself. Baba squeezed his shoulder and went off to get another drink, leaving Jeh and me huddled in a corner of the veranda, by a monstera with leaves as big as elephant ears, shooting furtive glances at Asha and Rhea.

"What do we do?" I said. "She's drinking!"

"Let's not panic," Jeh said, putting his glass down on a table. "Let's find out what's going on."

"Okay," I said, linking arms with my father.

Our shadows crept up the arm of the sofa Asha and Rhea were on and stuck to the wall behind them. Asha looked at us with a grin. "Hello, Tweedledee and Tweedledum."

"Asha," Jeh said, pointing to the champagne flute in her hand, "is that... ?"

Asha drained her glass and said, "I don't know what you're talking about."

Rhea gave a dismissive little smile. "One teeny glass of champagne won't hurt her."

"This will be your only drink," I said to Asha, my eyes rounded in warning.

"Of course," Asha said, flicking a grin up at Rhea, who'd gotten up and wandered off. In search of more champagne, probably. "Mother promise," she said, pinching the skin of her throat.

"Zal Papa and Lily Mama want this evening to go off without any drama, you know," Jeh said.

"It will, it will," Asha said, nodding vigorously. "I promise."

"Noomi," Jeh whispered, placing a hand on my back, "get your mother some food."

"Okay," I said. On the way to the kitchen, I noticed my grandparents staring, first at Asha, then at me. I flashed them a reassuring, we've-got-it-under-control smile. In the empty foyer, I leaned my head against the wall. I wished I could get a flute of champagne—or five. I felt a hand on my shoulder and turned with a start.

"Relax, it's me," Ammu said, taking a step back. "Didn't mean to scare you. I followed you back here. You looked very upset when you walked past."

"Oh, hi," I said, giving a little shiver. "I'm a bit stressed out, that's all." I gave her a hug. "Why haven't I seen you at the party? You didn't come here with your dad?"

"No, Baba got here earlier." Ammu glanced to her left. She had some-one in tow—a tall, young man with the most beautiful art-film face, like he'd stepped out of a Satyajit Ray movie. "This is Shiv," Ammu said, smiling.

"Hi, Noomi." Shiv seemed embarrassed.

"Hi," I said, shaking his warm, slim hand. "Nice to meet you. Shiv is short for something. Shiva?"

"It's short for Shivraj, actually," said Shiv, even more embarrassed. "I hate Shivraj, though."

"Shiv's a friend from London," Ammu said. "He moved to Bombay to start a media company. Hey," she yipped, as if an idea had just struck her, "aren't you looking for a feature writer, Shiv?" She smiled at me. "Noomi always won all the essay contests in school."

"Not *all* the contests," I said, brushing off the compliment. "Most of them."

"That's great," Shiv said. He looked at Ammu, who beamed her approval, so he went on. "I'd love to have someone like you writing for us. Here's my card." He produced a small rectangle from his kurta pocket. "If you're ever in town, come see me. My office is by Churchgate station."

"Thanks," I said, holding on to it. I pointed to the kitchen door. "I do have to get my mother some food. But hang around, have a drink." I smiled. "I'd love to learn more about your company."

Heading back into the party, I ran into a wall made of Lily Mama and Zal Papa, all raised eyebrows and anxious expressions. "Everything's fine," I said, lifting the plate of food to show them. "That was her one and only drink. She's promised."

"Why is Rhea here?" Zal Papa said.

"Her husband must be on a business trip."

"Rhea's my niece, Zal," Lily Mama said. "I invited her."

The three of us turned to look at Rhea and Asha clinging to each other on the sofa as if they were on a raft.

"Well, if she's going to be a problem, we should make sure the party wraps up soon," Zal Papa said. He looked for something to tell him the time. Lily Mama wore a gold watch with a mother-of-pearl face. He lifted her wrist to the non-stroke side of his face. "Have dinner served by nine P.M."

"Okay." I nodded.

Dinner was ready to be served, but the guests weren't interested in eating. All eyes were fixed on the scene unfolding in the living room. When drunk, Asha believed no one could be as charming as she, no one as interesting or intelligent. I couldn't cross the room fast enough to stop her from teetering over to the rich old woman in the gray sari with Binny, who was still buttering her up. Asha settled into a high-backed armchair and threw one leg over the other, eyes glittering as if she were running a fever. Mrs. Rao gave her an ambivalent smile; Binny, an unambivalent scowl.

"Hello, I don't believe we've ever met. I'm Reeti Rao."

"I was admiring the color of your sari," Asha said. "I thought I'd come over and ask where you bought it. The material—it's as if you wrapped a rain cloud around yourself."

"Oh, thank you." The old woman's eyes crinkled up. "It's a family heirloom. My mother's."

"I'd like to buy it," Asha said, and slapped her knee. "How much do you want for it? Name any price. I will pay whatever you ask for such a beautiful heirloom."

"Excuse me? You're out of your mind." Mrs. Rao laughed. "I told you, it was my mother's sari. Why would I sell it?" She looked toward Binny and chuckled. "I don't need your money."

"Mrs. Rao's husband," Binny sniffed, "owns most of the farmland south of Butibori."

"Oh, I'm sorry." Asha bowed her head. "Didn't realize I was in the presence of feudal royalty."

"Here's your food, Mom," I said, shoving the plate in my hands into Asha's and grabbing her arm. "Why don't you come sit with me. There's an empty table by the balcony. Let's get some fresh air."

"Do you know, Mrs. Rao," Asha said, setting the plate on the floor, "I've just returned from a *spa*?"

"Yes?" the old lady said, suppressing another giggle.

"It wasn't actually a spa!" Asha shouted. Heads turned in our direction. Asha laughed like a hyena. "It was"—she put one hand to the side of her mouth—"a rehab! For drunks!" She made her mouth into an O and stared at the old lady. "I was drying out there for a month."

"Asha." Binny rose from her seat and grabbed my mother's hands. "I think I saw Jeh looking for you a moment ago. Let's go and find him, shall we?" She motioned for me to get up.

A few moments later, Jeh and I stood over Asha in her bedroom. With an extravagant sigh, Asha stretched herself out on her bed, crossed her ankles, and put an arm behind her head. "The beds in that so-called spa were terrible," she said. "Hard, and so narrow. The room was always hot. No AC. It was like sleeping inside a baking tin."

"Asha," Jeh said, "why are you doing this? Why are you ruining everything? We planned this party so that people would *stop* gossiping about you." He placed his hands on his waist.

Asha, who'd been twisting about on the bed, sat up with an evil little smirk and rubbed one foot against the other. "You two thought there'd be no consequences to sending me away."

"Ma, we had to do it," I said. "Zal Papa basically gave us no choice."

Asha's face seemed to fall apart for a moment. Then it knit back together in a mask of spite. "There's always a fucking choice!" she screamed. "You could have chosen to grow a backbone." She threw a pillow at Jeh. "Do you know how they treat women in those places? They put us, turn by turn, inside a circle and hurled insults at us. Every day they told us we were depraved, base."

I peeked out the bedroom door to see if anyone had been listening. Binny, standing by the balcony door, was directing the help to clear up empty glasses and beer bottles. She seemed to have everything under control. Guests wandered toward the dining room. I turned back to see Jeh on the edge of Asha's bed, his face buried in his hands. Asha fumbled around for her pack of cigarettes, lit one, and blew a smoke ring that haloed his head.

The door opened and Binny popped in her head. "Jeh," she said, "your parents were tired, so they left. I told Shanta Bai to lay out dinner."

"Thanks, Binny," Jeh said. "Thank you so much. I'll be out very soon."

"Don't worry. Take all the time you need," Binny said, before closing the door with a nod.

Jeh turned back to Asha. "We'll have to start all over again. The Antabuse, the doctors."

"I realized," Asha said. She laughed—a loud, bitter cackle. "But your face when you saw me with the champagne in my hand. Priceless! Like I'd dumped a jug of water on your head. The look on your stupid fucking face!"

Asha was still shrieking when I left the bedroom. I needed to find a way to leave this place, this city, my family. I loved Jeh more than anything, but I couldn't go through that entire cycle again: the watching, the lies, the shame.

Ammu was talking to Shiv under the painting of gods and goddesses, the one I hated because it was joyful. Joy was uncomfortable, like a pair of ill-fitting shoes. Ammu broke off her conversation with Shiv and gathered me in a hug.

"What's up?" Ammu said. "Where are your parents?"

"Dad's inside with Mom," I sniffled.

"Oh, Noomi," Ammu said. She turned to Shiv. "What can we do to help?"

Shiv cleared his throat and tucked his hands into his armpits. "Yes, tell us."

"Let's make sure the party ends smoothly," Ammu said. "Shiv, can you manage the bar?"

"Of course." Shiv nodded and went off in the direction of the balcony. He turned back midstride and smiled at Ammu. I felt jealous at the absentminded way Ammu picked up love, the way a rabbit's pelt picks up burrs. I recalled a summer afternoon, when Ammu's brother plucked a flower from a vase and placed it behind Ammu's ear, while she, distracted, annoyed, buried her nose in a book.

The next day, just after dawn, I packed a bag and left the house while everyone was still asleep. I kept Shiv's business card inside my purse. If he didn't fire me, I'd freelance. It didn't pay much, but I wanted flexible hours. On the road in front of our gate, I managed to flag an autorickshaw to take me to the airport. A pink sun flipped up over the horizon.

PART TWO

PART
TWO

New Delhi's arid air shrouded me as I walked out the sliding glass doors of its snazzy, shiny airport. I clutched my handbag to my chest, a barrier between me and the men standing behind barricades, holding placards with travelers' names. They stared at me hungrily. It was half past midnight. I scanned the airport parking area, unsurprised that there were no women about at this hour. I hated this about Delhi. In Bombay, where I'd been working and living for a blissful three years, no matter the hour, women were everywhere: airports, restaurants, stations, tea stalls, even booze and paan shops. They made themselves known in the flash of silver sandals stepping out of a taxi, in the steady chopping sounds of a fish market, a wild shriek over the crash of waves at Marine Drive, in the clink of glass bangles at an all-night bazaar.

Veer stood in the pickup zone with flowers next to a fat white car with a red light on its roof. Before I could wave him over, a man in a white uniform had come forward to take my bags, which he proceeded to efficiently Tetris-load into the car's trunk.

"Welcome," Veer said, with the roses cradled in his arms like a child.

We couldn't kiss or even hug. The hungry men were watching us with too much interest. Veer held the car door open, and I slid in, dragging the roses after. In the back seat, once we were on our way, with the attendant's and driver's eyes on the road and not on us, Veer took my hand. Rubbing his thumb over my knuckles (a habit of his that I loved), he asked me, in his taciturn way, "Good flight?"

"I read a book," I said, resting my head on his shoulder.

He shifted uncomfortably. With a small nod, he indicated the front seat. I sat up straight and moved away.

"What's with all this?" I whispered, gesturing to the men.

"Oh, Dad said I could have his official car to pick you up," Veer said, beaming. "I think he wants you to be... suitably impressed." He let go of my hand and ran his thumb against the bristles on his chin.

In the first year of our relationship, Veer's parents had refused to meet me, protecting the family's brittle reputation from an unsuitable match. Veer told them that they might as well get used to the idea, because I wasn't going anywhere. Now here I was, in New Delhi, on my way to meet my future in-laws for the first time.

Veer's father was a high-ranking bureaucrat in the Indian government: a mover of files, a purveyor of kickbacks. I found this fact amusing—and also terrifying. Veer had grown up in an upper-middle-class New Delhi home, one filled with narrow minds and outsized ambition. When he was in school, his father would come at him with a belt if he ever scored less than 90 percent in his exams. His mother used her makeup to cover the marks.

Veer told me that the days following his father's violence were some of the most pleasant of his childhood. His dad would feel guilty. There'd be kebabs from Khan Market and long drives to Nirula's for ice cream. There'd be ill-afforded saris for Veer's mother, or an offer to help with the dishes when the cook took off early, while the radio played warbly songs into the evening.

Then there'd be too many long nights in a row at the office, or a jealous comment from a colleague. Veer's mother would burn dinner, or Veer would take a bit too long tying his shoelaces. A kick, a slap, a flying shoe, a belt strap to the calves. "Shh," Veer's mother would say. "Papa is just stressed."

Veer learned that one could use stress as a cover for all sorts of bad behavior. At his consulting firm, he developed a reputation for being obscenely hardworking, replying to his boss's emails seven days a week. Veer had once hated his parents. But now he seemed eager to impress them.

"My aunt is so excited to meet you," Veer said, lassoing my thoughts back inside the car. "She's waiting up for us."

"Oh," I said, alarmed. "Um, but why?"

"I guess she wants to make sure you'll be comfortable in her guest room," Veer said with a shrug of his eyebrows. "She's very particular."

Trucks rumbled past us on the Outer Ring Road—clumsy boxes that looked put together by a child with nails and a hammer. Swirls of dust slithered under their wheels like ghosts. They owned the road as shamelessly as bullies on a playground.

"*Her* guest room?" I stared at Veer in confusion. "Hold on, why am I staying at your aunt's place?"

"I've told you about her, haven't I?" Veer nodded. "My dad's older sister?" He pushed his glasses up his nose. "Listen, you know my parents are kind of traditional, right?" he said. "They feel it would be... I don't know"—he put up his hands—"inappropriate or something, if you stayed with us before the wedding." He avoided my stare, looking instead at the car's black window to fuss with his hair. Veer loved mirrors, and mirrors loved him back. His good looks and the doors they opened for him were our inside joke.

"That's ridiculous," I blurted out. The attendant in the passenger seat turned halfway and gave me a look. I ignored his eyes and rested my head on the window's cool glass.

"Of course you're right," Veer said, grabbing my hand. "But our parents' generation, kya karein, they're too set in their ways. Why be antagonistic right from the start, na? They're so excited to meet you. It's only a few days. Let's just make them happy."

The city flashed by outside my window. I thought back to when Veer and I had first met, two and a half years ago. I was still new to Bombay. Everything about it was fascinating. It was December and the shops glittered with holiday lights. Cool, dry inland air had temporarily pushed away the tropical mugginess. One lovely evening in Colaba, I decided to stroll down the Causeway after work, inspecting the street sellers' wares—bags, scarves, cheap but pretty jewelry, glass hookahs—on the way to Café Mondegar, or Mondy's, with its Mario Miranda walls, uncurious waiters, and extended happy hours. I walked under an old gulmohar blazing with orange flowers. Little boys, barefoot and dirty faced, pulled on my kurta: "Didi! We haven't eaten today. We're starving. Buy us some food." My purse had one fifty-rupee note. I gave it to the smallest boy, who snatched it and shot off. The others ran after him, shouting.

I was out of cash for beer. Luckily, there was an ATM around the corner from Mondy's. The machine was broken, but I didn't realize that until it swallowed my card. I turned to discover a huddle of annoyed people. Maintenance was on the way, a woman said to me. I went outside to smoke and wait. A man crossed the street and walked to the ATM. As he got closer, I noticed that he was good-looking in a Neanderthal-ish sort of way: large forehead and full lips. He was dressed in a gray suit with a gray tie. He loosened his tie and went around me with an apologetic smile. I considered warning him, but then he'd have walked away. I'd lose him to the city night. I watched quietly as the ATM swallowed his card. He let out a barrage of curse words.

"Someone's on the way to fix it," I said, walking back inside as my handsome Neanderthal stabbed at the buttons, muttering under his breath. I gave what I hoped was a dazzling smile. Perhaps it dawned on him that a not-bad-looking person wanted to flirt with him. Crow's feet appeared around his brown eyes.

"I'm Veer," he said, offering me his hand. I took it.

After we got our cards back, we walked over to Café Mondegar and drank beer until the waiters started to put chairs upside down on the tables. Sometime after 1:00 A.M., Veer snuck me into his sublet at Sassoon Docks, with its absinthe green walls and rickety furniture. The toilet tank had a chain flush. The whole place smelled like balchão, Bombay's signature odor. Veer's thin, shabby bed made his body look gorgeous, like a fancy car parked in a dingy alley. The sex we had that night, and the next morning, was exceptionally good.

In the afternoon, Veer stepped out to buy cigarettes and returned with a parcel. I tore open the soft, damp newspaper to find two red glass bangles. They clinked prettily.

"A woman was selling these on the side of the road." Veer scratched the back of his head and pointed at the bangles. "Thought that color would look good against your skin." These were the longest sentences he'd spoken thus far. "I thought just two, instead of the usual dozen."

I slipped the bangles on my wrist and smiled. "Parsi women wear a red bangle once they're married."

Veer ignored that information. "I'm starving. Let's get coffee and dosas."

"Okay," I said, rubbing my eyes, trying to remember the last time I felt this content.

We spent all winter going to bars, having sex, and lazing in bed on weekends. We explored the city like kids in a playground. With ships and ocean liners cruising in and out of its deepwater harbor, the busy wet docks, the floating casinos, and the noisy little ferries that start at the Gateway of India. Bombay is a nautical city whose spirit is reflected in the details of its architecture, with portholes, ship deck railings, and observatory towers common features of its art deco residential buildings. Bandra was sparkly and trendy Portuguese homes and palm-fronded lanes lit up with Christmas stars. At Mount Mary Basilica, you could buy a candle in the shape of a body part to light, with the hope that whatever ails it will be cured. I lit a candle in the shape of a heart.

I spoke about Asha to Veer in dribs and drabs, always bracing for the moment that he might turn away. He didn't. Finally, I let out a long, slow exhale. Veer was a mirror that made me seem beautiful. We kissed in a taxi hurtling down Marine Drive. The driver kept turning around to watch and almost drove us into the sea.

It was getting harder and harder to put up with the weird silence of the white government car, as it beetled across overpasses and past dusty construction sites, glistening glass buildings, and run-down tin shanties. Wobbly scooterists, cyclists, and pedestrians were forced to leap out of its path. I fell into a half sleep and was jerked back awake when the car stopped at Veer's aunt's address. The driver honked twice for the gate to be opened. I studied my exhausted reflection in the window, wiping smudged kohl from under my eyes, fixing my hair, swiping on lip gloss. Anxiety worked better than caffeine. A watchman, his face wrapped in a scarf, pulled open the iron gate.

A young man told us madam was waiting in the living room. Veer handed my bags to him. He walked me down a thin corridor. Dim lamps glowed orange in corners, throwing just enough light for us to see where we were going. In the living room, there was a white shag rug on the floor looking like spilled milk, maroon curtains with tasseled edges, and mahogany coffee tables that seemed to groan under the weight of crystal vases full of fake flowers and silver photo frames. It was an overcrowded room, as if the occupants were terrified of empty spaces, of negative capability.

Veer's aunt Kitty was scrolling through her cell phone on a sofa, in a velvet tracksuit and flip-flops. Chanel eyeglasses perched on top of her head were attached to a rope of small pearls. Her hair, with streaks of ash blond, was twisted up in a French knot. Almond-sized solitaires dripped from her earlobes; her wrists seemed weighed down with gold-and-diamond bangles; her index finger had a ruby surrounded by diamond baguettes.

"Hello, Aunty. Thank you so much for letting me stay with you," I said.

"Welcome, my dear. You can call me Kitty Aunty or Auntyji, if you'd like to be more formal," Kitty said, smiling warmly but keeping her arms folded. She looked as if she was waiting for me to do something. I scanned my sleep-deprived brain to see if I'd missed an important bit of etiquette. I was about to thank Kitty again, more profusely this time, when Veer dived as if fielding a cricket ball and touched Kitty's feet. My eyebrows shot up. I had no idea Veer did things like that. Did *I* need to do things like that? I didn't even know where to start. Veer had thrown me into the deep end of the pool.

Wanting her to like me, I stared at Kitty's manicured toenails. *Do I touch the toes or the whole foot? With my fingers or my palm?* I grabbed hold of her big toe for an awkward moment and shot back up, my face burning with embarrassment.

"Oh, so unnecessary," Kitty said with a chuckle. She pulled me up off the floor. Our faces grazed. Her skin felt like soft expensive kid leather. She smelled like a bowl of mangoes.

"Auntyji, would Monty Uncle like to meet Noomi?" Veer asked. "Or is he in bed?"

"Oh, I sent him off at midnight. He has a six A.M. tee-off at the Delhi Golf Club." Kitty rolled her eyes. "You know how he is about his golf."

"I'll see him tomorrow, then," Veer said, looking at his watch. "I should probably get going, Auntyji."

"Noomi, are you hungry? Do you want them to heat up some dinner?" Kitty said, turning toward me.

"I think I'll go straight to bed," I said, picking up my handbag, which had looked smart in the airport but now seemed quite shabby and old-fashioned among all this Dubai-level opulence.

"Of course," Kitty said.

She led us down the hallway to a bedroom with peach and pink furnishings.

"This is my daughter's old room. Make yourself comfortable," she said in a tone that conveyed the opposite.

Behind her head, Veer shaped his hand into a phone. "I'll call you," he mouthed, and left.

Alone in Kitty's daughter's old room, I tossed my bag in a corner, sat down on a pink armchair, and shucked off my shoes. Rubbing my aching feet, I looked around me. The bedroom, like the living room, was stuffed with furniture, pictures, and gewgaws. The ornately carved bed had a fat duvet, a mountain of frilly pillows, and a gauzy canopy. Kitty's daughter's photo stood on a bedside table. Her hair had ash-blond streaks too. Her eyes, in blue lenses, shot sexy death rays. I tossed all the frilly pillows to the floor, got into the bed, and read a few pages of my book, burrowed under the duvet. I was about to turn off the lamp when my cell phone began vibrating.

"Hey, what's up?" I whispered, and wondered why I was whispering.

"Hi, potato. Forgot to tell you—I'll be picking your parents up from the airport tomorrow," Veer said. "You can sleep in."

"That sounds great," I said, pulling the comforter to my chin. "But I'm sure *Auntyji* would not be pleased. Veer, listen, I'm not sure about this. Your aunt—she seems a bit intense. Would it be okay if I moved into a hotel or somewhere else, like a friend's place, tomorrow?"

"You're just tired," Veer said, and sighed. "Auntyji seems intimidating at first. But if you dig deep, she's a very loving person."

"Acha," I said with a half smile. "I might need one of those earth-boring machines to dig that deep."

"Poking fun at someone who just wants to make sure you're comfortable," Veer said. "Very polite."

"No offense to your aunt," I said, gritting my teeth, "I'd just be much more comfortable in a hotel."

A brief pause. "It's literally three days. Just play along? It'll look odd if you move into a hotel room after one night. You want to make a good impression, don't you? I mean, you wanted all of this marriage stuff. I was very happy with us living together."

"You were happy not committing."

Another sigh. When did Veer become such a sigher? "And you wanted a commitment," Veer said. "Why? Our relationship was doing fine, no? Why did you want the families to get involved?"

"I'm going to read you a line."

"A line?" Veer said. "What line?"

"A line from a book," I said.

"Which book?" Veer groaned. He wasn't much of a reader. "How long will this take? I'm tired."

"Which book?" I mimicked. "The one I was reading on the plane."

"Uh-huh, okay. Make it quick."

"It's poetry," I said, taking the book from my bedside and turning to a favorite page. "There's this line that keeps echoing in my head. It says..." I began reading, leaning toward the lamp on one elbow. "*I just want a humble, murderously simple thing: for a person to be happy when I enter a room.*" I lay back. "That's it. That's what I want."

"You lost me," Veer said after a pause. "Am I not always glad when you walk into the room?"

"Look, I don't know the exact reason why I want us to get married. My parents' marriage is destroying them, slowly, like termites eating a house. But ours will be different. Because I'm a nicer person with you around. Kinder, with softer edges, less angry."

"Less angry?" Veer teased.

"Shut up." I smiled.

"Okay, you're not angry. But you *are* starting to sound a bit loony. Get some sleep. I want you to look happy when you meet my parents."

"Shouldn't I *be* happy?"

"What did I say?"

"You said *look*. There's a difference between looking and being."

"Noomi"—I imagined Veer rubbing the bridge of his nose— "you'll probably deal with my family once or twice a year, max. Didn't we agree to play by the rules in Delhi? If you do the sanskari bahu bit around them, it'll make them more comfortable."

"All this sanskari bahu and playing by the rules," I said, "are tactics used to pressure women into having no boundaries. You'd know that, Veer, if you ever read a book."

"Noomi," Veer said, an edge creeping into his voice, "you're giving me a fucking headache."

"Okay, all right, whatever," I said, too tired to keep this going.

"You really think having a traditional Punjabi wedding will make you less enraged about the patriarchy?" Veer laughed. "Have you ever been to one?"

"Oh, just shut up," I said.

"Good night," Veer said. "I love you."

"Bye."

Too fidgety to fall asleep, I slid out of bed and walked over to my suitcase, bare feet dabbling the marble floor. From under my clothes, I took out a small bottle of vodka. Pleasing Kitty had made me feel like a court jester trying to entertain a bored queen. As I drank, I felt my confidence surge. Tomorrow would be better. I'd charm Veer's parents. I'd charm the hell out of them. I'd do the whole sanskari bit, become the perfect, obedient, charming daughter-in-law of their dreams. Yawning, I hid away the bottle, crept back under the comforter, and drifted off.

The alarm rang and I didn't know where I was. Then I did. New Delhi, Veer's aunt's house. The realization dropped like a pebble on my chest. I lay in bed, watching the fluffy duvet rise and fall with my breath. I looked around for the remote to turn off the AC. Today I'd finally meet Veer's parents. I wondered what they'd be like. Veer had said his mother was religious. How did she feel about the fact that I wasn't? Or had Veer not told her? What had he told them about me? Nothing? Everything? I headed to the shower, worrying questions multiplying like rabbits inside my mind.

Wrapped in a fluffy, nice-smelling towel, I laid a few outfits on the bed. Indian or Western? The sanskari thing, of course, was to wear Indian clothes when meeting one's future in-laws. But a salwar kameez made me look like a dowdy frump. I chose a pair of silk trousers with a loose cotton top. I hooked silver earrings through my ears and slid a pearl bracelet on to my wrist.

Once I was dressed, I wandered out into the living room. Kitty was seated in the same spot as the night before as if she'd never been to bed. The color of her kurta and the stacks of gold bangles on her wrists made her blend perfectly with the room. Kitty smiled at me. I smiled back. A smell of jasmine incense haunted the cool morning air.

"Good morning," Kitty said brightly. "Slept well? Everything was comfy?"

"Yes, thank you, Auntyji," I said, picking an apple out of a crystal bowl.

"There's cereal on the countertop," Kitty said, staring at her phone.

"Actually," I said, looking toward the kitchen, "could the cook make me an egg?"

Kitty, who'd been tapping out a message, looked up. "Today is Tuesday."

"Tuesday?" I was confused. "Okay, so..." *What happens on Tuesdays?*

Kitty looked at me sideways. "Our family doesn't eat non-veg on Tuesday." She made a dismissive gesture. "Really, Noomi, you should know all this. You did no homework on us?"

"Oh," I said, feeling stupid. "Of course, Veer did mention it. In that case, cereal is fine."

"Hello, pretty girl!" a man said.

Kitty's husband, presumably, from the way he ambled into the living room, as though everything inside of it, including the two women, was his. He took my hand, holding a pair of golf gloves in the other. Tufts of gray-white hair poked out from his ears.

"Noomi, this is Monty," Kitty said.

"Hello, Uncle," I said.

"Welcome to Delhi!" Monty said. I tried to get my hand back, but his grasp was firm. His goatee made his lips look oddly pouty. His eyes were an algae green, framed with thick eyelashes. He had a bulbous nose and made me think of a lecherous koala.

"Did you rest well, Noomi ji?" he asked. "Has Chubby given you any breakfast?" He called his wife "Chubby" even though she was as slim as a stork.

"Yes, thank you," I said, smiling, struggling to remove my hand from his grasp.

"Monty, please get ready, we're going to be late, and *she* just woke up." Kitty nodded in my direction.

I turned, surprised at the edge in Kitty's voice. "Oh, are we late? Veer said I could sleep in." I screamed inwardly at "Veer said." We weren't even engaged, and I needed him to sign off on staying in bed longer than what was considered acceptable by his relatives.

Kitty threw Monty a glance. "Aren't you worried about making a good impression on Veer's parents?"

"I guess it was a miscommunication," I said. In my head, I was breaking Kitty's furniture.

"Okay, ladies, I'll be out of the shower in a jiffy," Monty said. He gave me a twinkly wink and left.

"Oh, and"—Kitty looked me up and down—"is that what you're wearing? Don't you have a nice Indian outfit or something? My parents, Veer's grandparents, will be there. I don't think they would be very impressed by those tight trousers and that translucent shirt."

I returned to my room, my hands shaking. This promised to be a very long day, and I was already failing. Could Veer's idea of me change based on his family's first impression? I didn't know. As I changed from my trousers and top into a salwar kameez that I wore for work sometimes, the thought of canceling the wedding made me clench my jaw. I wasn't going to ruin this chance at a different kind of life. I took out my secret vodka and brought it into the bathroom, took two generous swigs. I brushed my teeth and my tongue, thinking I could be charming if I wanted to—I just needed a little help.

The sun was in the center of a cloudless sky when Kitty Ahuja's car turned down a narrow lane lined with Ashoka trees. It stopped outside a two-story home that looked a bit lost among the mansions in the Malhotras' posh South Delhi neighborhood. Veer's grandfather had built his house in the 1960s, when that part of the city was forest land. But Delhi had grown and spread like moss, and the famous Colony Market, full of expensive restaurants and kirana stores selling foreign goods, was only a five-minute walk from the house. Veer's granddad's name, C. M. Malhotra, was spelled out on the mailbox in gold. Two cars were parked bumper to bumper in the driveway, next to a patchy little lawn, the kind my grandmother would turn up her nose at. Its balding grass was bordered with red bricks embedded into the ground.

A woman in a pink chiffon salwar kameez stood framed in the front doorway. Her fluffy hair fell to below her chin. When she smiled, little crow's feet appeared around her eyes, like they did around Veer's. A big red bindi marked her forehead, and a mangalsutra hung around her neck. How many signs marked a married woman, while a man didn't even need to wear a wedding ring. As we approached, the woman, Veer's mother, dropped her gaze and folded her hands in a namaste. Her gold bangles were not as heavy or numerous as Kitty's, and her fingers were adorned with only two rings: one was a single ruby set in gold, the other a pearl flanked with small brownish diamonds.

I approached with a smile. She held me lightly by the shoulders, cocked her head, and regarded my outfit, her gaze dripping with honeyed impersonality. "Noomi, welcome, welcome! I'm Veer's mummy," she said.

I smiled again mutely. It felt like I'd stepped into a play but had forgotten my lines.

"All okay? We expected you a bit sooner. Didi, Jeejaji! How are you?" Rita Malhotra—that was her name, I remembered now—greeted the Ahujas with a namaste.

"Hallo, Rita Rani," Monty said. "How are you, my beauty? Always lovely to see you."

"Sorry, Rita," Kitty said. "Noomi here took her sweet time." She gave a mean chuckle.

"I'm so sorry," I said, pushing down my anger. "Veer said I could sleep in."

"Oh ho. Anyway, never mind," Rita said with a slight bow of her head. "Come in, the family's eager to meet you."

She smiled. With her hand at the small of my back, she waltzed me through the door, into the house.

An assortment of relatives, like chocolates in a box, was seated in the Malhotras' living room, which looked like a budget-conscious version of Kitty's: maroon curtains, white rug, knickknacks and artificial flowers. In one corner, a refrigerator hummed next to a dining table covered in an eyelet-patterned plastic tablecloth. Rita led me to Veer's grandparents, seated side by side on a sofa like aging gods. C. M. Malhotra wore a blue cravat arranged around his sagging throat. His bottom lip stuck out, as if he was displeased about being seated next to his wife. They'd been married fifty years and had probably run out of things to talk about. Veer's grandmother reminded me of a small brown hen, with a beaked nose protruding out of her soft, round face. Her pink satin kurta was taut and shiny over the mound of her belly.

Next to the old couple, with his hands resting on the back of their sofa, was a compact-looking man with very good, attentive posture, who looked to be in his late fifties. His short salt-and-pepper hair had been aggressively combed over, and he bounced on the balls of his feet like a child waiting for his turn to speak.

"Hello, Noomi," the gentleman said. "Welcome. We are so very pleased to have you in our home."

"This is Veer's daddy, Mr. Sanjay Malhotra." Rita spoke her husband's name like an awards show hostess. "And here," she said, turning to the old couple, "are most respected Mummyji and Daddyji."

"Namaste," I said, joining my hands.

"How was your stay last night?" Mr. Malhotra asked. "Very comfortable, I'm sure?"

"Yes, very comfortable." I smiled.

"My sister has been spoiling you a lot, hmm?" Mr. Malhotra said. "She loves to spoil us, I tell you."

"Oh yes, spoiled rotten," I said. "Auntyji has such a beautiful home."

"Very loving, Kitty Didi is. Hain na, Rita?" He turned to his wife.

"Absolutely," Rita confirmed.

"She dotes on our parents. Last summer, she took them to Europe for a month. A month! Stayed in the best hotels. Let Mummyji shop and shop to her heart's content." Mr. Malhotra spread his arms wide and beamed. "Let me introduce you to them," he said. "Veer calls his grandpa Bade Papa. And my mother is Badi Mummy."

"Namaste, Bade Papa, Badi Mummy," I said.

Once again, the expectant pause, like a music note suspended in the air. I added an enchanted smile to my face and bent to touch the grandparents' feet.

"God bless. May you have a long and happy life," Bade Papa said gruffly. He thumped my shoulder—a signal that I could stop bending.

"Your daughter-in-law is so quaint," Kitty chirruped. "Always touching everyone's feet."

"A traditional girl ji," Monty roared. "A rare commodity these days."

I imagined my father holding his sides, laughing.

"God bless," Badi Mummy wheezed, and patted the cozy space between her and Bade Papa. "Come, sit."

"Please," Rita said. "What can we offer you? Something to drink? Tea, coffee, juice?"

"No thank you," I said, squeezing in between Veer's grandparents. My answer displeased them. I was in a play, and I'd veered off script. "I mean"—I cleared my throat—"if you have juice of any kind, that would be lovely, thank you." I turned up the wattage of my smile.

"Bring madam some *fresh* lychee juice," Mr. Malhotra, emphasizing the "fresh" very hard for some reason, ordered a young man hovering at the edge of our little tableau. He dashed off and returned with a tiny glass in the center of a large silver tray.

"Thank you," I said. "Do you know when Veer will get here?" I asked with another polite smile. In response, Badi Mummy picked my hand up and plopped it into her lap. Her thin fingers felt like chicken bones covered with soft, loose skin, on which her cold rings moved up and down.

"You are sweet," Bade Papa said, looking me over. "Small and cute. How tall are you?"

"Five-two," I said.

"And how old are you?" Bade Papa continued.

"Um. Twenty-six."

"Slightly old. Less than average in height," Bade Papa said. "But you'll make an attractive couple. Our Veer is six-two. You two will look like Amitabh and Jaya Bachchan."

"Thank you, Bade Papa," I said. Jaya Bachchan indeed. I sat up straighter and made it a point to speak more clearly, like a beauty pageant contestant.

"Veer is handsome, smart, earning well. You'll be able to enjoy." Badi Mummy squeezed my hand tighter. "Lucky girl"—she patted my cheek hard—"you've found a real diamond!"

"Indeed," I said. "I feel so very lucky. I thank god every day."

"Good, good," Bade Papa said, nodding.

I took my hand away, pretending I needed to scratch a mosquito bite on my leg. I closed my eyes. According to Bade Papa and Badi Mummy, I'd been sitting around, waiting for Veer or some other man to crash a champagne bottle on the ship of my life. In reality, I'd taken a taxi to the airport straight from the courts. Because people were more likely to talk freely with a woman, Shiv had given me a tough beat. That day, I'd covered a trial where three men were charged with rape. The men— the boys, rather—yelled threats at the magistrate as she read out their sentence. The boys' families blocked my way in the corridor. They took out hospital bills, exam papers—anything to prove their sons had been elsewhere. Love stretched far beyond the borders of morality.

Jeh and I would speak on the phone every night; sometimes I'd read out my latest article. It's surprising what you find out about yourself when there's no one around to tell you who you are. In the anonymity that came with living in a big city, I bloomed. I made friends. We lived three women to a flat in Bandra. Much to our landlady's horror, the flat was littered with cigarettes, bottles of alcohol. We spoke like banshees. The building across the road faced ours. On the second floor lived a woman who had a lover visit every Tuesday night. We'd make our drinks and gather to watch. The lover would enter and throw his briefcase and, if it was raining, his umbrella to the floor, and they would begin kissing in the hall of her long railroad-style flat. As they made their way from hall to bedroom, so would the three of us, carrying our bottles and ashtrays, running from one window to the next until the couple finally leaped onto the bed, flopping about like dying fish.

There were evenings when Veer and I would go smoke hookahs at the rooftop bar of a seedy hotel, or share a joint in his room and go watch a terrible Bollywood movie at the Regal Cinema. We were always broke; drinking at posh bars was unsustainable. No matter. Unlike in Kamalpur, you needn't be rich to have fun in Bombay, just young.

I was good at my job as a reporter. Shivraj turned out to be an excellent boss. He gave me the freedom to cover a trial from any angle I chose, without the fear of being hauled up for contempt. I became known on my beat; sources trusted me and fed me leads. My cell phone contained the contacts of powerful people: commissioners, politicians, bankers, a Bollywood actor or two. My job was the thing, Veer said, that he found most interesting about me.

As I plotted my escape from Badi Mummy's chicken-bone grasp, Veer, the diamond, walked into the living room. He'd picked my parents up from the airport. Jeh walked in after, in office khakis, jacket draped over his arm. My brain flooded with relief. I was even glad to see Asha, who, in her silk shirt and pressed trousers, made a refreshing contrast to Rita's overabundance of flowy chiffon. I'd kept a self-preserving distance from my mother. We spoke on the phone once in a while, but never about anything important. She'd ask me questions about my life, but I always slipped out from them like hands from a cat's cradle. The details of my life were mine alone, they were my treasure to share with those whom I trusted. I didn't ask her if she was sober; for the most part, I didn't care.

I hugged them both. No discernible smell of alcohol or cigarettes on Asha. Veer had decided his family could be given information on a need-to-know basis. I'd given up caring, but I knew that the Malhotras' ears would prick up if they heard a single word of Kamalpur gossip. Before I could whisper my warning, Mr. Malhotra had bounded up to my parents, hands outstretched.

"Welcome, sir!" he said, shaking Jeh's hand. "And, madamji, welcome! I'm Sanjay Malhotra. This is my lovely wife, Rita."

Head bowed, Rita folded her hands. "Welcome ji," she said. "So glad to finally meet you in person. Please come meet the rest of our lovely family: this is Kitty Didi and Monty Jeejaji."

A round of compliments and counter-compliments began afresh and ended when Bade Papa ordered lunch be served.

At the table, Rita flipped a hot, puffed roti onto my plate. I looked up, smiling like a Samoyed. The women sat on one side of the dining table, the men on the opposite, and Bade Papa at the head. Rita remained standing to continuously pile food onto everyone's plates. I covered mine with my hands. Rita, it seemed, was not one to give up so easily.

"Noomi? Wouldn't you like some more curry?"

"No thank you, er, Aunty," I said.

"Some dal then?"

"I already have some, thank you."

"Paneer?"

"Maybe a little later?"

"Yogurt?"

"There's still some on my plate," I pleaded.

"Then have some fruit?"

"I'll help myself, thank you!" I hadn't wanted to sound irritated. Chatter pulled to a record-scratch stop. Veer shot me a look from across the table. I shot a guilty one back at him.

"I mean," I amended. "I wouldn't want to waste."

"Rita, what is this? You're only serving," Kitty said. "Come, come, come, *chalo*, please sit down, relax, eat. I'll make sure everyone gets enough rotis." She grabbed Rita's serving dish.

"Please, Didi! Don't get up!" Rita sounded panicked. "I'll eat once everyone's eaten."

"Arey, come on." Kitty snatched up a large bowl and began to ladle yellow dal on Bade Papa's plate until he grunted for her to stop. Rita offered him a roti, which he took and didn't say thank you. She offered one to her husband, who also took it and didn't say thank you.

"It's the bloody sanskari Olympics," Jeh whispered, making me stifle a snorty guffaw. I took the napkin from my lap and threw it at him. Bade Papa looked up at us with a pouty frown.

"Very badly brought up, this one," Jeh said, smiling and pointing a thumb at me. "Bashes up her own dad."

"Don't worry," Bade Papa said, looking very serious. "Once she's a Malhotra, we will fix her."

After lunch we returned to the living room. I was about to fill Jeh in on everything that had happened when Veer threw me a look over his shoulder. I should be helping Rita out in the kitchen, the look suggested, not lolling about on the sofas with my father. I went and brought back a tray laden with bowls of fruit custard.

"So how big is... what's the name of your town again? Kamalabad or something?" Kitty asked.

"Kamalpur. It's not big at all, everyone knows everyone," Asha said, blowing on the face of her coffee.

"Are there good hotels?" Kitty grimaced, looking from Asha to Jeh. "Where will you put up our guests?"

Our guests? From behind his aunt, Veer gestured for me to calm down.

"Dad could arrange a place," Veer offered. "At a government guest-house, perhaps?"

"Nonsense," Monty said. "The girl's family always pays for everything." He gave Veer's head a light tap. "It's tradition. Don't try to be modern-shodern, son. Let the elders do the planning."

"Happy to arrange hotel rooms for your guests, Malhotra sahib," Jeh said, "once you tell us how many." He put on his bifocals and took out a notepad. I glared at Veer.

Veer's father clasped his hands between his knees. "Dekho Jeh, we Malhotras are not old-fashioned. I mean, we don't ask for dowry." He nodded encouragingly, as if to say, *That's modern of us, right? To not sell our son?* A breeze from the window upset his comb-over. He quickly patted it down. "But," he added with a smile, "our relatives... they must get gifts. Only to keep face, you understand. And for Veer, we'd like a few new suits, maybe a nice watch?"

"Okay, okay," Jeh said, jotting everything down. "Relatives: gifts. Veer: suits, watch."

"Dad," I said, putting a hand on Jeh's shoulder. "Can we discuss this?"

"What's there to discuss?" Kitty said. "This is nothing compared to what we'd have got if Veer was marrying a Punjabi girl." She put her custard bowl on the table. "But then, we wouldn't have such an embarrassingly frank discussion. It would've all been understood." Kitty threw up her hands. "Bhaiya darling, I noticed that you didn't include our parents in your list. You don't have to include me, but they should be given respect. They are the elders of our family." She nodded at Jeh, who scribbled another note.

Mr. Malhotra turned to his sister. "Oh, come on, Didi. As if Jeh would do such a thing." He turned to Jeh. "It goes without saying that my sister is very important in the family."

"Of course, of course," Jeh said.

"Dad."

"Your son is so good to our daughter," Asha said. "We worried that Noomi would never get married."

"Mom!"

"Oh ho, that's so sweet, Asha ji," Rita said, and smiled beatifically. "It's been wonderful meeting you and Jeh. We wish you weren't leaving tomorrow." She turned to me. "Noomi, do you know what tomorrow is?"

"Wednesday?" I offered.

"Ha!" Kitty said.

"Silly girl, it's the most important day of the year! We wives must fast all day for our husbands' health and long life." Giggles escaped her lips like bubbles. "I have an unconventional request: we want you to keep your first fast for Veer with me." Rita beamed like this was a special treat. "Asha, if you can change your ticket, Kitty Didi offered to host a kirtan in the evening. We break our fast after the moon rises."

"Oh, thank you so much, Rita," Asha replied, smirking. "But I think I'll let you and Noomi bond."

Alarmed, I glanced over at Veer, who made an encouraging kissy face.

"I'd love to," I said with a big fake smile.

Bade Papa and Badi Mummy retired to their room for a siesta. Veer's father, followed by his gaggle of attendants, said his goodbyes, got into the white car with the red light, and drove off to his office somewhere in the labyrinth of Lutyens' Delhi. Asha made Jeh take her shopping. Not in any hurry to head back to Kitty's, I asked Veer if he'd like to show me around the family market. The sun was low in the dusty sky. We held hands, walking down a road that curved through the neighborhood. Tramping on brittle yellow leaves and sticks, we passed under the curious stares of drivers and chowkidars, who'd escaped their houses in the afternoon lull to chew tobacco and play cards.

The market looked best in the evening: gleaming cars in the parking lot, and well-dressed South Delhiites going in and out of the restaurants and shops. College students in colorful kurtas and silver jewelry hanging around outside dive bars, smoking and arguing politics. The evening shadows were forgiving; not so the afternoon sun. Daylight exposed cracked and unpainted sidewalks, electrical wires that looped and sagged crisscross over trees, cigarette butts and shopping bags that collected in corners and clogged the gutters.

A gang of street dogs rummaged through garbage to find food. They whined and barked at the gooter-gooing pigeons across a small dusty lawn, scratching their dirty fur with their hind paws, mouths stretched in silly grins. Tiny fat puppies followed a mother with huge, heavy teats.

We stepped into a cookie-scented bakery and found a table. Veer ordered us coffee.

I looked out the window, feeling more than a little depressed. "It's a funny thing about dogs."

"What is?" Veer said. He turned the pages of a thin plastic menu.

"They're hierarchical animals. The pack can't function without an alpha."

"Acha?"

"Yeah." I nodded. "They need to know who they can boss over and who bosses over them."

"Interesting."

"Some people are like that too, don't you think?" I looked over at him.

"So, what's up?" Veer said, raising his eyebrows with a little smile. "You don't look happy."

"What do you mean?" I said.

"Why are you so sad?" Veer frowned. "I thought everything went off really well."

"I'm not," I said, looking into my coffee. "I'm just... it's just... all of this has been too much."

"What has?"

"All of it," I said, waving my hands in front of my face. "Delhi, your aunt, your parents. I don't know. I don't think I could ever fit in with them... with the Malhotras." I drummed the scarred wood table with my fingernails. "They are so... different. Now this fast thing. And you're, like, suddenly okay with me fasting all day for your long life?"

"You know I don't believe in all that stuff," Veer said. "But if it makes my mom happy..." He showed me his hands. "I mean, it's harmless, isn't it? It's a way for women to bond with each other."

"Why can't we bond like normal people—over shared traumas and suchlike?"

"Potato," Veer said, fixing me in place with a stare, "if you do this it'll make my mother very happy."

"Okay, why don't you fast with me then?" I said, crossing my arms. "For *my* long life."

"No chance." Veer let out a bark of laughter. "Women are used to starving yourselves with your dieting and whatnot. I would pass out."

"I'll do it." I nodded, squeezing the sides of my face. "Only because I want them to like me."

"They like you a lot already! You were amazing today." Veer smiled, pulling my hands away from my head. He opened my palms and kissed them.

"Yeah, that wasn't me," I said. "They don't like *me*, they like their ideal of a daughter-in-law. They like a lie." I took my hands back from Veer and covered my face. "I had to worry about everything I said or did. I felt like some kind of jewel thief, twisting this way and that to avoid those laser beams that set off alarms."

"Well, then fucking relax!" Veer said. "You don't need to be perfect. In fact, it made you come across as a bit snotty at times. Like, at the dining table, you didn't have to be so rude to my mom."

"What are you talking about?" I balked. "Snotty? When?"

"At lunch. You gave her such a look, like you thought she was an imbecile. You've got to control your face, Noomi. You didn't have to put my mother down like that. She's a simple woman. Food is just how she shows affection." He stood up and put money on the table.

"Veer, I didn't give any look," I said. "She wouldn't stop tossing rotis onto my plate. It felt like a domination thing."

"Be yourself," Veer said. "They will love you as much as I do."

"They'll never love me."

A brown puppy and its mother had settled under the shop's steps. The pup was chubby, his brown fur full of ticks. He rolled around in the dirt. His mother lay on her side. The puppy flipped over to tug at her ear. The mother's flank rose and fell as she snoozed in the late-afternoon sun. She let her pup nibble and pull at her ears for a while, then lifted one paw to delicately roll him away, a little ball of fur and dust. I sat down on the steps, not wanting to leave yet, and watched them play. Veer turned around and called out. I had to follow him back to the house.

*O*nce upon a time, there was a queen with seven older brothers who doted on her more than on their own wives. Her husband, the king, was at war. The queen went to her maternal home to fast for his long life. On the day of the fast, the queen's brothers returned home to find their sister collapsed on the floor, weak with hunger and thirst.

"Why do you starve yourself?" they asked her. "Come, eat and drink with us."

"I am fasting for my husband's victory in battle," the queen said. "Only once the moon has risen and I make offerings to it will I eat."

Unable to see her suffer, the youngest brother went out into the garden and placed a lamp in front of a mirror on the branch of a peepul tree.

Running back, he told his sister, "The moon has risen!"

The queen went to the terrace. After praying to the false moon, she came downstairs and broke her fast. With her first morsel, she sneezed; with her second, she found a hair; with her third morsel, a maidservant came running in—soldiers had arrived to say that the king, her husband, had died in a skirmish with his enemy.

"You've angered the gods," sneered her brothers' wives, who had not yet broken their own fasts. They were waiting for the true moon to rise. "Your brother lied to you."

The queen left her mother's home and rode with her guards until she reached the battle. She searched all over the corpse-strewn field and finally found her husband's body stuck with hundreds of arrows. Crying, she made a vow to not let a priest perform his last rites. She would bring him back to life with her devotion. For one year, the queen guarded the king's body. Each day she pulled out an arrow from it. When the day of the fast came around, only a single arrow remained.

Not wanting to leave anything to chance, the queen kept a fast so strict, she did not even swallow her own spit. When the moon rose, she looked at it through a veil, and then, satisfied that she'd fulfilled her duty, she left her husband's body in the care of her maidservant and went to find water to break her fast. The gods would surely take pity and give back the king's life. While the queen was away, the maidservant, wishing to end her good mistress's misery, pulled the last arrow from the king's body. He opened his eyes and, upon seeing the beautiful maidservant, took her for his wife. When the queen returned to the king, she was sent into the kitchen. The maidservant became the new queen.

An old woman sat upon a bunch of pillows on the marble floor in Kitty's living room, reciting this katha into a microphone, surrounded by a perfumed crowd—young and old—all dressed in red and pink, like brides. The bar was emptied of alcohol bottles and turned into a shrine covered with brocades, upon which sat gods and goddesses in silk and jewels. The smell of flowers, sandalwood incense, and, maddeningly, food floated above the floral scents of the women. The katha lady had henna-red hair and paan-stained lips. She closed her eyes and shook her head from side to side at the queen's sad folly.

According to the meteorological department, whose website I refreshed every few minutes, the moon was supposed to rise in another half hour or so. I'd had no water or food since Kitty woke me up at 5:00 A.M. that morning. Rubbing my barely open eyes, I'd followed her into the living room. I found Rita, fully dressed in bridal wear and makeup, waiting with a plate of sargi, which she wished to feed me by hand. There is something unnerving about discovering your future mother-in-law dressed to the nines before dawn. I touched her feet and then Kitty's feet. By the day's end, it felt like I'd touched everyone's feet.

"What gift are you giving your new mother today?" Badi Mummy asked. She was dressed in a red salwar kurta with gold flowers down the front. Her wrists were weighed down with bracelets that made noise whenever she moved, crashing and clanking like dishes in a sink.

"A sari?" I mumbled dizzily. More than twelve hours of no food or water made my head hurt. My stomach felt like it was being gnawed at. Laughter wafted in from the terrace. Veer, his father, and the other husbands were "keeping watch" for the moon, fortified by whisky and chicken tikkas, the smell of which made me want to claw off my nose. A thread of saliva dribbled from the side of my mouth.

"Bas?" Badi Mummy clucked her disapproval. "Arey, you're supposed to give your mother-in-law many things. Money, clothes, jewelry. After all, she has given you your life's happiness."

"She has?"

"Yes, you're marrying her son. Veer is a diamond!"

If Veer were really a diamond, I thought, I would've gladly sold him for some chicken tikka. I managed to keep this thought private. Instead, I mustered up a smile for Veer's grandmother.

"Excuse me, Badi Mummyji," I said. "I need to reapply my lipstick."

The peachy canopy over Kitty's daughter's bed glowed with light coming in from the street. I leaned against the bedroom door. Bursts of chatter and laughter buffeted it from the outside. I went over to my suitcase and scrambled through the mess of clothes for the hidden vodka bottle. I took a swig. By doing so, I'd technically broken my fast. Veer might be shot full of arrows. I took another swig and vodka dribbled down on my kurta. There was a knock at the door. I tucked the vodka bottle back into the suitcase, tossing a pile of clothes on top.

"Who is it?"

"It's me, sweetie," Rita said, jiggling the doorknob. "We were wondering where you ran off to?"

"I spilled water on my kurta. I'll be right out," I said.

"The moon is out," Rita said, sounding inspired. "Come quick. We'll break our fast together!"

"Oh, wonderful, give me two minutes," I said glumly. I peeled off my kurta, which wasn't stained but smelled like vodka. As did my breath. In the bathroom, I brushed my teeth until my gums bled. *Come on*, I told myself, slapping, pinching my cheeks. *Let's be pretty for the Malhotras.*

I hadn't packed another Indian outfit. All I had left were jeans and T-shirts. I looked in Kitty's daughter's closet. The doors slid open to reveal saris, salwars, dupattas, and stoles in all colors: lavender, fuchsia, chartreuse, orange, pink—all embellished with plastic gemstones, silver embroidery, sequins, beads, or tassels. The outfits were sealed in individual plastic bags, like items in a shop. I couldn't bring myself to tear off the plastic; besides, Kitty would surely mind if I borrowed her daughter's clothes. I had no option but to wear the lunchtime outfit that Kitty had ordered me to change out of yesterday. I wore the blouse and pants, ran a brush through my hair. With a long breath to clear my head, I walked out of the bedroom.

"Ah, there she is," said Mr. Malhotra, beaming. "Our sweet little bride."

They'd gathered on the terrace. The unpunctual moon wafted up from the branch of a tree. Rita walked over to me, holding a sieve as if it were a steering wheel. I was supposed to look at the moon through it and then at Veer's face, breaking my fast with a sip of water. Rita approached with that alarmingly beatific smile of hers. All of a sudden, the smile melted off her face. In its place was a glassy, surprised stare. She blinked once, twice.

"Noomi," she said, looking me over, a furrow in her forehead. *"What are you wearing?"*

Everyone craned their necks to see. I looked down at myself, wondering if there was a button missing on my top or a tear in the seat of my pants that I hadn't noticed. But there wasn't.

"My kurta got dirty," I said. "Didn't pack a spare. This was all I had left in my suitcase."

Rita made a little squeak of disappointment. "But you're supposed to be a... a *bride!*"

"I'm sorry," I said. "I didn't know there would be so many occasions for fancy Indian clothes."

"Didn't your mother advise you on what to pack?" Kitty arched her eyebrows.

"My mother doesn't advise me on anything." I was going to say something ruder, but I felt a hand on my shoulder.

"Let's move on," Veer said. "Noomi doesn't know all these little things yet. Finish this ritual, so that you ladies can eat." He held my hand, smiling. "You must be starving."

"Oh, how sweet," Rita said. "We're very used to it. I don't even notice that I'm fasting."

"Well, I do," I said, grabbing the sieve from Rita's hands. "Come on, Veer, let's see if this makes you any more handsome." I held the sieve up to Veer's face, then moved him aside and looked at the moon. I lifted a glass of water and drank it greedily, spilling it on my shirt.

"Well done, Noomi," said Mr. Malhotra, clapping. "Your first fast is a great success!"

"Not yet," Rita interrupted with a small, girlish giggle. "There is one last thing."

"What?"

"Noomi, you must touch Veer's feet."

"What?!"

"It's tradition." Rita pointed at Veer's feet in case I didn't know where to find them.

A pause. "I'm sorry," I said.

"Sorry?" Rita smiled and frowned at the same time.

"Yes, I'm sorry. I can't do that." I shook my head.

"I don't want her to," Veer added hastily.

Another pause. I fixed my gaze on a terrace tile with thin, lacy cracks; I could feel everyone's stares on the back of my neck. A lizard, taking advantage of the distraction, slithered across into a pink bougainvillea. If Rita asked me to touch Veer's feet one more time, I'd take the next flight out of Delhi.

"Okay," Rita said. Although it was clear that she was annoyed, her tone stayed as pleasant as ever. "How about you touch Veer's daddy's feet, then?"

How about I lock myself in the bedroom and drink to oblivion? Veer's family wanted me to grovel at their feet! If I'd been less insecure—if I wasn't desperate to believe that Veer and I had something worth groveling for—I would've walked out. I should've walked out.

"Okay," I said. Sounds of relief from the crowd. I went to my future father-in-law and touched his feet.

"God bless," Veer's father said. I straightened back up with a smile. He grabbed my face and planted an unwanted kiss on my forehead, then wrapped his arms around me. I placed my hands on his chest and pushed away gently. He didn't let go.

"Okay, okay, great," Kitty said, sarcastically clapping. "Dinner is served. Come on, everyone."

We came in from the terrace through a pair of French doors. The dining room was lit with dimmed ocher lamps. The moon's watery light cast our shadows across the marble floor.

Dinner was laid out on the glass dining table in long silver dishes: kofta curry; fried okra and eggplant; a salad with almonds, walnuts, and raisins; vegetable pasta with a white sauce; and vegetable biryani. The servers circulated with pooris and parathas. For dessert, there were gulab jamuns, dark as bruises; glistening jalebis; and kheer with slivered almonds.

"So proud of you, Noomi!" Mr. Malhotra exclaimed. "Our good little bride."

"With a good little appetite," Kitty said, glancing down at my plate.

A server offered me a fresh, hot poori; I waved it away.

Kitty went on: "Dear, if you keep eating, how will you fit into your wedding outfits, hmm? Oh, that reminds me." She grabbed Rita's hand. "I want you both to stay back after dinner. I'm getting outfits made for you, Noomi. I don't really get your taste." She looked me up and down, reading my clothes. "It would be better if you picked the designs yourself."

"Thank you," I said. "That's so kind. You don't have to do that."

"I'm not doing it for you. Veer is my nephew, I want do this for *him*," Kitty said. Kitty's insults were like cat shit, buried in conversations, but they left behind a powerful stink.

Once the other guests left, Veer, his father, and Monty had a drink on the terrace. Kitty, Rita, and I sat down at the dining table, now cleared of dishes and wiped down. Kitty spread out magazines and piles of fabric, beads, sequins, and plastic gemstones.

"I thought we could take this," Kitty said, holding up a sequined swathe of fuchsia silk, "and add these to the neckline and to the collar." She smiled, tossing egg-sized blue-and-silver plastic gemstones onto the cloth.

"Wow, Didi! That's a great idea. So creative," Rita said.

"Very nice," I said. The idea of wearing outfits festooned with plastic jewels made me want to die.

"And then I thought," Kitty went on, pleased with her fashion-designing skills, "we could make this"—she held up a bit of staticky satin embroidered with giant sunflowers—"into that type of Anarkali." She pointed to a picture in a magazine. "Although Noomi is short," she added, biting on a thumbnail, "so I don't know if it will suit her."

"No, no. It'll look very nice, Didi," Rita assured her. "Noomi can wear high heels."

I would have to wear these outfits, giant sunflowers and all, at the wedding. In public. I smiled and nodded, smiled and nodded. Inside my heart screamed and howled.

After it was over, I crept into my bedroom and locked the door. From my suitcase, I took out my vodka bottle and set it gently, like a lover, on the canopy bed. The house was silent. Everyone had gone home or to bed. What would happen if I called off the wedding and spent my life in a room with only alcohol, cigarettes, and books for company? I twisted off the bottle cap, poured three fingers of vodka into a glass, and drank it down. The evening fell from my skin like leeches dowsed with salt. *I can handle it,* I thought, pouring myself another.

My cell phone buzzed, and Veer's name flashed on the screen. "Hi," I said unenthusiastically.

"Hey, you were amazing tonight," Veer shouted over loud, pulsating music. "You were brilliant. My parents were super impressed. Good job!"

"Thanks," I said, frowning. "Wait, where are you? What's with the loud music?"

"Well, Mom sent me to the market to order flowers for Auntyji, you know, to say thank you for tonight. I ran into some friends," Veer shouted. "They were drinking at 4S. I told them we'd just got engaged, so they dragged me to this nightclub to celebrate. Don't worry, I know I have to pick you up crazy early tomorrow for your flight. I'll be heading home soon."

"Wait, why don't you come pick me up now?" I said. "I could do with a night out."

"Nooms, it's late at night," Veer said. "Auntyji would think it was inappropriate."

"What's so inappropriate about taking me out to a club?" I yelled into the phone. "We're engaged."

"Don't be idiotic, Noomi," Veer said.

"Fuck you, Veer," I said. "This is like being married into a convent. I'm a nun now."

"I'll let that go," Veer said in his best calm, corporate-guy voice. "You've had a rough day. Now tomorrow I'll pick you up at—"

I cut the call. Fine, I'd make my own nightclub. The vodka bottle sloshed about as I carried it by the neck into the bathroom. I took my cigarette pack out from its hiding place in a laundry basket. I took a swig and sat down on the floor. My cell phone lit up through the thin cotton of my pocket. I took it out and looked at the screen.

A text from Veer: *PLZ DONT BE ANGRY. ILU. C U 2MORO.*

"Fuck you," I told the message. I swiped through my last dialed list. I called my father, even though he was probably asleep.

"Hello?" Jeh sounded like he'd been raised from the dead. "Noomi, is everything okay?"

"Everything is terrible."

"What happened?" Jeh said. I could tell that what he meant was: *What did you do?*

"I'm at Kitty's house," I said. "Nothing happened, okay? Relax."

"You've been crying."

"I'm not crying," I said, weeping. "The evening was a disaster."

"What's wrong, Piglet?" Jeh asked. "Talk to me."

"Dad, Veer's family, they're *insane*. His aunt won't stop criticizing every fucking thing I do. I was starving all day, and then they wanted me to touch Veer's feet!"

"Noomi, Noomi, you sound hysterical," Jeh said. I imagined him pulling at his hair, the way he did when he worried. "Just try and make them happy. You won't see them again after the wedding."

"You're telling me to lie down and take it." I raised myself up off the floor.

"Peace at all costs," he said. "Peace at all costs. That's always been my motto."

"Fuck peace! Who gets peace? Why is it never me?" I screamed. My damp soles slid on the floor. I slipped forward. "I'm asking you to have my back. Instead you're telling me to bend and grovel."

"In life, be like a coconut tree. It bends so it won't break. Veer's a good man. Don't be self-destructive, Noomi. Try to please his family. Play the game for a bit."

"Go back to sleep. Sorry I bothered you."

"Promise me you'll behave," Jeh pleaded. "I don't want you to miss this chance at being happy."

"I'm leaving in the morning. There's no time to misbehave," I said.

"But—"

"Good night."

I put the cell phone on the sink counter and pushed it away; it caromed across the granite top and crashed against the mirror. I looked at my swollen eyelids. I was ugly, and the vodka bottle was almost empty. I lay down on my side on the floor, a towel under my head, taking small sips to make it last longer. The hard marble hurt against my hip bone.

I must've passed out. When I woke up, the light outside the bathroom's small window had become a powdery, predawn blue. Still drunk, I stood under the shower for as long as I could stand the hot water. I brushed my teeth and sprayed perfume all over my body, hoping it would mask the smell of vodka that seemed to leak from my pores. I placed the bottle inside my suitcase and laid my clothes on top of it. I looked around to check if there was anything else that I needed to hide. So much time and energy spent hiding, lying about who I was. I'd left my cell phone in the bathroom. It began to ring, rattled to the sink's edge, and fell off. The screen cracked. *Veer calling,* it flashed.

In the car on the way to the airport, I pretended to nap. But Veer didn't seem eager to talk; he was on his laptop, already in work mode. If he smelled the vodka on me, he didn't comment. I didn't ask him what time he got home from the nightclub. I didn't care. My mind made a picture of what being married to Veer would be like. I opened one eye and looked out the window. Delhi slid past in a nauseating blur. I groaned and shut it out.

Veer and I would marry in my grandparents' garden. Lily Mama and I sat on the veranda on a winter afternoon, the sunshine sweet and soft, our heads together over a goldsmith's sketches for my wedding necklace. I held a stone, the size of my pinkie nail, up to the light. It was full of green fire. I brought it close to my eye.

"Remember," Lily Mama scolded, "emeralds are brittle. They crack easily."

"Where did you get these?" I asked, setting the emerald down gently on the blue velvet cloth.

"They were my mother's." Lily Mama smiled. "I set them aside for you on the day you were born."

Love squeezed my ribs. Lily Mama was good at hiding how much she cared. We looked out at the garden in comfortable silence. A green bird the size of a ping-pong ball, with opalescent wings and a ruler-straight tail, landed on the terra-cotta birdbath by the rosebushes, admired its reflection for a moment, and then flew off.

"Uff-oh, this new gardener has made it his life's mission to ruin my roses," Lily Mama said. She trundled off into the lawn, barking orders in her broken, mangled Hindi, looking large and pure in the yellow morning sunshine, like a fat, gracious angel. A greater coucal, a crow pheasant, hopped onto the lawn, copper wings burnished in the sunlight. Its eyes were tiny red flames in its oil-black head. It saw Lily Mama and took off, letting out a *whoop-whoop-whoop*. In remote parts of the country, like the village Shanta Bai grew up in, the coucal's call was a bad omen. I'd always thought of it as a sign of good luck.

I pointed out the coucal to Lily Mama and said, "Look, my lucky bird."

"He doesn't belong to you," Lily Mama said. "Luck is a wild, untamable thing."

I remember being in the kitchen when Lily Mama showed Asha how to make Jeh's favorite dessert, malida—made of wheat, ghee, cardamom, almonds, and sugar. Asha slivered the almonds with a long knife and tossed them into a sizzling pan of ghee, as Lily Mama watched, arms crossed. "No, no, you're supposed to wait until they're golden brown." I saw Asha's eyes begin to tear up, her smile collapse under the weight of disapproval. The knife slipped out of her hand

and clattered to the floor by Lily Mama's feet. "Well, come on, pick it up," Lily Mama said. "Pick it up!" she roared. Asha dived to the floor. She lifted the knife; it flashed in my eyes. My mother too was a brittle gemstone; she too cracked easily.

The coucal flew into the bamboo thicket. I found him perched on a gray stone. Puffing up his throat, the bird let out a few whoops. I bowed. He flew off without returning the greeting.

"Did you put aside gemstones for the other baby?" I said to Lily Mama, coming out of the thicket. "He died, so can I have his share too?" I blinked until my eyes adjusted to the sunlight, putting one hand over my forehead like a visor to cut the glare.

Lily Mama was bent over, big bottom in the air, pulling dead leaves out with her hands. She turned and said, "What?" then went back to stripping the rosebush.

I strolled up with my hands clasped behind my back. "A few years ago, Shanta Bai told me my mother had a second baby, born when I was six. He didn't survive." I studied Lily Mama's alabaster face. Something bright and green flashed in the corner of my vision. I turned to watch a flock of parrots alight on a bare tree and turn into its leaves. They took off again when the dogs ran helter-skelter on the lawn, barking.

Lily Mama straightened up and squinted at me. "He looked like you," she said. "A tiny thing." She cupped her hands and brought them together. "Asha was out of control, screaming, shouting." She looked down at the grass. "His little lungs couldn't work. Only lived for a few days."

I remember when my mother would lie still on the bed and let me paint her arms and legs with my Camlin colors set. I made flowers on her arms, vines that twisted around her long, beautiful legs. I had only a few happy memories with Asha after the age of six. I took Lily Mama's hands, plump as madeleine cakes, in mine. "I'm sorry," I said.

Lily Mama smiled. "Pudding," she said. "You're going to be okay."

A tailorbird flew down to the birdbath. I took the emerald out of its velvet bag and held it out.

"Look," I said to the bird. "This color is you."

"Noomi! What did I say about being careful with those emeralds?"

Startled, the tailorbird took off, a jewel flying away in the pale winter sky.

The groom's party was late to the mehendi. They would be late to everything. Veer's aunts, uncles, and cousins walked through carrying a basket of gifts. We rounded up the herd of relatives and handed them presents. Jeh had borrowed money to pay for the jewelry and saris for Rita, Kitty, and Badi Mummy and watches for Mr. Malhotra and Bade Papa. Jeh said weddings and funerals were times to place family unity ahead of individual feelings. I wasn't happy about any of it.

Rita ushered me onto a sofa. "Sit," she ordered. I sat. As the relatives watched on, she placed a velvet case on my lap. "For our new daughter," she said, opening it with a flourish to display a gold rope necklace with matching earrings and a set of gold bangles with dodgy-looking diamonds.

"Now," Rita said. "Let's see how our Malhotra jewelry looks on you."

Rita unclasped the necklace with Lily Mama's emeralds and laid it on a table. She hung the thick gold rope around my neck. Veer's Auntyji, smiling, pushed a red fabric bundle of clothes, bangles, sindoor, bindis, et cetetra into my arms. I should've smiled more—pretended to be grateful for all the fuss. That afternoon, I learned violence could be transmitted by actions that might , to a bystander, appear entirely innocent. Kind, even. When Rita took off my grandmother's gift, I couldn't protest or I'd come off as rude in front of all the fawning relatives. She took away my necklace and, with it, my voice.

The next day was a break before the actual wedding, so I dragged Jeh off the lawn. He'd spent all morning on a white plastic chair, smoking cigarettes, the butts of which he'd pill up and put in his pocket, as he yelled at the boys stringing up lights in the trees. We left the house without telling anyone and drove out to Seminary Hills. Jeh and I often walked on a secret path starting at the foot of the hills. I parked in our usual spot outside of Our Lady of Lourdes Grotto. Back when I was little, the parking lot had a wire enclosure to one side where the priests kept big bright pink pigs like the ones in Enid Blyton's stories. They were not like the bristled walking nightmares you saw rooting about in the garbage around town, scary and mean. These pigs let you pet them. The highlight of my childhood Sundays used to be petting the happy Catholic pigs.

Leading away from the grotto, hidden behind a mud wall, a narrow footpath climbed up the hill and twisted around the back of the Gymkhana Club's tennis courts, went through a shallow ravine, ran along the toy train tracks by the deer park, skirted around the Parsi cemetery, and ended down at the Japanese Garden.

I lit a candle and placed it at the feet of Lourd Mata, as she was known locally, who stood on a pedestal with baby Jesus in her arms. She looked bored, the way mothers of small children often do. From the corner of my eye, I caught Jeh praying, eyes closed, lips moving. I took his hand. His fingers, fat and warm, laced with mine.

"Come on," I said. "It's starting to get a bit muggy out here."

Jeh paused at the beginning of the path to type on his BlackBerry. He looked so sweet in his khaki shorts, like a chubby, middle-aged boy scout. I snatched the phone. He looked up in surprise.

"No phones allowed," I said, crashing into him with my shoulder.

"Disrespectful," he said with a good-humored smile.

We trudged up the dirt path. For the first time, I felt like things might turn out okay. The day was hot but beautiful. The path was steeper than I remembered. Sweat slid down my temple; I wiped it with the back of my hand. My stomach gave a loud gurgle.

"One foot in front of the other, Piglet," Jeh said as I started to lag behind. When I was a child, he'd swing me up by my armpits and perch me on his shoulders if I got tired. We'd continue our walk. I'd pull leaves, large as elephant ears, from the teak trees as we went under their branches.

"Look," I said, pointing at the cloud-mobbed sky. Huge birds, wings outstretched, were circling above our heads, like planes in a holding pattern. "Are those eagles?"

"Hmm," Jeh said, holding a pair of binoculars to his face. He was part of a conservation group that met at the Gymkhana Club. "See the white breast? And those black wingtips? Brahminy kites." He let out a low whistle. "I haven't seen these many in a long time. They're dying because of all the pesticides farmers use these days. Literally falling out of the sky."

Jeh sat down on a rock. The kites wheeled around in the sky like sentinels for a god. A strong breeze lifted the dead leaves from the ground and made them dance. I placed my hand on Jeh's shoulder. All was silent except for the rustle and creak of the forest.

"You seem fascinated," I said, squeezing onto the rock next to him.

Jeh gripped the hand I'd put on his shoulder. "Do you remember Baba Amte's ashram?"

Below us, on Rani Lake, a herd of white-tailed chital deer ran down the banks, startled by the scent of something. A predator. I hoped it was a tiger. Sometimes a tiger would wander too far from a nearby wildlife sanctuary in search of a mate or food. Once a female and her cub had wandered into the Kamalpur power plant. The workers had fled in panic. They refused to return—the entire city was without electricity for a week—until the tiger was darted and taken back. Jeh took me to see the cub at Baba Amte's ashram. I remember its coat was the softest thing I'd ever touched, far softer and more beautiful than cats' fur. The cub had slashed Baba Amte's arm. Streaks of blood ran down onto a black rexine sofa. I remember its metallic smell, mixed with the aroma of dinner cooking in the kitchen. The cub started crying for its mother. I wanted to go home. "Don't be scared, Piglet," Jeh had said. "I won't let anything happen to you."

"Baba Amte, the old man who rescues animals," I said.

"That's the one," Jeh said. "When I was a little boy, my father took me to the ashram on my—what was it?—my tenth birthday. He said he wanted to show me something. I remember being so excited. He wouldn't tell me what we were going to see. 'It's a special surprise,' he said."

I thought of the old pictures I'd seen of Jeh as a boy. His little overbite and his side part. Lily Mama used to dress him like Pinocchio, in small shorts and suspenders. "I'm guessing the surprise was..." I squinted up at the sky.

Jeh nodded. "Baba Amte's foreman brought a Brahminy kite, wearing a hood, into the courtyard." He smiled at me. "When they took off the hood, the bird was startled, her pinion feathers ruffled up. She hadn't expected to be surrounded by people. Her eyes, they were wondrous. I saw an intelligence far deeper, far more ancient, than mine. It stole my breath."

"What happened next?" I asked.

"Well, I started crying," Jeh said. "Such a gaze that bird had. I was overwhelmed. My father thought I was scared. He said, 'Come on, Jeh, don't be a sissy.' But I couldn't stop."

"Zal Papa was a very modern father."

Jeh gave me the binoculars. "Take a look," he said. "What do you see?"

"Um. Kites and sky."

"Yes," Jeh said. "We see just the kites. But the kites see us, they see the trees, the hill, the grotto, the city. We are just a small part of their world. A mere speck."

"What's so great about being a speck?" I said, feeling sad.

"Well," Jeh said, shifting his weight from one side of his bottom to the other, "it's comforting, isn't it? To be a speck. To know that all this"—he gestured to the trees, the sky—"can carry on, *will* carry on, without you."

"I suppose."

Jeh sighed. A rich, contented sigh. "I feel so much lighter now that you've found Veer."

"He's not a speck on you, though," I said, resting my cheek on Jeh's shoulder. "I still need you."

Jeh absentmindedly brushed my face. "In my next life, I want to be born a bird."

On the night of my wedding, tea lights turned the trees into shimmery creatures swaying to some secret music. An unexpected chill descended on the garden, making the guests pull on shawls over their wedding finery. The air smelled like marigold flowers and rose water.

Standing in front of a mirror, I rubbed my arms to warm up. My midriff was bare. My hair was yanked tight across my scalp and bundled with hundreds of bobby pins that bit into my head like tiny teeth. A maang-tika sat on my forehead, its delicate chain along the middle part in my hair. A dupatta with gold roses was draped over my head. I looked down at my hands full of henna, my wrists full of red-and-white bangles.

Three knocks at the door and Jeh popped his head in. "All decent?" he asked. "Can I come in?"

"Sit for a minute," I said, frowning at my reflection.

"Everything is running smoothly," Jeh said. He walked into the bedroom and sat on my bed. "Not bad work by dear old dad." He smiled, laid his ankle across his knee, and shivered his foot.

Struggling to keep my dupatta on my head, I nodded. "Great job. Now help me pin this."

Jeh held the dupatta in place, smiling. I fastened it with another thousand gold pins.

"Is Mom giving you any trouble?"

Jeh placed his palm gently on the top of my head. "Everything is fine as long as you are happy, Piglet."

"We've had to put up this dog and pony show for the Malhotras. That's... They're awful. Veer and I aren't right for each other, Dad. I don't think I can walk out there tonight."

Jeh held my shoulders. "You're not marrying the family." His smile was filled to the brim with love. "Don't give up now. It'll be over before you know it."

I turned back to the mirror. "I should finish getting ready," I said, dabbing my mascara.

"I'll send Ammu to bring you out when the baraat arrives," Jeh said.

I watched his reflection leave. He paused for a moment at the door, arranged his features, and stepped out.

The next knock wasn't Ammu, but Asha. She pushed the door ajar and held out a plate. "Hungry?" she asked. "I brought you a nice fat aloo paratha to eat."

"How can I eat," I said, showing her my hands, "with this mehendi all the way up to my elbows?"

"Oh," Asha said, looking down at the paratha as if it might provide an answer. "Shall I feed you?"

"No thanks," I said, smoothing my clothes. "I'm too nervous. I'll eat after the ceremony."

"Come on," Asha said, tearing off a morsel and bringing it to my face. "Let me feed you."

The smell of alcohol clung to her like a sloth. "Stop it," I said, pushing the edge of the plate away. "You'll get food all over my lehenga." I closed my eyes. "I need to get ready."

Asha slammed the plate down on my dressing table. "You are," she began, "a rude, ungrateful person. I am trying so hard to be a loving mother to you—all I get is your hate."

"You always do this, Ma. If there's an important moment in my life, you've managed to make it all about you. You've not given me much to be grateful for," I said, sitting on the bed to exchange slippers for high heels. "I suppose I should be glad to be alive. Not all your children were that lucky, na?"

In old movies, when someone is stabbed, there's a moment when their eyes open wide in wonder, as if death were a magic trick. That's what Asha's face was like. She took the plate from the dressing table and tried to smash it over my head. I caught her arm. I took the plate away and threw it on the floor, where it shattered.

"Are you fucking crazy?" I said.

"Now you see how that feels," Asha said, tilting her head to one side. She raised her open hand, as if she were about to slap me. "You are cruel. I hope you lose a child. You have no idea how I struggled. I almost died in that hospital. Did you know that?"

"Look," I said with a placatory movement, "I can't get into this right now."

A knock at the door. "Noomi?" Ammu said. The army of awful Malhotras with Veer leading them on a white mare must have arrived. "Uncle wants you at the mandap in about fifteen minutes. Aunty"— Ammu turned toward my mother—"you need to be at the front gate right now."

Muttering under her breath, Asha yanked a tissue out of the box on my dresser, scrubbed her cheeks, and walked off. We watched as the bedroom door swung closed with a bang.

"How do I look?" I asked, turning to Ammu shakily. "This is one of Kitty Auntyji's lovely designs."

"A bit like the Barbie dolls we used to play with," Ammu said, and grinned. "Sanskari bride Barbie."

"Shut up," I said, smiling. "You're just jealous you're not wearing an outfit that says your zamindar husband regularly bankrupts his farmer serfs."

"Thakurain chic." Ammu giggled and looked down. She saw the shattered plate and looked at me. I shrugged. Ammu kneeled on the floor to arrange the fall of my lehenga. It was a loving gesture, something I imagined a mother would perform.

"Thank you," I said, trying not to cry.

We heard music as Veer's baraat got closer and closer. My heart bumped along with the dholak. I sat stiffly on my bed, waiting, like a dessert, to be brought out at the right moment. At the front gate, my family stood with garlands for the groomsmen. Veer would be brought down off his mare. My mother would paint a red tika on his forehead.

"Look what I have." Ammu pulled out a cigarette from her purse.

"Oh god, yes," I said. "Quickly, before I have to go out."

"Cigarette before the firing squad?" Ammu raised her eyebrows. "So dramatic, Noomi."

"Hurry up and light it."

Ammu lit the cigarette and gave it to me, pinched between thumb and forefinger.

"Shit, I can't have the smell on my hands," I said, tilting up my face. "Give me a few drags, please."

Ammu put the cigarette to my lips. The tip glowed brighter when I inhaled. I could feel the smoke creep into the empty places in my stomach. I couldn't remember the last time I'd eaten. The baraat sounded louder. The dholak made my heart go pitter-patter, pitter-patter.

"Are you happy to finally become Mrs. Malhotra?" Ammu asked.

I winced at the sound of my married name and took another drag from the cigarette.

"People act weird at weddings, you know," Ammu said. "There's pressure to put on a show." She crushed the cigarette on her heel. "It'll get much better once it's just you and Veer."

"I hope you're right." I frowned.

A folk song, filled with quivering women's voices, was the cue for me to walk out under a net of flowers to Veer waiting at the pavilion. The flower net was held up by my male relatives: Adil and some distant ones, whose names eluded me in my state of nerves. If my baby brother had lived, he would probably have been holding up a corner. Perhaps he would've had a lover watching him from the crowd, who'd have been teased about being next. I imagined Jeh feeling proud of his son, of the way he spoke to people, of the way people spoke to him.

Veer and I exchanged our milni garlands to oohs and aahs and posed for photographs. We were guided to a pavilion, where the pandit sat cross-legged, impatient to marry us. The pavilion was made of silver fabric gathered with orchids, dusted with tea lights, and crowned with rococo arrangements of carnations, lilies, and long, twisted silver twigs. Lily Mama's design.

The priest, humming his Sanskrit prayers, set the sandalwood fire ablaze. The serious and sober business of getting married had begun. Puffed rice and sandalwood chips were tossed into the fire so its smoke got thick and fragrant. Soon, my face began to feel hot, feverish; sweat gathered on my forehead. The garland of fragrant roses began to feel like a steel cable. The priest told me to bend my head. Veer took a ring filled with sindoor, moved my maang-tika aside, and rolled it over the part in my hair, making a red mark. He placed a mangalsutra around my neck. The ceremony took an hour to complete, and by the end of it we were married. Yoked together by stoles, Veer and I were made to touch everyone's feet. Crushed under the weight of my clothes and the garland around my neck, tired from the smiling and bending, I felt a rush of relief when they untethered me from my husband. I ran back to my room to wipe off the sweat before our reception.

I lay down, savoring the coolness of my pillow, the comforting smell of my sheets. A writer I loved once said that dressing up a bride was like polishing firewood. I'd never fully understood that sentence until today. "I am firewood," I said to the ceiling fan. Summoning all my willpower, I stood up, took a deep breath, looked at my room, my beloved objects—photographs, the poems on my mirror—for what felt like the last time, and went out the door. Veer was in the driveway, looking handsome and a little confused, as if he'd wandered into the wedding and they'd asked if he'd like to be the groom. We were taken by our relatives to a car, whose hood had been decorated with a mountainous bouquet of orchids.

The streets in Kamalpur empty out after sunset. The car paused at a red light beside a van filled with children. A girl with gravity-defying pigtails stared at me, her nose pressed white against the glass, her face lit with awe. She curled her fingers in a wave.

"So, Mrs. Malhotra, how do you feel?" Veer asked cheerfully.

"Don't think I'll change my name," I said, waving back at the girl. She stuck her tongue out.

"We don't have to get into that right now," Veer said. "How do you feel? Happy? Sad?"

"Are you happy?" I asked, sticking my tongue out at the girl, who giggled.

"Everything went off perfectly, don't you think? My parents are so proud of us." Veer gave a satisfied yawn.

"Yes, but," I said, taking his hand, "didn't you feel like it got out of hand?"

"It was overwhelming." Veer nodded. "But it made our families happy. That's what matters." He searched my face to see if I agreed with him. Was he worried that I might throw some sort of tantrum? "Are you wearing comfortable shoes? We'll be standing for a few hours, you know."

"*Of course* I'm not wearing comfortable shoes," I snapped.

Veer looked out the window. "Turn right here," he said to the driver.

"I'm sorry. I'll be fine once this"—I pointed at the entrance to our reception, decorated with lights and flowers—"is over."

"Almost at the finish line." Veer gave my hand a squeeze.

The guests had already started lining up. Veer's father led us to a stage decorated with gold fabric and roses that matched my dupatta. The guests began their procession, entering on the right with an envelope of money or a silver item—or, in some annoying cases, a heavy kitchen appliance—smiling for a few photos and exiting stage left. A few felt put-upon to make a comment. "Congratulations! You've been promoted from bahu to mother-in-law!" said one woman to Rita, who stood beside me, palms joined. "Your status has gone up in the world!"

"Thank you for blessing the new couple," Rita said.

For hours, I stood, smiling, shifting from one aching foot to the other. My lehenga felt like it was made of lead. I stole envious looks at Veer in his comfortable dress shoes and brushed wool suit, effortlessly charming all the aunties. I didn't want to smile at anyone ever again.

Jeh weaved, like an autorickshaw driver in heavy traffic, through the twisting buffet line, receiving envelopes full of money, shaking hands. Asha wasn't with him. I looked around the photographer moving in for a close-up of my jewelry and scanned the crowd for my mother. A few minutes later, Asha rushed up onstage, holding her sari above her ankles. The line of guests scattered like marching ants as she broke through and grabbed me, sobbing. I could smell the vodka on her breath, in her hair, on her skin. She buried her head in my clothes. I heard a rip in my gold dupatta.

"You can hate me all you want," Asha blubbered, pawing my face, kissing me. "But I'll always be your mother."

I scrubbed my mother's kisses away with the back of my hand. This made her grab my face and plant more of them, wet, appalling. My forehead was covered in lipstick marks. The Malhotras looked stricken but also puzzled, as if Asha had sprouted tentacles from her head. Veer stared at the floor. An embarrassed giggle escaped my lips. I began laughing uncontrollably. Shrieking, really. People kept walking onto the stage. They stared. The bride? Laughing? Unthinkable. Brides were supposed to be serious and sad. From under her tears, Asha looked at me. She began to wail louder and louder, like an ambulance. This made me laugh even harder, with no idea what I found so hilarious. Maybe it was my in-laws' faces as they slowly realized Asha was drunk. Jeh and I had pulled off a massive scam.

In the midst of this chaos, Jeh rushed up onto the stage and pried Asha away. He led her down the steps, muttering excuses and apologies. I looked at Veer and giggled, enjoying the light shade of salmon pink flushing up from under his shirt collar. We were let go to mingle with the guests. I went to a sofa and slumped down like a bag of laundry. A waiter brought over some food and a glass of water. I drank it off. The food was standard club buffet fare. I pushed it around with a fork, wishing with all my heart that I could have something to drink. Veer sailed by, carrying a plate to a table occupied by his friends.

"Mrs. Malhotra!" Ammu came up, smiling, holding hands with Shiv. She plonked down next to me, looking more than a little tipsy. "Do you feel different now that all is official and state sanctioned?"

"I feel tired," I said. Her sweat smelled like rose water. And alcohol.

"Congrats, Noomi. And my compliments to your dad. This wedding has been super fun." Shiv grinned.

"Adil had a bar in the trunk of his car in the parking lot," Ammu laughed. "He was playing loud Punjabi music with the windows rolled down. We had a dance party."

"Apparently my mom found that bar," I said. I stood up. Buds of pain shot up into my feet.

"Where are you going?" Ammu called after me.

"To get Veer," I said over my shoulder. "I want to leave."

Veer sat with a bunch of his old college buddies around a table under a gaudily lit-up palm tree. A waiter went back and forth with drinks and snacks. These were his pakki yaari, brothers from another mother. I waved for Veer's attention. He smiled, waved back, then turned, rolled his eyes, laughed, resumed talking to his friends. I waved with both hands. He seemed determined to ignore me.

"Veer," I said. "Come here for a minute." Veer's friends stopped talking and stared, smiling, in my direction. I felt like a clingy child.

"Oye hoye," said one, raising his glass. "Paapey's married less than half an hour and already in the hot seat. That's got to be some kind of record."

The others laughed and clinked their beer bottles. Veer dragged himself from his chair like a teenager. He threw his napkin on the ground.

I tapped one foot on the grass. "Hot seat." "Paapey." Fucking... idiots.

"Can we go?" I said. "I'm tired. I haven't slept in three days. If I don't get some rest, I'm going to collapse."

"In a while." Veer patted my arm. "Let me finish eating dinner with my friends."

"I want to leave *now*," I said.

"I can't right now, okay? The guys are all flying back tomorrow. You know how important they are to me." Veer tipped his head up and let out a frustrated sound. "You're being so selfish. Grow up."

"I'm selfish?" I said. "It's our *wedding*. You're more concerned about your friends' feelings." I poured all my contempt into the word "friends." I pulled on his arm. "Don't you care if I'm happy? Put me first."

"Noomi," Veer said, pulling away. "This isn't just about you, okay? It's a celebration for our family, our friends. They've worked hard to make it special. Stop being a brat."

I swallowed the pebble in my throat. I was lost in an undiscovered country; no one spoke my language here. I was eight years old, watching from my garden hideout, as Veer walked back to his friends.

Much later, in the car heading to the hotel, Veer leaned over to kiss me. I turned my face away.

"What the fuck?" Veer's voice went a bit shrill when he felt embarrassed. "I can't kiss my wife?"

I stared out the window. "This is a disaster," I said dramatically.

"Oh god, grow up," Veer said. He rolled down the window and lit a cigarette.

"I need us to be alone. Will someone be waiting at the hotel room?"

"Maybe, I'm not sure," Veer said. He took a long drag. "Knowing my mother and her love for doing things the 'right way,' probably yes."

"Veer, please, tell your mother we'll see her in the morning?"

"Okay," Veer agreed after a pause. He took out his cell phone. "Hi... yeah, Mom? Everything's fine. Are you... are you, you know, at the hotel room? It's just... Noomi says she's feeling very tired." Another pause. "Uh, okay," he said, and cut the call. "Sorry, sweetie." Veer turned to me. "Mom's excited to give you some gifts... or something like that." He began fussing with his hair.

Rita was there to greet us in front of our room. Standing on tiptoes, she held the sides of Veer's forehead and kissed it. I bent down to touch her feet.

"Kitty Auntyji decorated your bed. Isn't it lovely?" Rita led me by the hand to the bed strewn with red rose petals. I began to feel nauseated. "And this," Rita said, holding up a sari wrapped in cellophane with a big red bow, "is for my new daughter-in-law! We are so..."

I sat down on the bed, tore off my dupatta, and tossed it to the floor. Slowly, with shaking hands, I began plucking out the hundreds of bobby pins stuck in my hair.

"Oho! Why is she crying?" Rita asked Veer, looking worried. She reached out her hand and then drew it back, as if I might bite her. "Was it something I said?"

"She's tired." Veer came up to me, stroking my head like I was his pet. "She needs to sleep."

"Oho, beta, don't cry, smile! Come, please, give me a smile. You look much prettier when you..."

I cried—louder and louder—until, finally giving up, Rita went away, closing the door behind her.

PART THREE

PART
THREE

"Remind me again now, how long have you been married?"

"About two years."

"And you're happy?"

"I'm not... miserable."

"He's not abusive."

"No."

"He has a good job? He can support a family?"

"Yes."

"So then, explain to me one more time, why do you want to end this pregnancy?"

Dr. Roosi Mistry, a kindly old Parsi doctor, liked to steeple his fingers and chew on his lower lip. He listened to my tearful assay of my situation with the trademark indifference of a longtime Mumbaikar. Then he put on his gold spectacles and looked again at my sonogram, which showed a small blob the size and shape of a kidney bean.

"I'm depressed," I said, stacking the plastic ovaries and uterus on his table as if they were Lego blocks. "I'm not in any condition to look after a baby. I can barely look after myself."

That was half the truth. The other half was that I couldn't—no, I *wouldn't* stop drinking. Not for a baby. Stone-cold sobriety for a whole nine months and change wasn't in the realm of likelihood. And Veer wasn't of any help. If we weren't out getting smashed, he'd spend his evenings nursing a beer or two on the sofa, watching TV. If I tried to start a conversation, ask him about work, tell him about something from my day, he'd give me this look—I placed it between boredom and irritation.

I'd call his cell phone and he wouldn't pick up or call back. I began to haunt our Bandra apartment, unseen and unheard. I walked around in my pajamas and drank vodka out of a coffee mug. The only time Veer appeared interested in me was when we were around other people. Like the time his boss came home for dinner. The boss had just married. Sitting in our small warm living room, drinks in hand, he and his wife stared at the towers of books against our walls. Veer, puffed up with pride, explained that I was a poet.

"She even gets published in foreign journals," he'd said, taking his boss's glass to pour him a drink.

"Well," I said, smiling, "I got a poem published once, in *Granta*. But that was probably a fluke."

"Noomi's read every book in this house," Veer said, dropping down on the sofa. He held up his whisky glass to indicate the stacks. "She's spent more time between pages than setting up this apartment. That's why we don't have bookshelves, ha-ha."

"Well, it's good to keep busy," Veer's boss's wife said, "till you have children." She took out a fancy phone from her purse. The wallpaper was a picture of a boy and a girl in matching pajamas. "These two are my whole life." She smiled and blew a kiss to the phone. "My niece and nephew, Arya and Karan. I can't wait to have two of my own."

"No thanks. But having a few book-children might be nice," I said. "Probably more rewarding."

The boss's wife looked at her husband, who looked at Veer, who looked at me. I stepped into the kitchen, on the pretext of frying up some kebabs, and took a swig from the bottle I kept in the freezer. When I came out, the boss was talking about their summer trip to Italy and Paris, while his wife was taking selfies with my books in the background.

The boss and his wife left around midnight. Veer went to shower, and I helped our cook clean up. Later on, I stuck my head into the bedroom. Veer was lying on his side of the bed, staring at his phone.

"That was nice of you," I said. "I didn't know you cared that much about my writing."

"Uh-huh," Veer said, swiping his finger on the screen.

"Do you want to read the poem?" I said, stepping into the room. "The *Granta* one? It's online."

Veer's eyelids flickered up and down as he scrolled on his phone.

"Veer," I said, walking up to him. "Veer?" I shook his shoulder rather violently. "Hello?"

"For fuck's sake, what?" he snapped. "I'm in the middle of an article."

"Never mind," I said, turning away from him. "I'm going to make myself another drink. Night."

"Good night," Veer said. "Tell the cook that I want breakfast at eight thirty tomorrow. Eggs."

I'll never forget how Veer looked at me when I made up my mind to do it. To have an abortion. With unfettered relief. We scheduled the procedure for two weeks before we were supposed to visit his parents in New Delhi. Veer even missed half a day of work to take me to the clinic.

"It's okay," Dr. Mistry said wryly, scribbling on a pad. "India's population is too large anyway."

I gave a weak laugh and balled my kurta in my sweaty fists. "I've never had one."

"Will it hurt?" Veer asked, looking pale.

"Not really," Dr. Mistry said. "A chemical termination feels like period cramps." He glanced again at the scan. "Only more painful." He took my clammy hands in his two warm, dry hands, shook them, and stood up. "Follow me," he said, shuffling out the door. Veer was told to find a seat in the waiting room.

Dr. Mistry never accepted a patient unless she was married, and even then, he didn't examine his patients himself. He handed me off to a lady ob-gyn in a starched blue sari and lab coat. "My associate, Geeta, will do the procedure," he said, walking out immediately. "Good luck!"

Geeta checked my pulse, blood pressure, and temperature. She made me lie down on the table and, covering me with a sheet, instructed me to take off my underwear. Then, without preamble, she inserted two fingers into my vagina.

"Cervix is nice and *spawngey*. You are definitely pregnant," she said.

"I know," I said, looking up at the tube lights embedded in the ceiling, wincing.

"Everything looks good. You're having a girl?" Geeta asked, pushing down hard on my belly. "Is that why you are wanting to terminate?" She smiled and, one by one, squeezed my nipples.

"What? No... I don't know. It... it doesn't even have a heartbeat yet," I said, looking at her.

"Okay," Geeta said, putting on another pair of gloves. "Many times, we are doing termination because the families are wanting a boy instead of girl." She bobbled her head, smiling. "Of course, we cannot reveal the sex because that is illegal," she assured me. "But other ways are there, to find out."

"I don't want a boy or a girl," I said, fighting back sour tears. "I don't want a baby at all."

"Of course," Geeta continued, "with IVF, nowadays they can simply pick male embryos, like choosing eggs from a grocery basket."

She smiled and pushed two suppositories into me. After I put on my underwear, she gave me another two pills to swallow with water that had a faint chlorine smell to it.

"It will start in a few hours," Geeta said. "You'll have somebody with you?"

"My husband is with me," I replied.

"Have someone prepare you a hot water bottle. Take this painkiller if it gets too bad. Good luck." She patted my shoulder with a bright smile.

In the waiting room, Veer flipped through a magazine, shaking his leg. I went over and touched his shoulder. He shot out of his seat.

"How bad did it hurt?" he said, hugging me. "You look all right, surprisingly."

"It hasn't started yet," I said, pushing him away. "Don't squeeze me, I feel sick."

The sea was smooth and glistening, like a tub of Vaseline. As the cab crossed Worli Sea Face, Veer told the taxi driver to turn right. The car slowed to a stop by a beige building, stippled with bands of sea light. Veer gathered his laptop bag and prepared to get out of the cab. He kissed me on the forehead. "See you later," he said.

"What the fuck?! What are you doing, Veer?" I asked, grabbing his shirtsleeve.

"My boss wants me to meet this new client," Veer said, slowly disentangling his arm.

"The doctor said I shouldn't be alone right now. When the cramps start."

Veer said that I wouldn't be; he'd called our cook and told her to stay over. And besides, I looked fine to him. Couldn't I manage for a few hours? "I'll see you soon, potato. I love you."

"I feel full of death," I said, hugging my stomach.

"Noomi," Veer said, poking his head into the car window, "get a hold of yourself. You'll be fine."

The cramps began as the cab climbed up our lane. By the time we arrived at my apartment building, the fetus was an animal clawing the inside of my body, trying to get out. I had to ask the watchman to help me into the lift. The cook left me curled on my bed with a hot water bottle. I took the painkillers and went into the bathroom to sit on the toilet. A few minutes later, I felt something slide into the pot. I looked. A betta fish of blood and tissue floated peacefully in the white porcelain bowl. The pain went away. In its place were relief and exhaustion. I took an ice-cold shower to rinse off the sweat. With my hair still wet and dripping, I turned the AC up as high as it would go, got under the covers, and fell into a dark, dreamless sleep.

A week later, Veer took me out to dinner as a tepid attempt to cheer me up. By the time we got to the restaurant, I was so drunk, I could barely taste the seafood served on platters decorated with lemon-peel roses. Next came shots at a strobe-lit nightclub inside a Juhu hotel. I danced shoulder to shoulder beside a woman with a tattoo of roses on her cleavage. Veer peeled me off just as I was starting to have fun. He said it was getting late. He had to work the next day. I didn't want to leave, so he dragged me outside by my arm. On the street, we smoked cigarettes and fought while waiting for an autorickshaw. Veer was the kind of easygoing guy who picked up friends how the wind picks up leaves. He endeared himself to aunties by being a good eater, full of compliments for every dish on their dinner table. Uncles loved him because he was a "strapping young man" who "reminded them of themselves at that age." His bosses valued his ability to work like a sheep herding dog. Only I knew how to burrow under his skin like a tick. I slapped him across the face.

"Stop or I'll hit you back," Veer said. He twisted my arm behind my shoulder.

A policeman strolled over, his bamboo lathi scraping along the road. In Marathi, he asked Veer what was going on. Veer replied, in

Hindi, that it was none of his business. The policeman looked at Veer as if he'd called his mother a whore. A sly meanness crept into his face. He turned to me and tapped my bottom, like he was testing the ripeness of a watermelon.

"Come on, go home. You North Indians are ruining this city," he said in Marathi. "Go back to UP."

"I'm from Delhi, motherfucker," Veer said.

The policeman assessed Veer's six-foot frame and realized he'd get pulverized in a one-on-one. Calmly, he raised his walkie-talkie to his mouth. The situation was turning dangerous. I placed a hand on the policeman's arm and gave him a dazzling smile.

"Please ignore my brother," I said, tottering on my heels. I made a loop with a forefinger near my temple. "He's mentally not all there." I took whatever cash I had in my purse, folded it, and stuffed it into the policeman's palm. He took the money, then waited, staring, for me to beg some more. I obliged him by shedding a few tears.

The policeman left, swinging his lathi. I flagged down an auto-rickshaw. We stopped once and bought kathi rolls, then ate them as the auto jostled us over the potholed lanes. Then we stopped again and bought cigarettes from a boy selling them on a bicycle.

"Why'd you tell that thulla that I was your brother," Veer asked, wiping his mouth with the back of his hand.

I pushed a strand of hair off my damp face and took a drag from my cigarette. "That's what it feels like nowadays," I said, "like we're brother and sister." I flicked ash to the rickshaw's floor. The driver had DON'T CALL ME BHAIYA scrawled in bright paint across the back flap.

"You were coming on to that woman with the tattoos," Veer said.

"Was I? I don't remember that." I said. "Sorry."

"It was hot," Veer said, slipping his hand into my shirt.

We got home just as the sky turned sunburn pink. In the bedroom, Veer pulled me toward him. We kissed, fumbling with each other's smelly, sweaty clothes. The red betta fish from the toilet bowl swam into my head. I pushed Veer off me. He looked at me wearily. He was sick and tired of my being miserable all the time. He pulled the covers over himself and slept. I wanted to say something. I didn't know how to put the feeling into words. I turned away from him and closed my eyes.

We flew to Delhi a week later. Thanks to a protocol only for high-ranking government officials, my in-laws received us as soon as we stepped out of the aerobridge. Rita wore three rows of pearls (at ten in the morning!), while Mr. Malhotra had on a spiffy beige suit with a peacock-hued cravat. I smiled at them, feeling a little bit like how one feels in the dentist's waiting room, knowing an assuredly unpleasant encounter lay ahead.

"My children!" my father-in-law said, his arms open. "Welcome, welcome home!"

A young man walked out from behind him with a bunch of pink roses tied with a giant pink bow. His face was solemn, as if giving pink bouquets were part of his official government duties. I took it with a polite bobblehead nod and smile.

"Thank you very much," I said.

"See," Rita said to no one in particular, "the flowers perfectly match Noomi's fair complexion."

"Cool," Veer said.

"Thank you. They're beautiful," I said, and bent down.

"Oh, so nice, god bless you," Rita said. "May you have a long and happy life." Rita expected me to be servile in my greeting of her, yet she managed to act surprised whenever I touched her feet.

"Come, come," my father-in-law said, ushering us out. "Veer, I want to show you my lovely new car!"

The lackeys surrounding my father-in-law had multiplied, like bacteria, since our last visit to Delhi. It was clear that Veer's dad, by way of a recent high-profile promotion, had reached the pinnacle of his career. This meant all sorts of perks: club memberships, a new car, and fancy government quarters. Ever pragmatic, the Malhotras had put their house on rent and moved into a gracious bungalow on Willingdon Crescent. Mr. Malhotra was escorted by men carrying Kalashnikovs to a shiny black bulletproof SUV. Delhi-wallahs, perennially enamored by power and its trappings, bobbed backward out of their path. A driver jumped out of the SUV and ran around to open the doors. Veer sat up front like an excited kid. I squeezed in the back. A chap with a Kalashnikov sat in the cargo seat, the muzzle of his gun disconcertingly close to my head.

The coming weekend was Independence Day; the SUVs in our cavalcade had tiny Indian flags. They elbowed aside civilian cars, two-wheelers, and cyclists on the way to Lutyens' Delhi, a nest of Raj-era bungalows with Raj-era lawns dotted with Raj-era peacocks. Throughout the hour-long journey, Veer praised his father's car, pressing all the shiny buttons, making the side mirrors flap back and forth like cows' ears when we were stopped at security checkpoints. We drove down a tree-lined avenue into a large compound. A brass band started up next to the portico.

The house was abuzz with men in white epauleted uniforms. They brought out government canapés: canned pineapple skewered with a cube of cheese, baked beans on tiny pieces of toast.

"Come, you must be hungry," Rita said. "We'll take tea in the veranda."

"Um, could we go to our room first?" I asked. "I'd like to freshen up a bit."

"There'll be plenty of time after tea," Rita insisted. "Come, come. I want you to meet the new staff."

Two secretaries with their wives waited in the foyer, arms full of flower bouquets. They handed all the flowers to me, then we made small talk: "How was your flight?" "Doesn't Mr. Malhotra's car drive well over our terrible Delhi roads?" "How kind of him to come personally to pick you up!"

"Noomi darling, could you please take this around?" Veer's mother said. We'd settled on the rattan sofas on the veranda that overlooked the peacock-dotted lawn. Rita pointed a pink-nailed finger to a plate full of paneer cubes with toothpicks sticking out of them. "Just offer it to everyone. Start with Dad."

I looked down at my cup of tea and sandwich. "Can't one of those fellows do it?" I pleaded.

"Noomi, it would be *so nice* if you could serve everyone. You are our new bahu." Rita smiled.

"Bhaiya," I called out to a young man on the lawn. He jogged up to the veranda. "Could you show this around to our guests, please." I handed him the tray of paneer and smiled at my mother-in-law.

"No, Noomi," Rita said, shaking her head at the young man, who backed away. "It has to be you."

Rita always sounded like a fairy godmother—soft and pretty—even when she had her foot on my neck. I tried to catch Veer's eye. He was chatting with my father-in-law's secretaries, senior and junior, while their wives hovered over Rita like a pair of mosquitoes. Rita cleared her throat and nodded at the tray of canapés. The secretaries' wives turned their heads in my direction. I beamed and showed it around, suddenly desperate for a smoke.

Once tea was over, we were led to our guest room. There was a king bed piled with frilly pillows, a basket of fruit, and a neatly organized his-and-her dressing area. The bathroom had his-and-her toiletries, plus a bag full of makeup for me: eyeliner, pink lipstick, and a packet of red bindis, all still wrapped in plastic. I locked myself in the bathroom and took the metal trash can from next to the sink, turned it over, stood on top, and blew cigarette smoke into the exhaust. I couldn't let my in-laws find out I smoked. They didn't even know Veer smoked. He became a different person around his parents—formal, circumspect. He treated me like a boss with his new intern. His eyes lost their soft, warm light, like windows of a shop temporarily closed for business.

Sometimes, I thought about what made me stay with Veer. Maybe it was that having a leaky roof over your head is better than being in the rain. Or maybe it was those moments when we were alone, doing everyday stuff, and a sense of peace would descend over me like clouds on a hill. There was this one morning on vacation when Veer and I snuggled deep under a winter blanket. A space heater was next to the bed. I'd poke one foot out to warm it. We didn't talk or have sex. We lay curled up inside the blanket like squirrels, too snug to get up even for food or coffee. I put my head on Veer's chest and listened to the bop of his heart. Happy memories are like cash in the bank.

"What's taking you so long?" Veer said, knocking on the bathroom door.

I hopped off the trash can, threw my cigarette into the commode, flushed. I spritzed perfume in the air. The butt didn't go down. "Just a minute!" I called, flushing again.

Veer had dumped out his suitcase on the bed. "Hey, where are my yellow socks?"

"I don't know," I said. I picked up a pile of shirts and found him a pair of argyles.

"Were you smoking in there?" he asked.

"Yeah," I said, and pushed all his clothes to one side to lie down.

"Noomi, you know you can't smoke here. You know that." Veer frowned. "And you can't nap right now either. Get dressed. Dad wants to take us all to the Golf Club for lunch."

I turned over onto my stomach and put a pillow over my head. "Ugh. We just ate."

Veer lobbed a pair of socks at me. "It's the Golf Club, babe. The food isn't the point."

"Can't I close my eyes for a bit while you put away your stuff?" I asked from under the pillow.

Veer smacked my bottom. "Feisty potato," he said. "I like your bum. Seriously, though, get dressed."

"Okay, fine," I relented. I looked for an outfit that was right for the most obnoxious country club in Delhi. "But shouldn't we put our clothes in the closet first?" I asked Veer. "Your parents strike me as the type who value neatness."

"Oh, Dad's flunkies will fold up my shit," Veer said. He slipped a shirt with a polo pony over his head, popped the collar, then stepped into a pair of jeans.

"Oh, good," I said, emptying my suitcase. "My salwar kurta needs to be ironed and hung."

"Well," Veer said, spritzing cologne, "remember, these are all young men. They might find it weird to handle a woman's clothes. Especially all your skimpy things. Sorry, sweetie. You'll have to manage."

"Are you serious? You get five-star service and I'm supposed to do everything myself?"

"It's not just you." Veer rolled his eyes. I was being a difficult woman again, a pain in the ass who wanted to be treated the same way he was. "Mom manages her own clothes too. She'll teach you to iron your salwar and all the other stuff."

"Arrgh!" I said, and walked off. "This is bullshit."

At the Golf Club, we were seated at a table overlooking a slim, long green lawn dotted with Mughal ruins, ancient tree canopies, and the occasional golfer. Around us sat South Delhi—the women in oversized sunglasses with designer handbags displayed on their tables, the men wearing polo shirts and mirrored aviators. Everyone looked fresh from the salon. No one smiled at or even made eye contact with the waiters. With movie stars and politicians jostling for a spot on its waiting list, the club wasn't a friendly place. I recalled a news story about a nanny who'd accompanied children to the Golf Club for a birthday party, who was told she couldn't enter the main dining room as her clothes looked like "maid's attire."

"Bloody Marys for the men," Mr. Malhotra said to a waiter, and thumped Veer on the back. "I'm going to have a drink with my son." He turned to us. "Rita, what would you ladies like?"

"Nothing for me," Rita said, smiling. "Only some warm water with lemon."

"Yes, good idea, warm water with lemon for me too," the senior secretary's wife said quickly.

"Same here," said the junior secretary's pretty, plump little wife.

"I'll have a Diet Coke," I said.

The senior secretary's wife threw me a smile. "Diet-shiet? When we were younger there was no such thing as a Diet Coke. Are you concerned about your figure? Now that you're married, you must put on a little bit of weight." She smiled again. Rita had introduced her as Mandira. "But you can call me Mandy Aunty," she'd said between air-kisses.

"If you want to put on some weight, Nooms," Veer said, "this is the right place." He studied the menu. "These kakori kebabs look outstanding! I wonder if they'd let me have the recipe."

"Veer is an excellent cook," I said to the secretaries' wives, senior and junior.

"Oh." Veer's father, from across the table, looked at his son, worried. "You mean after a long day in the office, you come home and cook?" He looked at me. "Why doesn't Noomi do the cooking?"

"Well, I don't do it every day. We have a cook who comes in to make rotis, sabzi, whatever. It relaxes me," Veer said. "It's a hobby. I like trying new recipes for Noomi and me to taste."

"Haw-haw, look at this son of mine," Mr. Malhotra chuckled to his secretaries, who began to chuckle too. "Cooking? A hobby? Now *eating*—that's a worthwhile hobby!" He laughed. The secretaries laughed.

"Why would I want to put on weight?" I asked, turning toward Mandy.

"Oh ho, because a little bit of weight helps to"—Mandy mimicked rocking an infant—"you know. Look at Tanya here, already in the family way." She gestured toward the junior secretary's wife, who gave us a shy smile.

"Well done," Veer's father said. He grabbed the bespectacled junior secretary's hand and shook it so hard, the young man's glasses slid down his nose. "Waiter! Another round of Bloody Marys."

"I don't think I'm ready," I said, looking down, folding and unfolding my napkin. "For children."

"You mean," Tanya said, "no children ever? But then who will look after you in old age?"

"It's a child, not a pension fund," I said. Tanya looked embarrassed. I softened my tone. "I don't think never. Just not right now. I'm not ready yet."

"Nonsense," Mandy scoffed. "Who is ever ready for a baby, silly? Don't you agree, ma'am?"

"By god's grace," Rita said, staring heavenward, "all will happen when it is the right time."

"Ma'am is too nice to say anything," Mandy said, "but I'm toh a very frank person." She held her palm up and shook her head. "Nowadays youngsters don't want to make their parents happy."

"Aunty." Veer's voice floated over to us from the men's side, above the restaurant's chatter and din. "That is nobody's business but ours. Mine and Noomi's." He smiled and took a sip of his drink.

This didn't sit too well with my father-in-law. "What do you mean it's nobody's business?" he said, vibrating like a teakettle about to whistle. "It's my business! And your mother's! It's everyone's business!" He was so angry, his comb-over slid to his forehead. I waited to hear what Veer would say. But Veer merely took more sips of his Bloody Mary.

My heart sank into my shoes.

"What are you yelling about, bhaiya?" Kitty Ahuja had walked in, dressed head to toe in Burberry, her ears barnacled with diamonds. Monty, her husband, followed behind.

"Brother-in-lawji," Monty said, shaking his hand. "Great to see you. And beautiful Rita Rani too." He pulled up a chair for himself without offering one to his wife. His shoes had discreet heels to make him appear taller. "Chubby, take a seat with the ladies."

"Let's make some room for Kitty Didi," Rita said. As wife of the junior secretary, pregnant Tanya was about to give up her seat, until a waiter ran over with a chair for Kitty.

"We can't stay," Kitty said, looking at the chair. "We have plans. But I came over to invite you for lunch tomorrow." She looked over at me. "Oh, Noomi, I didn't notice you."

"Hello, Auntyji." I stood up to touch Kitty's feet, assuming that's what she wanted me to do.

"Oh god, what're you doing?" Kitty said. "People will think I'm some kind of old-fashioned behenji."

"Sorry," I said, feeling embarrassed. I sat back down and resumed fidgeting with my napkin.

"Rita," Kitty said, making large eyes at my mother-in-law, "train her *better*."

"Ma'am is doing her best," Mandy said loyally.

What would Mandy say, I wondered, *if I went to the men's side of the table, picked up their pitcher of Bloody Marys, poured myself a drink, and gulped it down?*

"Okayji, we must be off," Monty said. He stood up. The men shook hands. Kitty gave Rita a hug. "Chubby and I can't keep our friends waiting. See you at our place tomorrow, twelve noon sharp."

I'd snuck a bottle of gin in my suitcase. Gin always made me feel like shit the next day. I woke up with a headache and a racing heart. In a few hours, it would be time for Kitty's lunch party. And there was a problem. Kitty, who liked to make everything into an occasion, loved color themes. Today she wanted us to dress in yellow.

"I have nothing yellow to wear," I said to Veer, guzzling a bottle of ice-cold water.

"You're hungover?" Veer said. "Noomi, you promised you wouldn't drink on this trip."

"Why do you get to drink, then?" I said.

"I'm drinking?" Veer looked around him. "Where's my glass?"

"Who drank those Bloody Marys at the Golf Club?" I crossed my arms and stared at him.

"That's different," Veer said, sounding irritated. "That was bonding with my father."

I rolled my eyes. "What do I do about this fucking theme?" I asked, squeezing my forehead. "Where am I supposed to find something yellow to wear."

"Borrow something from my mom," Veer said. "She'll have lots of things in yellow, I'm sure. She's a big one for bright colors. Now don't bother me until it's time to leave. I need to send out some emails." Light from his laptop glinted off his glasses. He banged on his keyboard. "Go."

A fit of nausea walloped me in the stomach. "I think I might be dying," I groaned.

"Throw up, then," Veer said. "Don't drink gin if it makes you sick."

Over the toilet, I stuck two fingers into my mouth and heaved up a string of bile. I flushed, closed the lid, and sat on it, taking my phone from the edge of the sink. I called my father.

"Hi, baby!" Jeh said, answering on the second ring.

"Hi, Daddy," I said. "I miss you. What's going on? We're in Delhi. I hate it."

"Oh, that's right. I forgot. Are you behaving yourself?"

"Yes." A pause. "No."

"Oof, Piglet."

"I don't want to get into it. Tell me, what've you been up to?"

"Well, nothing much. We might have a small thing at the Gymkhana, for Independence Day."

"Oh, nice," I said. "That's this weekend, right? Why don't Veer and I come? We can all be together."

"I'd actually love that," Jeh said. "But... would you be able to find tickets on such short notice?"

"My father-in-law can get us train tickets, I'm pretty sure," I said, staring at my splotchy face in the mirror. I would need so much makeup to hide the bags under my eyes. "I'll ask Veer if he can take a few more days off." I wondered how long it would be before someone began yelling at me to get ready. "Is Mom being good these days?"

"Asha found a therapist. She's been going, uh, once a week. One sec." Jeh began coughing and then wheezed like he couldn't breathe. "Sorry," he continued. "Yeah, she's doing a lot better, actually."

"What the hell was that? You sound like a bagpipe. Are you okay?"

"Yeah, yeah."

"Have you seen the doctor?"

"Don't worry about me, I'm fine," Jeh said. "I just have to remember to take my heart medication."

Fear crawled up my arm like a furry spider and closed its spidery legs around my throat.

There was a tap on the door. "Noomi, are you ready?" Rita trilled. "I brought a few outfits for you to try on. I'll leave them here on the bed." I heard her walk away. "Hurry up, dear!"

"I'll be right out!" Into my phone, I whispered, "I have to go. Love you."

"Love you, Piglet."

I chose a high-collared mustard silk kurta with flowers embroidered down the front. I slipped the kurta over my head. It fit me surprisingly well. The color added a touch of gold to my face. Apart from the itchy embroidery and the fact that it was a little too warm for the August humidity, it was a lovely outfit.

"You look beautiful," Veer said, shrugging on his jacket. "See? Nothing to worry about."

"I guess so," I said, smiling.

The weather was mild and cloudy, if not exactly cool. Kitty had her French doors open to the terrace of her condo, which overlooked a broad, leafy street. The clouds parted once in a while; a friendly light danced on the glass dining table with its massive arrangement of flowers. Whenever the kitchen door swung open, one heard the clatter of pans and a hissing pressure cooker. Seated on the sofa, in a silk kurta and expensive sandals, Kitty spoke in blocks of fast sentences about a wedding she'd recently attended. "Oh, they must have spent a bomb," she said, putting a hand up to her forehead. "Pakistani girl, very pretty. Fair, tall. My friend Lavi's daughter."

She turned to Rita, who looked fascinated.

"Anyway, what was her name?" She stared at the ceiling. "Ah, Heena, that's it. She took me upstairs. I had to use the powder room. On the bed"—Kitty made a shape with her arms—"there were a dozen toosh shawls, each one probably costing more than a Gucci purse, okay? Heena says to me, "Dekho, Aunty, this is my trousseau. It's my ambition to buy a toosh shawl in every color.' I smiled at her, but to myself, I thought, *What a dumb ambition*." Kitty rolled her eyes. "My children would never want anything so stupid. I'm so proud of them both. They're too busy in their careers."

"By god's grace," Rita said, "Your children are a great credit to you and Monty Jeejaji."

"Thank you." Kitty settled like a cat in a spot of sunshine. "Only I wish they'd hurry up and marry."

"Um, Auntyji, when will lunch be served?" Dizzy and sick, I looked over at Veer, who stood with his father and the secretaries senior and junior, listening to Monty expound on some whisky that he was pouring into their glasses. I thought I was over my hangover. Evidently not.

"We'll eat when the men are done with their drinks," Kitty said coolly.

Without food, soon my hands began to shake. Sweat pooled in my armpits. I wished I'd taken something to settle my stomach. Someone brought around a tray of coffee. I took a cup and filled it with milk and sugar. The coffee made my heart race even more.

"Excuse me," I said to Rita, and walked over to Veer. I yanked on the tail of his jacket. He didn't turn. I tapped his shoulder. Still nothing. "Hey!" I poked him hard in his ribs. "Am I invisible?"

"What?" Veer snapped. The men fell silent. I looked away, em-barrassed.

"I'm not feeling well," I said in a small voice.

"Okay, give me a minute," Veer said, and then turned back around. I waited, but he kept talking.

"Chubby," Monty said, holding a bottle of beer in one hand and a tall, frosted glass in the other. "We are getting too drunk. I think you should serve us some food. Brother-in-lawji, what do you think?"

"Yes," Veer's father said, clinking glasses with Monty. "Ladies, please put lunch on the table."

"Don't bother yourself, Didi." Rita shot up before Kitty could move. "Noomi and I will make sure that lunch is served. You just relax and chat with your guests."

"Thank you, Rita," Kitty said. "You're more like a sister than a sister-in-law."

"Oh, not at all, Didi," Rita said, blushing like a teenager. "It's our pleasure to help."

Since Kitty went to her kitchen only to give orders, it was no surprise that she'd spent little money or time on making it a comfortable place to cook. The ventilation came from a small window near the ceiling, fitted with an exhaust. The stoves and oven were old and leaky. The kitchen seemed permanently steamed up from the various bubbling pots on the stove—maa ki dal, saag paneer, biryani, vegetable korma, et cetera.

I pulled at my kurta's high collar, suddenly feeling very light-headed.

Rita ordered the dishes placed on the counter, where a flurry of hands filled them up. The cook made rotis and flipped them onto a plate, while the servers marched out with the food.

"Noomi, you take that bowl of dahi out to the guests," Rita said, pointing to a crystal bowl filled with ice-cold yogurt. "And then come back inside to help with the rotis."

A damp breeze from the French doors greeted me as I brought the dahi over to the dining table. A coolness spread slowly between my shoulders; I realized that I'd sweated through my kurta. An unsightly stain, I imagined, was blooming down my back. The embroidery caused an unbearable itch. The urge to scratch almost made me drop the bowl in my hands. The dahi wobbled in a way that was nauseating. I was about to put it down on the dining table and rush to the bathroom, when my father-in-law gestured for me to come over to him.

The only sounds in the dining room were of marrow being sucked from bones, the smacking of lips, the licking of fingers, a few appreciative burps from the men, whose dinner plates were a salmagundi of yellow, brown, and green. As I bent to serve my father-in-law, pain struck my head like a cudgel. My mouth flooded with spit. Drops of sweat collected at the backs of my ears. Without any warning, I snatched the yogurt bowl from my father-in-law's hands and retched into it. I heard the sound of chairs being pushed away. I looked up. Disgust was pasted upon everyone's face. "Sorry," I muttered. Cradling the sour-smelling bowl in my arms, I hurried into a bathroom to dump my sick in the toilet, ignoring Veer's bewildered questions from the other side and Rita's offers of help.

"When you locked yourself in Auntyji's bathroom, my mom got quite excited," Veer said. "She kept asking me if you weren't pregnant." He gave me a sidelong look. "All afternoon, she was like, 'Are you sure, Veer? Are you very sure?' Isn't that funny?"

The Delhi-Kamalpur Shatabdi began lurching into the station. I pulled the dirty train curtain from the window to feel the sun's heat on the tempered yellow glass. A porter hopped into our compartment, dragging all the station smells inside—sweat, urine, spices, oil, smoke.

"You should've told her about the abortion," I said.

"Right," Veer snorted. "Didn't you hear my father going off at the Golf Club? I wish you didn't drink so much, Noomi. My parents aren't fools, you know. They figure things out eventually."

"There's nothing to do but drink," I said, leaning my forehead on the warm glass. It felt like there was a small child inside of me, always howling. When I drank, she fell quiet. Then I was like a mother who'd put her baby down for a nap and could spend a few hours alone. I remember how my mother would enter a party on the verge of tears, and then, as if by magic, I'd pass by her later and she'd be laughing, a drink in hand, her face glowing like a lamp.

Veer asked the porter to carry our bags; the man said it would cost two hundred rupees per suitcase. That wasn't cheap, but Veer never bargained with someone poor. The porter took off his gamcha from his neck and coiled it into a pillow. He squatted so that we could pile our suitcases on his head. Then he stuck out an arm for Veer to hang a duffel bag. Our platform was far away, ninth from the exit. He walked ahead of us gracefully, swaying for balance, like a dancer. A rat ran across the platform, and I leaped to avoid it. We briefly lost sight of the porter in the crowd. I was alarmed. Then he reappeared, a dark strip of sweat down the back of his red shirt.

The exit was swarming with cars, taxis, and autorickshaws picking up passengers, tossing up clouds of ocher dust. A flow of pedestrians weaved through the traffic. I spotted Jeh's Jeep and directed the porter toward it. Jeh was sitting in the driver's seat with the door open. I jogged up and gave him a hug. He hadn't shaved; his bristles poked my face. He smelled, not in an unpleasant way, of dead leaves and moss. I felt calm envelop me like a shawl.

"I'm so happy we're here," I said. "Where's Mom? Is she waiting for us at home?"

"I snuck out without telling her." Jeh grinned. He gave Veer a hug. "I wanted to be the first one to welcome you and Noomi home."

"Thanks, Dad," Veer said. "Noomi has been talking nonstop about coming home. She misses you a lot."

"Dad, after lunch today, let's take Veer to our old walk up Seminary Hills. I want to show him the spot where we watched the kites that day, remember?" I hugged him again.

The porter put the luggage in the back. Jeh gave him a large tip. "Here you go, boss."

I pushed Jeh and got into the driver's seat. "I'm driving."

With Jeh next to me and Veer crammed in the back, I drove the Jeep out of the station lot, careful of the crowds of pedestrians. At an intersection not far from home, we stopped to let a funeral procession pass. Mourners carried a body covered in flowers on a stretcher over their heads. A man shouted, "Ram naam satya hai." *The name of God is the truth.* In reply, a coucal whooped from a neem tree.

I killed the car's motor and turned, drumming the steering wheel. "So, what's today's plan again?"

"Lunch is at Lily Mama's," Jeh said, lighting a cigarette. "For dinner, we could go to a restaurant if you like." It took only a few puffs for him to start coughing. His skin turned a worrisome gray.

"Dad," I said, and plucked the cigarette from his mouth. I tossed it out the window. "You're fifty-three years old and you smoke more than I do."

As the last stragglers from the funeral walked past, the havaldar in charge of the intersection blew his whistle and motioned for the traffic to move. I honked at a sputtering autorickshaw blocking my way. Traffic began to unsnarl. I looked in the rearview mirror at Veer. He'd been very quiet.

"Hey, babe," I said. "You want to stop and buy some flowers or something for Lily Mama?"

"Later," Veer said. His folded-up legs looked cramped in the back. "I need to get out of this car."

Milo, our dog, a golden retriever—fat, joyful, and dumb—began barking as soon as he heard us arrive. A glutton for affection, he'd sidle up to anyone for a pet. If you stopped petting him, he'd scooch closer and put his paw on your leg. He ruined our clothes with his slobber. He followed us up the stairs, whining and knocking over vases and ashtrays with his excited tail.

"This numbskull," Jeh said, pulling Milo's neck so his ears waggled.

Asha emerged in an orange kaftan, trailing cigarette smoke. She came toward us, stretching her arms for a hug. "Your father didn't even tell me before he left to pick you up," she said. "You didn't bother to call me to say you were coming. I've been so excited. I couldn't sleep last night."

"You were asleep when I left," Jeh said. He crouched and gave Milo a belly rub. Milo's pink tongue hung over the side of his open mouth; he moaned like he was going into labor.

"Don't start guilt-tripping Dad as soon as he walks in the door," I said, wheeling my suitcase to my bedroom. "I'm sure we'll have lots of time to catch up."

I turned, waiting for Veer to follow. He went up to Asha and folded his arms around her.

"Hi, Mom," he said, planting a small kiss on her cheek. "You look good. I like your kaftan."

Veer never made Asha feel as if she didn't matter. A few months ago, when Asha wanted his advice for a project at the orphanage, Veer went through her presentation, slide by painful slide, offering input on how to improve it. The orphanage was the only place where Asha felt important. Jeh said she spent most of her time there these days.

In Lily Mama's drawing room, the ceiling had lamps that looked like drop earrings, the billowy curtains were stained with yellow sunlight. A painting of the Himalayas hung above a dining table inlayed with mother-of-pearl chrysanthemums. When Lily Mama and Zal Papa retired for the afternoon, as children, Adil and I would climb on the table and pretend the painting was a secret map. I'd point up at the farthest mountain: "That's where the treasure's buried." In the garden, the "treasure" was a big flake of mica, or a feather, or a pile of leftover bricks we pretended was made of gold.

Our memories are contaminated with our emotions. The past is a fable we teach to ourselves. I tried to recall the good memories, but bad ones, like dirty water after a storm, kept seeping back into my mind. Still, I was happy to be home that afternoon and with my family. Not even Zal Papa's habitual barbs could put me off.

"Noomi dear, I hope you're keeping your lord and master happy." Zal Papa leaned back, hands on his knees. A mug of beer sat on a side table within easy reach. His gray beard looked freshly trimmed. Zal Papa's eyes held affection lit up only by little sparks of anger.

"Ask him yourself when he comes back with my beer," I said, perching myself on Jeh's knee.

"Aren't you a little old to sit on your father's lap?" Lily Mama chuckled. "And heavy, also?"

"She'll never be too old to sit on my lap," Jeh said, hugging me. "Even when she's a mother herself."

"Kids aren't in the timeline," Veer said, sauntering back from the kitchen. He gave me a beer.

"Thanks, babe," I said. Veer gave me a look. The beer was against his better judgment, the look said. I tried to reassure him with a smile. He turned away. It struck me that I might lose him if I didn't stop drinking. I'd worry about that tomorrow. I took a sip and felt instantly more cheerful.

Veer pulled his chair close to Asha. "Mom, you've been very quiet this afternoon. Everything okay?"

"I'm watching," Asha said, pointing her chin at Jeh and me, "the daddy-daughter act. Very charming." The orange chair she sat on didn't match Lily Mama's beige sofas. Asha was still wearing her orange kaftan from the morning, and she blended with the armchair like a chameleon. She crossed her legs, dangling a slipper off one foot. In her hand was a glass of lemonade full of ice cubes. Asha was being good, while we drank beer. I could feel the resentment rising from her like heat from an oven. It played out like this: sobriety, resentment, then seething, pulsating anger and relapse. I hoped that Veer and I would be long gone before the final stage.

Lily Mama looked at Asha the way I'd seen her look at the aphids eating her rose plants. "Asha dear," Lily Mama said, "your kaftan needs a slip. I can practically see your underwear. It's so vulgar."

It was as if Lily Mama had stood up, walked behind Asha's chair, tipped it, and sent her crashing to the floor. Asha gathered her kaftan in her lap, muttering about a faulty lining. It irritated me to see her cut down so effortlessly. I looked over at Jeh, hoping he'd speak up. At the same moment, I knew he wouldn't, and that if it were me in Asha's place, Veer wouldn't either. They say girls want to marry their fathers— I certainly had.

"Want to know something funny? Veer's mom's never worn a skirt above her calves in her entire life," I said viciously. "She feels it's too scandalous. Imagine."

I took Jeh's beer and poured it into my glass. A muscle in Veer's face twitched, but he stayed quiet. He hated it when I spoke about his mother as if she were a village prude.

"I'll get you a new one," I said when Jeh grumbled about his beer. I stood up and went into the kitchen.

A pot of dhansak sat spattering on the kitchen stove. I took up a ladle and swirled the dal until I found a cube of mutton to pop into my mouth. Shanta Bai appeared from Lily Mama's pantry and tapped the back of my hand. "Wait until lunch is served." I smiled and gave her a hug.

"What do you think about my nowra?" I asked, smiling. "Does he look like Chunky Panday?"

"Changla," she said, and nodded. "Little bit soft-spined," she added after a few moments' consideration.

"True," I said, looking in the fridge. The beers were stashed behind a chocolate cake with WELCOME HOME VEER AND NOOMI! frosted on its face. I dug a finger into the icing.

Back in the living room, my grandparents were ready for lunch. Asha's chair was empty.

"Did Mom leave already?" I asked Jeh.

"She went to lie down," Jeh said. "Asked me to bring up a plate for her later."

I looked at Asha's empty orange chair. "Shall we have lunch then? I'm hungry."

"Shanta Bai! Lunch!" Lily Mama said.

Zal Papa sat, as usual, at the head of the table. Veer had the place of high honor on his right. I sat between Lily Mama and Jeh. Shanta Bai's dhansak arrived in a huge bowl, hot and delicious. Its aroma cast a reverent silence around the dining table.

"Hey, Dad," I said, breaking the spell. "Don't forget. We're taking Veer on a walk after lunch."

"Haven't forgotten," Jeh said, and turned to his father. "Daddy, would you like to come with us?"

"Where, son?" Zal Papa sprinkled salt on his food and then threw a little bit over his shoulder.

"You know, the old walk, up Seminary Hills."

Zal Papa shook his head. "Oh no, that slope is too steep. My heart won't take the strain."

"We'll have to go soon," I said, looking out the window. "It looks like it might rain."

"It'll be nice to see the kites again." Jeh smiled, he turned his head to stare dreamily out the window.

We heard a coucal calling from the trees. *Whoop-whoop-whoop!* Its cry was otherworldly.

"Bad omen!" Shanta Bai hurried out of the kitchen. "Hut! Hut! Hut!" she shouted, leaning out so far I was afraid she might fall into the garden.

My heart was beating fast when we reached the summit. Jeh was bent over, hands on his knees. Breathing hard, he sat down on a flat brown boulder.

"Dad, are you okay?" I asked, noticing a tinge of blue to his lips, his pale face.

"I'm fine," Jeh said. "Just winded." He smiled. "Shanta Bai should make her dhansak less rich."

"Perhaps we should rest. Why don't you sit here? I'll catch up with Veer."

"Good idea," Jeh said. "I wanted to have a good look at these kites anyway." Scrunching up his face, he took the pair of binoculars from a pocket and put them to his eyes. "You go ahead," he said with a reassuring smile. "I'll catch up in a bit."

"We'll wait for you down at the ravine," I said, and hurried after Veer, who'd long ago lost interest in the birds and walked on.

The ground crunched under my shoes. I looked forward to finding the bruises I always got on my calves from the scrubby brush. Veer stopped to tie his shoelaces. He looked smug as I caught up with him, even more out of breath. Competitive guy. Then he craned his neck and looked around me. A shadow of worry crossed his face.

"What's wrong with your dad?" Veer asked.

Before I could turn around, Veer sprinted back up the hill, scudding with his new sneakers over rocks and dirt. I ran after him. Jeh had fallen from the boulder, arms to his sides. I dropped to my knees in the dirt beside him. Veer pulled out a cell phone and began punching in numbers.

"Is he having a heart attack?" I watched my father's mouth open and close like a fish on dry land.

"No network here," Veer shouted. "I'm going down to get help."

"Dad... can you speak?" I asked. "What happened?"

Jeh stared at the sky in amazement, as if the kites had, through the patterns of their flight, given him the answers to a riddle. His eyelids fluttered when I said his name. Cold rain fell inside my T-shirt. My brain stopped working. I forgot which side the heart was and did compressions in the wrong spot. As he died, my father let out a sound that I can still hear sometimes when I'm alone. The earth held his still body in her brown palm, like a small offering.

The rest of my memories from that day appear to me like scenes from a movie I'd watched long ago. Veer running up followed by priests from the seminary, cassocks flapping; driving on the wrong side of the road to get to the hospital; the sickening whine of a defibrillator; Asha rocking back and forth, back and forth, on a chair, praying loudly, something I'd never seen her do; Lily Mama, standing next to Jeh's bed with his hand in hers.

"Tumka deemag nahi chalta hai kya!" she screamed at the nurse in her awful Hindi. *Is your brain not working? This is my son. Don't cover his face! Are you stupid? How will he breathe?*

Zal Papa, crumpled on a hospital chair, looking like he'd watched his house burn down, pieces of ash fluttering everywhere like butterflies. "Jeh, Jeh," he said, as his old hands slowly found their way to his old face. His shoulders moved with sobs.

Fate stalks our lives like a tiger from downwind. But she is patient and won't act before time. Two days ago, we'd walked behind my father's body. A day earlier, he'd smiled. Alive. Awake. Now I was driving to a crematorium to pick up his ashes. It was late afternoon. Shadows on the tar road had begun to stretch out like soft wax. The humid August air smelled of decay, of earth. I put my hand out the window and sieved the cottony breeze. How did I get here? I looked back on the years sewn together by the presence or the absence of a bottle in my mother's hands—in my hands.

The crematorium prided itself on accommodating both traditional and modern funerals. There were pyres—long cement blocks, some with embers glowing—and there was also the electric crematorium, tucked away inside a shed. It was cool and dank with the smell of cement like a construction site. When he saw us walking in, a thin man with soot up to his elbows, like opera gloves, opened a hatch and used a trowel to noisily scrape out ashes into a rough iron bowl. Bones were mixed with the ash and made a solid clunking sound as they fell in. Ash flew out in thin licks into my nose.

"Careful, the bones are still hot," the man warned as he put the bowl on the floor.

There was Jeh, then, in that bowl.

I took a bottle of sedatives out of my handbag and swallowed two. The man brought a scraggly little garland, incense, and a square of red cloth. He tossed the flowers and incense into the bowl, laid the cloth on the floor, put the bowl on it, and tied the corners. My gruesome gift. He held out the bundle to me—my knees started to buckle. Veer took the bundle and balanced it on his hips. He held me up with one arm.

"It's okay," he said.

The furnace had opened its metal jaws and licked Jeh's corpse with its tongue of flames. And now, in that iron bowl, mixed with Jeh's ashes was the dimple on his left cheek when he smiled; was Sinatra's "My Way," which Jeh liked to sing along to when he was drunk; was his favorite flower the mogra—night jasmine; was the year he split his pocket money with his friend whose dad lost his job; was chocolate; was rice straight from the cooker, packed into Jeh's palm; was the color red; was the way Jeh hassled little babies because he thought they looked cuter when they cried.

To balance out breaking from Parsi tradition by honoring Jeh's wish to be cremated instead of buried, Zal Papa wanted all other funeral rituals and prayers—no shortcuts. A shamiana was set up in the lawn for guests who'd begun to stream in once the news spread about town. Funerals and weddings, I thought, weren't too different: the fire, the prayers, the people who offered condolences instead of congratulations.

"Jeh was so caring," said an elderly neighbor. "When I was sick, he'd visit the hospital every day. When he found out I needed an urgent blood transfusion, he rolled up his sleeve without hesitation."

"When I needed a loan for my new business, no one would help until Jeh used his goodwill with the local banks. He put a roof over my family's head. I owe him everything."

They cleared Lily Mama's hall of furniture and put down a rug. In its center burned a sandalwood fire inside an afarganyu, a brass fire urn. Around it sat five priests in muslin robes, mouths hidden behind masks to keep their breath from polluting the sacred fire. The fat, fragrant smoke made our eyes burn. They hummed prayers that, like bees, flew around our heads in a swarm, surrounding, blurring the outlines between our mourning bodies. They hummed and hummed and hummed for hours. Then they stood up. Like surgeons after an operation, the priests changed out of their white robes and dumped them in a cloudy pile. They slipped shirts over their bellies and turned back into ordinary men.

Someone brought out tea, fresh fruit, and biscuits on wooden trays. There was a gathering to celebrate Jeh's life, followed by farewells. Then a silent house. I squeezed shut my eyes, swollen and pink from the smoke. A desire to get blind drunk took over me, and my shame quieted it down.

The world was ending. Invisible thumbs pushed into the soft cartilage of my throat. My breath came out ragged, fighting up from my chest. The road that I was driving on seemed to sway back and forth. Sweat dripped from my upper lip into my mouth. My heart scampered about like a startled rabbit.

You're dying, said my mind. *This is what dying feels like. This is it.*

I swerved my car to the side of the Sea Link bridge to cries and insults from cars charging across the suspended freeway. The noise was deafening. A taxi slowed down next to me. A man in the back seat rolled down his window halfway. He wore sunglasses the color of dragonfly wings. I thought he was going to help. "Crazy bitch!" he yelled. "Learn to drive." He motioned for his taxi driver to go.

It was late August. A year since Jeh died. The sea was gray and motionless. The bridge vibrated with moving cars. The low-tide stench made it even harder to breathe—it was worse than the drying fish smell that hung over Sassoon Docks. Birds screamed in the air. The sky was full of big-bellied clouds, so low one could almost poke them.

I took out my cell phone and searched for a number. I pressed the call button, hugging my chest with one arm, praying that Natasha wasn't busy with another client.

"Hi? Noomi?" Natasha sounded older on the phone. Not that I knew her age; she never revealed any personal details during our sessions. I'd received a shock the first time I'd walked into her office. A therapist should have a few white hairs, no? This one was alarmingly youthful. I'd nicknamed her Jung. She'd stood up and extended a small, neat hand. I shook it with a skeptical glare. Still, there was something honest about Jung's eyes when she smiled.

"I'm hah-ing a panih attah," I mumbled. My mouth felt full of marbles. I hoped Jung could understand what I was saying over the din of seabirds and traffic.

"You're having a panic attack?"

"Yeh."

"Where are you right now?"

"Sea Lick."

"You're on the Sea Link?"

"Yeh."

"What?"

"YES," I said. "And"—I sat back in my seat—"I'm having trouble breathing."

"Be mindful of the breath," Jung said. She always said *the* breath instead of *your* breath, as if it had nothing to do with my lungs. "Let the panic flow through you. Once you start feeling better—*which you will*, Noomi, I promise—drive your car back across and get in a cab."

"Can I come over?" I said.

There was a short pause. I heard something being put away, papers being shuffled.

"Okay, I have a cancellation at one thirty. If you leave now, you'll make it."

"I couldn't turn on the bridge," I said, plonking my purse on the tiled floor at 2:00 P.M. I fell onto the comfortable, bowl-shaped rattan chair in Jung's office.

"We have twenty minutes, okay?" Jung said. Her tone was what one might use with a toddler threatening a tantrum, gentle but unyielding. "Maybe we can have two sessions next week?"

"I'm not in town," I said "Flying home to Kamalpur. For," I began digging into my purse for my cigarettes, "the first anniversary of my father's death." I lit one. "They're having prayers," I continued, blowing out smoke, waggling the cigarette about in a circle. "I don't know the details yet. The entire family is going to be there."

Jung looked at me. "It's been a year since he died." She tilted her head. "How do you feel?"

"It's... hard to believe, sometimes, that I won't ever see him again," I said, pulling on the cigarette.

Jung made what I thought of as her therapy-dog face: her eyes big and soulful, her brow furrowed, her head cocked to one side. "How do you feel?" she asked again.

I shrugged. "I suppose I should feel sad. I should be grieving."

"You talk a lot about how you should or shouldn't feel. How do you actually feel?"

"I feel... exposed, somehow. Like a hermit crab with no shell, just vulnerable flesh."

Jung uncrossed her slim, churidar-clad legs, shifted her weight, and recrossed them. "Are you afraid?"

"Obviously."

"Could it be possible that your panic attack today was related to going back home?"

"Um, yes, again, obviously," I said, and enjoyed seeing Jung's irritation peek out from under her smooth mask. "I have to deal with my family at home. I have to deal with my mother."

"Will Veer be joining you?"

"He'll fly in later. He can't get out of his *work commitments*."

"And how do you feel about that?"

"Hmm. Angry I guess."

"What makes you angry?"

I let out a plume of smoke and scratched a mosquito bite on the back of my neck. "I don't know, Natasha. I'm fucking angry. At least when I'm angry, I'm not scared. And when I'm drunk, I'm not scared."

"Have you heard of the term 'referred pain'?" Jung asked.

"Yes," I said, rubbing my face. "I mean..." I looked at her. "No. Not really."

"It simply means pain that you feel in one part of your body, when there is an injury in another part."

"Oh," I said. "Like how I got those earaches as a kid, when actually I had a sinus infection."

"Yes, exactly." Jung nodded. "You can medicate the pain away, temporarily. But if you don't treat the underlying problem, it will always come back."

"Ah," I said, smiling at her. "I can see where you are going with this."

"Anger," Jung said, "can be a referred emotion."

"What about anxiety?" I said.

"Same." Jung clicked her ballpoint pen. "Tell me, do you think Veer loves you? Or that you love him?"

I considered the question. "I don't know," I said. "I've never understood the idea of romantic love. I know that when I hear a good song, discover a recipe, watch a great movie, pet a cute cat or dog, hear a joke—the first person I want to tell is Veer. Is that love?"

Jung made another small note. "Let's return to your panic attacks."

"Yesterday, I put my head on Veer's chest. I felt terrified his heart would just stop. I waited for it to stop. The waiting made me feel sick with panic." I puffed on my cigarette. "I felt like I needed to get out of bed and get really, really drunk."

"Have you been drinking a lot as a way to cope?"

"I've always liked to drink," I said. "I drink so that I can believe that the universe isn't malevolent. And it's the only way I can be around other people," I massaged my temples, "without wanting to scream."

Jung gave a smile. "I had a teacher who loved George Eliot. Have you read *Middlemarch*?"

"Not yet," I said, sliding down in my chair.

"We lived in Juhu, but my school was in South Bombay. I had a long ride home. My teacher gave me *Middlemarch* to read on the bus. There's a line in there that I painted on a strip of silk: 'What loneliness is more lonely than distrust?' I think that's what made me want to become a therapist. To teach people how to trust."

"That's the first time you've ever told me anything about yourself," I said.

"Well," Jung said, "I only share things from my personal life if I think it might help."

Sadness is a lake. If you explored its depths, it swallowed you. Anger, on the other hand, is a cliff. At its edge, things seem smaller, farther away. But cliffs are dangerous too.

I t was pouring the night I returned to Kamalpur. The rain fell in straight lines like a running stitch, creating torrents down the roadsides, cleaning them of trash: plastic bags, food cartons, a rat, a gelatinous condom. Adil had to take the long way home from the airport. The overpasses had turned, by the evening, into rivers suspended in the air. I put my feet on the car's dashboard. Pressing my toe to the fogged-up glass, I drew a smiley face.

"Could you not do that?" Adil said. "Seriously, I just bought this car."

"So touchy," I said, putting my feet down. "New car, huh? Business is good, I see."

"It's great," Adil said.

He switched the indicator on to turn. *Ticktock, ticktock.* His face was spotted with the shadows of raindrops. *Ticktock* went his little green arrow.

"By the way," he said, looking at me, "I'm not sure if you know this, but we had to fire Mr. Murthy."

"You fired Daddy's secretary?" I stared. "Old Murthy? Why, Adil? He was always so nice."

"It didn't work out," Adil said. "He refused to adapt to my style of doing business."

"But he's been with the company for thirty years," I said. "He still sends me birthday cards." I drew an angry face in the window. "Dad was so fond of him. Mr. Doubting Thomas Murthy."

"It's not personal, Nooms," Adil said. "I took over Uncle Jeh's work. I need to have a secretary that I can get along with. Isn't that fair?"

After Jeh died, they made Adil, only twenty-five, a director in the family business. They gave him Jeh's old office and his staff. They took Jeh's car away from Asha, as the company owned it, and gave that to Adil as well. Asha and I had no say in the matter. Adil claimed that he'd done it for Zal Papa, who still couldn't speak my father's name without breaking down. Having Adil around was the only thing that kept him together.

At home, in the house Zal Papa built, a garland of marigolds adorned my bedroom door. I reached up and plucked one. I pressed it to my nose, breathing in its watery scent. It told me that Lily Mama had been upstairs today, to make sure my bed had been made up with freshly laundered sheets, the house and kitchen swept clean, all my favorite foods stocked in the fridge.

I took my clothes out of my suitcase and laid them on the bed. There was a tiny knock at the door. Asha poked her head through the gap. She gave a little smile, then came in and sat on my bed, on top of my clothes. Looking around for something to do, she picked up a T-shirt to fold, even though it was already folded. Her hands shook a little.

"Shanta Bai told me you were in your room," Asha said. "I'd waited up for you."

"The roads were flooded," I said, pulling out a pair of slippers from my suitcase. I threw them on the floor. The loud slapping sound made Asha jump. "We took a detour."

"I thought you'd at least come in to tell me that you're home."

"Didn't think you'd care." I yanked a pair of pants from under Asha's bottom.

Asha stretched her arms out to me in a way that reminded me of how, as a child, I'd reach up to her for a hug, right after she had slapped me for making noise inside a restaurant, or annoying her with too many questions, or for back-talking in front of strangers. If there is no other option, children will seek comfort from those who hurt them, like a dog wagging its tail at the owner who feeds it but also beats it with a stick.

"Prayers start at seven in the morning tomorrow," I said, giving Asha a hug, suppressing a remark at the alcohol hidden in her breath. "Zal Papa will be angry if we're late."

"I promise not to be late," Asha said, and left.

A memory flooded my mind: a bright orange sun, the creaking of a playground swing. Asha was late picking me up from school. My teacher in fourth grade—I'd forgotten her name... Miss Sharma? Miss Kumar?—sat on a bench in the playground, propping her head up with a fist. Birds chittered in the trees. The sun dipped below the horizon, leaving the evening sky aglow with winter light.

"I've never had a parent be five hours late to pick up a child," my teacher said. "Where could your mom be?"

"Don't worry, miss," I'd said. "She'll be here soon."

I swung higher and higher. The goal was to touch the setting sun with my foot. I loved the butterflies in my stomach on the way down.

Asha arrived, drunk, apologetic. She hugged me and breathed vodka into my ear. "So sorry, so very sorry," she said to my teacher. "Lost track of time completely."

I could tell my teacher did not believe her. But she was tired and wanted to go home. She looked at me, and I gave her a nod to say, *I'll be okay.*

"Please make sure this never happens again," she said, staring at my mother.

"I promise not to be late." My mother pinched her neck and smiled. "Mother promise."

We got into the car. Asha threw my bag in the back, lit a cigarette, and pushed a tape into the deck. A pop song played through the speakers—chirpy, upbeat music.

"I'm sorry, baby. Tell me, how can I make it up to you?" she said.

"Let me try that," I said, pointing to her cigarette. "I want to see why you like it so much."

"What?" Asha snorted. "No way. Cigarettes are bad for kids, stupid girl."

"Then why do you smoke when I'm around? I'm breathing it in, aren't I?"

"That's different," Asha said, looking irritated.

"I'll tell Daddy you forgot me at school for five hours."

Asha shifted gears and looked at me. Trees and cars whizzed past. The sky was bluish purple.

"Come on," I pleaded. "One little puff."

Asha narrowed her eyes. "Okay," she said with a sigh, handing the cigarette to me. "Don't tell anyone."

"I promise." I licked my lips and took a tiny puff. I began coughing immediately. "This is so disgusting!" I said, passing the cigarette back to my mother. She laughed. I stuck my head out the window and spat away the taste.

"Serves you right," Asha said. "Now you know better."

I laughed too. We were friends now. Partners in crime.

"I'll never smoke again," I said, pinching my neck the way I'd seen her do. "Mother promise."

We hit a stretch of empty road. Relaxing in her seat, my mother sped up. She flipped the tape in the deck to side A. I stuck my head out the window and screamed along with the song. There were butterflies in my stomach. I'd discovered the pleasure in falling very far, very fast.

As with anything the Wadias did, the prayers began precisely on time. The priests in white robes sat around the fire, murmuring gathas for Jeh's departed soul and for the health and well-being of his family. I sat cross-legged on the floor, my back against the hard wooden leg of a chair. I felt myself rising like a balloon over my body, until I bumped up against the wedding-cake ceiling of Lily Mama's stately living room.

Lily Mama had on a pale yellow sari, its diaphanous pallu covering her head. Her face was beautiful, inscrutable, like a marble statue. On the other end of the sofa sat Zal Papa, his face all emotions and twitching muscles. Too scrutable. He looked as if grief had shrunk him. His collar seemed too big for his neck. Friends commented that he'd lost his enthusiasm for meddling in their lives. In fact, nowadays, they said, Zal Papa barely stepped out of the house.

Binny sat between my grandparents. Her husband, Cyrus, Jeh's older brother, stood behind them. He joined heads with Adil, whispering something to do with the priests' fees. Binny gave Zal Papa's arm a comforting pat. Tears glazed his face every time the priests said Jeh's name. I'd heard that Binny had been planting seeds in Zal Papa's head and gardening them diligently. They'd begun looking for a wife for Adil; he would need a house to start a family. He'd already taken over Jeh's role in the family business, so why not his flat too? Asha didn't need three huge bedrooms now that she was all by herself. Besides, their marriage had been a sham. Everyone knew. Jeh was too weak-willed to get a divorce. Everyone knew. One might even go so far as to say that Asha was the reason Jeh's heart gave out—her constant drinking, her breakdowns, her tantrums.

Everyone knew.

I looked at my wristwatch. It was half past noon. The watch was a gift; Veer had bought it for me for our first wedding anniversary. He'd taken me to the store to choose it. The salesman tried to nudge me to get a more feminine style. "That's not her," Veer had told him. He'd be here in two days' time. I had to keep going until then. From a corner, I heard a little sound. Asha had covered her mouth with her dupatta. Tears dripped onto her hand. I wasn't sure if it was grief or if it was smoke from the fire that made her eyes leak. Perhaps both.

Sheila Sehgal arrived with Sid once the prayers had ended, at the head of a retinue carrying food. Sheila hugged Binny. They'd been close friends since high school: good-looking girls who knew they amplified each other's good looks. Sheila swished past Asha with a nod, swooping her hair over one shoulder. Gracefully, she touched my grandparents' feet. Sid did too. He and Adil hugged, the way young men hug, smashing into each other.

The next to arrive were Ammu and her parents. Ammu took my hands in her own. I noticed a diamond the size of a chickpea on her ring finger. My mouth fell open like a ventriloquist dummy's.

"That's quite the rock on your hand," I pointed out.

"Yeah, I got engaged." Ammu said, running her fingers through her fine hair.

"When? Why didn't you say anything?" I said, staring at her, taking in her face. "Who is it?"

"I didn't know what to say," Ammu said. "To be honest, I'm a little embarrassed."

"Is it Shiv?"

"Of course it's Shiv." She laughed.

"You'll be happy," I said, a band of jealousy tightening around my heart.

"Oh, I'll do okay," Ammu said, grinning, tucking a wisp of hair behind her ear. "I want to tell you more, but you should go see to guests. I have to say hello to your mom. Chat later."

Ammu's life was like a bullet train. It arrived at every station on time. It was clean, neat, and quiet and had a team of experts to keep it running at peak efficiency. My life must have been run by Indian Railways.

I should've been happy for Ammu. I wasn't. In a mood to irritate, I slinked off. Sid was at the lunch table, debating hard between an aloo or a gobi paratha. He saw me and smoothed down the sides of his hair. I imagined him as an old man, still preening for every woman who gave him a second look. I didn't need to turn to know that Sheila was boring her eyes into my skull.

"The dal looks really good," I said. It looked horrible. "It's making me hungry. Nice of your mom to bring all these dishes over. Her kitchen staff must've worked for days."

"Well, you know, Mom pays the best rate in town," Sid said, slapping an aloo paratha onto his plate. "And hires the best cooks. Anushka is obsessed with the maa ki dal in our house."

"Where is Anushka?" I asked, looking around.

Sid tore a piece of the paratha and began to chew on it. "Where's your hubby?"

"He'll be here Friday," I said. "It's the middle of a workweek, you know, Sid. Everyone doesn't have a corner office in Papa's factory."

"I've heard your husband is a corporate big shot. Do you guys have an amazing place in Bombay?" Sid said, scratching his stubble. "Where's he from again? Agra... or Lucknow?"

"Delhi," I said. "His dad is very close with the home minister."

"Oh?"

"Oh yeah, he's got, like, a bungalow near India Gate and everything," I said, hating how I sounded.

"Really," Sid said, pulling the word long like putty. "I guess you've moved up in the world, huh?"

I wondered if Sid practiced in a mirror until he found the most disaffected way to say these things. "So anyway, where's Anushka?" I said, picking off all the coriander from my oily potatoes.

"I saw Anushka with her mom yesterday," Ammu said, strolling over with a plate. "Shopping for baby clothes."

"Nushki is pregnant." Sid smiled at Ammu. "She's at her parents' until the baby comes. It's a boy." He relayed the news as if it were relatively uninteresting, hooking his arm around my shoulders. "Hey, since we're all in town, let's celebrate with a little get-together. What are your plans for tonight?" He looked at me. "Adil's dropping by around nine. Why don't you tag along? You should come too, Ammu. I haven't hung out with you since your engagement, I think."

"Oh no, I can't make it tonight." Ammu smiled. "I have plans with Shiv after work."

"Sexy plans?" I asked, turning around. Sheila and Binny were on the beige sofas, tittering like wicked sisters in a fable. Asha was on the orange armchair, at a distance, by herself. Fury boiled in my head like a cumulous cloud.

"Noomi, don't be crude," Ammu said, flustered.

"Sounds good," I said to Sid, raising my glass of nimbu paani. "I could use a real drink."

"See you tonight," Sid said, cocking a finger gun at me. "I have to get back to work."

Adil didn't like this plan at all. "It doesn't look right," he said. "The first anniversary of Uncle Jeh's death, and you're out drinking? What will people say?"

"Fuck what people say," I snapped, pulling on my cigarette. The car stopped in front of Sid's massive front gate. "Why do you get to drink and go out? He was your uncle, after all."

"Don't act all naive," Adil said. "You know there are different rules—"

"For men and women," I said, cutting him off. "Yes. Yes, I know. I also know that if I don't have a drink soon, I think I might die."

Adil parked next to Sid's sleek car in the driveway. The chowkidar directed us to the gazebo. Sid looked rich and free of care in his Gucci loafers. Industrial-strength hair gel protected his Johnny Bravo pompadour against the oppressive monsoon humidity. Sid was a generous host. The alcohol was top shelf: Japanese whiskies, artisanal gins. Loud and expensive speakers played Punjabi hits, which Bollywood churned out faster than Sid's factory did low-grade cement.

I was neither very rich nor very pretty, and so, I wasn't supposed to talk much. That was okay. I was happy sucking on drink after drink overfilled with ice. Adil lit Sid's cigarettes and laughed a bit too hard at his jokes. The topic of conversation was money—who had it, who did not. Women came up often too. Acquaintances' wives and girlfriends rarely escaped without having their social media pictures pulled up, their bodies neatly dismembered and appraised for value. Breasts, legs, ass, waist.

"Women are real estate," Adil said, swirling the ice cubes in his drink. "Like, in Bombay. At twenty, they're a Colaba penthouse. At twenty-five, a three BHK in Bandra." He grinned. "At thirty and beyond, well, then we're looking at Andheri or Juhu. Not bad, but no status symbol either."

I kept my face politely blank and wondered what was left of the sweet kid Adil had once been. Many monsoons ago, our garden was overrun with swallowtails. A large blue one landed on Adil's shoulder. It didn't fly away, so he named it "Buttsy." Adil, who was six or seven years old at the time, showed Buttsy off to his friends. "I have a pet butterfly!" he said. Life cycle over, Buttsy died. Adil lifted his butterfly up by its dusty wings and placed it in a matchbox coffin lined with a tissue. We buried it next to a mogra bush. At the funeral, Adil insisted we all say something nice.

"What does that make you then, Noomi?" Sid laughed. "A sublet in Malad?"

"Fuck you, Sid," I said.

"Relax," Sid said, stretching his legs out on the sofa. "I'm just teasing. You're still hot."

Adil looked slowly from Sid to me and said, "I think it's time to head home." He grabbed his car keys from the coffee table, stood, stretched out his arms with a yawn. "Come on, Noomi. We have to get up early for prayers."

With his palm on the glass door, he turned, wondering why I hadn't followed.

"Chalo, Noomi," he said, and jerked his head toward the lawn. "Let's go home. Chop-chop."

Sid poured out tequila shots. I drank one down and felt it burn pleasantly in my throat. Three gin and tonics later, I was still thirsty. "Go ahead," I said to Adil. "I'm not tired yet."

Adil jangled his car keys like a jailor. "You'll never get up on time for tomorrow."

"Stop acting like my babysitter," I said. "*I'm* the older cousin, remember?"

"Chill the fuck out, uncle," Sid said, handing me another tequila shot. "I'll drop Noomi home."

A look crossed Adil's face. "Fine," he said. He pushed open the door and loped off across the lawn. I tossed back a tequila shot and watched as he got smaller and smaller, until the garden, and the night, swallowed him.

The next morning, my skull pounded with a steady, dull throb. My mouth tasted like an ashtray; my sweat reeked of alcohol. I wobbled over to the bathroom to splash cold water on my face. Wiping off my streaky mascara, I turned and threw up into the toilet. My heart bounced like a beach ball in my chest. I brushed my teeth and flung my toothbrush at the sink, mashing the heel of my hand into my eyes. My head was filled with pieces of memory that didn't quite fit together, like a jigsaw puzzle left in the rain.

Adil left. Sid and I moved on from tequila to sharing a joint. We began talking about the past. The talking led to kissing. It was almost lovely. Then Sid said wouldn't it be a thrill if I blew him, right there in the open? He unzipped his pants and pulled out his penis, a fleshy stamen between denim petals. I thought of corpse flowers that give off a rotting stench when they bloom. Then my father's dead face, gray and waxen like a strange doll, floated before my eyes.

"Sid," I said, moving away, "I want to go home."

Sid grabbed my wrist and pulled my hand toward his penis. "Okay, get me off. I'll take you home. I haven't had sex in months. Anushka won't let me touch her because of the baby. Come on."

"I'm serious," I said, "I'm going to be sick."

Vomit erupted from my mouth right onto Sid's lap.

"What the fuck?!" Sid said, grabbing a napkin to wipe off the tequila-smelling puke.

He looked so disgusted and upset. I giggled.

This made Sid angry. He grabbed the back of my neck. "You think this is fucking funny? You're a piece of trash. And you're insane. Girls like you should come with a 'use me' sign."

"Sid, let go," I said. "Please."

"No," he said.

He pushed my face down. I didn't know what else to do, so I bit his thigh. Sid let go with a yelp. I whipped my head up and hit him in the nose. There was a wet, crunching sound. Drops of blood spilled all over the white sofa.

I came out of the bathroom and went through my handbag. I found my phone. Five unanswered calls to Veer at 3:17 A.M. Then a call back from him. I shut my eyes. What had I told him? Blank. I took a deep breath and dialed his number.

"Hey, potato, you're up already?" Veer sounded concerned but not worried.

"Um, yeah," I said, sitting down on the bed. "Did... did we talk last night?"

"Yeah, I was going to call you later. I thought you'd still be asleep. You sounded pretty upset last night," he said. I closed my eyes. "You missed your dad. Then you started crying, saying your family's going to kick your mom out of the house—something like that. You weren't making a lot of sense."

"I need help to stop drinking. Antabuse, or some other way, Veer. I can't do it by myself."

"That's a bit dramatic, no?" Veer said. "Everybody binges once in a while." I heard a car honking in the background. " Just learn how to control yourself."

"I can't, okay?" I said, wiping away tears. "Veer, I think"—I sat up straight—"I think I'm in trouble."

"You're beginning to sound hysterical," Veer said, his voice calm but dismissive.

"You don't understand," I said. "Last night, I..." But I didn't have the guts to tell him.

"Listen, I've got to go. I've changed my flight to tomorrow. I'll be there soon, okay? Take it easy. Stay *out* of trouble."

Veer hung up. My stomach made an angry noise. I went to the kitchen to cut up some fruit and took it back to my room with a glass of water. Passing by Asha's door, I looked in. Her bed was neat, bare, like it belonged to someone who'd just died. At least one of us had made it to morning prayers.

I turned my laptop on and typed "Can a hangover kill you?" in the search bar. The answers were crazy. I typed "Alcoholics Anonymous." Taking a bite of an apple, its flesh a little tart, metallic, I looked through AA locations in Worli, Panvel, Byculla, et cetera. Too close by, too far, too crowded. I clicked the minimize button, sighed, slammed the lid shut, and stretched toward my phone. Jung's number was in the emergency contacts list. I pressed call. It rang and rang. No one picked up. I texted: *Need help. Can you prescribe Antabuse? If yes, send prescription via email.*

A knock at the door. Asha, dressed in white, smelling like sandalwood smoke. She walked in and sat at the foot of my bed, crossing, in a deliberate way, one leg over the other. I sat up, uncomfortable.

"What is it?" I said. "Why are you looking at me like that?" I crossed my arms.

"They were asking about you." Asha looked me over. "Adil told us what happened last night." She shook her head. "You were screaming, he said. You broke Sid's nose."

I tried to put last night in the proper order. Adil had come back. He'd forklifted me off the ground by my armpits. What else, what else? Oh god. I'd thrown up on Sid's sofas and gone out into the garden, screaming for Jeh. Oh, fuck. Sheila had come out wrapped in a dressing gown, her cell phone to her ear.

"Do... do Lily Mama and Zal Papa know?"

"Know?" Asha snorted. "Zal Papa yelled at *me*. Like I'd made you into this... this person." Asha's eyes glazed over. "You could think about me for once, Noomi. They'll kick me out of this house for sure now."

If anyone could elevate making everything about herself into an art form, it was Asha. I wanted to scream at her, but she already looked so terrified. I swallowed my anger.

"I won't let them do anything like that," I said. "This is *our* house."

"Zal Papa wants to have a talk with you when he gets up from his afternoon nap," she said.

I'd sat in Zal Papa's office with Jeh and watched him bully, cajole, and wear down my father into sending Asha away. If Zal Papa wanted something to happen, it happened. Fear held me in its spidery embrace. Everything started to blur. My breath caught in my throat.

"What's wrong?" Asha said, grabbing hold of me.

"Nothing," I said, shaking.

"Noomi, talk to me, what's happening?" Asha shook me gently.

"Panic attack," I choked out, slumping sideways. The fear-spider wrapped its legs around me.

Asha pulled my head to the place where her collarbone met her neck. "Shh, everything's okay."

"Stop it," I said. "You're making it hard to breathe."

"You need to sleep it off," she said, hurt but trying to hide it. She took a sheet of pills from her purse. "Here, take two of these." She handed me the glass of water on my bedside.

"Thanks," I said. I didn't ask her what kind of pills they were. If they could help me calm down, I'd take a hundred.

"I'll leave the rest here, just in case," Asha said. "Okay?"

I put my head on a pillow. Slowly, the knots in my neck and back came loose. The spider let go. I covered myself with the duvet and welcomed sleep like an old friend. The last thing I heard was Asha shutting the bedroom door with a click.

My dreams are cliché, as if my subconscious were run by a washed-up novelist. In this one, I struggle to finish a math test, but the ink evaporates from the page. I am drunk, and it is hot in the cramped classroom. Being drunk in a dream feels weird; all dreams are based on drunk logic. The numbers on the test keep jumping about, like grasshoppers. I sweat alcohol through my clothes. My papers are snatched away. The final bell sounds like a telephone.

It turns out to be my cell phone.

"Hello?" I answered in a dry-mouthed whisper.

"I saw that you'd called me a few times. Is everything all right?" Jung said.

"One second." My eyelids felt glued together. For a moment, I thought I was back in my Bandra flat. But I was in my room, at home, in Kamalpur. I heard birds squabbling in the trees outside my window. The setting sun dyed my walls orange. I squinted at my phone. It was seven o'clock. I'd missed my meeting with Zal Papa.

"Can I call you in a bit?" I said, getting up. "My grandfather wants to talk to me about something."

"Sure," Jung said. "Before you hang up, I can't prescribe you any medication. I'm not a psychiatrist. Even if I could, I wouldn't recommend Antabuse." A pause. "You don't need to punish yourself like that."

"Are you an idiot or something?" I yelled. "You think I have a choice? That I *want* to be on Antabuse? Do you have any idea how hard it is to stop drinking?"

Silence.

"Fuck," I said. "Sorry. I'm so scared." I flung a pillow to the floor. "I don't know what my grandfather wants to talk about. Mom keeps saying that he wants her out of the house."

"Noomi, before you go downstairs, do me a favor. Look at yourself in a mirror. You're not an eight-year-old anymore," Natasha said. "You grandfather doesn't have the same power over you."

"I really have to go," I said.

"You're back on Monday, right?"

"I hope so."

"Well, I have a cancellation on Tuesday. Would you like to come in?"

"Yes."

"Okay, great. And, Noomi?"

"Yes?"

"Please don't yell at me like that again."

"I know. I'm sorry." I grabbed my forehead. "I'm really, really anxious."

"I'm here for you, but don't do that, okay?"

"Okay."

I swung my head under my bed to look for my slippers. I saw Milo's little red ball, glowing like the tip of a cigarette. My cheek pressed against the floor, I stretched my hand out for it. Milo loved Jeh. Every night, he would bark his head off when he heard Jeh's car at the gate. Jeh would push open the passenger-side door and Milo would hop in. Together, they'd drive into the garage. A few months after Jeh died, Milo was run over. The driver was an old man on his way to visit his wife in the hospital. He kept apologizing as he helped the chowkidar carry Milo into the house. We thought that—perhaps when Jeh stopped coming home, Milo went out to look for him. We laid poor, sweet, greedy Milo to rest in the garden with a candy bar between his paws.

Tossing the red ball from one hand to another, I went across the hall to Jeh's bedroom. It was a museum of the last day Jeh was alive. Lily Mama had it cleaned and the bed made every day. She and Asha were feuding about Jeh's things. Jeh had laid a shirt on a chair to be ironed; it was still there. So were his slippers. The book he'd been reading was still on his bedside; he'd used his glasses for a bookmark. The book's cover said it had won many prizes. I went to the closet and wrenched it open. The smell of Jeh's cologne pulled my face into his clothes. I crawled in and closed the doors.

Z al Papa was in the glass sunroom he'd installed in the veranda. The room was soundproof, not by accident. Lily Mama had a habit of shouting at the gardener, at her cook, at the drivers, continuing to shout long after they'd hurried away. Zal Papa liked reading his newspapers in peace. He was sitting at a table, turning the pages of a magazine, resting one hand on his knee. Next to him, looking over a stack of office files, was Cyrus.

I dragged up a chair and sat down.

"Glad you took time out of your busy drinking schedule to meet with me." Zal Papa looked up. "I'll get right to it." He stabbed a finger at the file in Cyrus's hands. "This appears to be Jeh's will."

"Okay," I said.

"But it isn't signed," Cyrus added. He turned the papers toward me.

"So then who cares?" I said. "You don't want to carry out his wishes."

"Be respectful," Zal Papa warned, "or I'll take my chappal off and thrash you."

"Noomi." Uncle Cyrus's voice, high and nasal, made everything he said sound like a complaint. "Your father never told you, but he had a lot of debt, mostly because of your wedding, and some because of Asha's stints in rehabs. He passed away before he could pay our company back."

"Yes," Zal Papa began to blubber. "My Cyrus was kind enough to wipe it out."

"Thank you, Uncle," I said, without an ounce of gratitude. Zal Papa used to think his elder son was too soft. Too weak. As a boy, Cyrus had been very attached to his mother. Jeh said Cyrus liked to sit on Lily Mama's lap at the breakfast table. When teasing and snide comments didn't work, Zal Papa pulled Cyrus off with a whack and shouted, "What're you, a bloody pansy?" Jeh, on the other hand, was Zal Papa's little man. He picked fights with the boys in his class, he played football, he played rugby, he walked about in the garden, shirtless and potbellied, claiming, "I'm Sandow!" When Jeh was around four, Zal Papa was knocked unconscious by a loose roof tile during one of his absurd home remodels. Lily Mama took the boys to see him in the hospital. Cyrus, sobbing, held on to his father's hand, while Jeh said, frowning curiously, "Bloody fellow is dead or what?"

Zal Papa wanted Jeh to be a man and control his wife. Asha's very public struggles had emasculated him, in Zal Papa's eyes, made him seem lacking in a certain ruthlessness that was needed to appear respectable in society. It was the great disappointment of Zal Papa's life.

"We understand the word 'respectful' a bit differently, I think," I said, looking over at Zal Papa. "You mean 'respect my authority.' But to me"—I opened my palms on the table—"respect means treating a person with dignity." I flipped them downward. "Why do I have to accept your absolute authority for you to even consider treating me with dignity?"

Zal Papa leaned forward in his chair. "Really?" he said with a bitter smile. "You demand that we treat you with dignity. When you behave like a madwoman." He let out an angry bark. "Where was your dignity last night, huh? You're lucky the Sehgals didn't decide to call the police." He jabbed the air with his forefinger. "Your behavior reflects at all times on the family."

"That's ridiculous," I said.

Cyrus cleared his throat and shuffled papers.

"We've discussed it," Zal Papa continued. "It's best that you don't come back to Kamalpur unless your husband comes with you. We cannot take responsibility for you anymore."

"What? You can't do that. This is my home !" I slammed my hands on the table.

"This isn't your home anymore," Zal Papa said. "You live with your husband."

"Please, Daddy," Cyrus said, indicating the will. "Let's get back to why we called this meeting."

"Go on, son," Zal Papa said. "You tell her."

Here it comes, I thought, bracing myself. They were going to tell Asha to get out.

"Noomi," Cyrus said, "in this will, which is unsigned, Jeh said that he would like to leave his flat to you and Asha." He opened his palms and tipped his head to one side. "We don't think it was his final intention. We know he wasn't happy with your mother."

"Should've never married Asha. Should never have," Zal Papa said. His chin wrinkled as the corners of his mouth were pulled down. He began to blubber. "My poor son. Poor, poor boy."

"Daddy, calm, please," Cyrus said with a hand on Zal Papa's shoulder. He turned to me. "The house still belongs to Zal Papa. And frankly, he doesn't want Asha having a claim on the property." He rubbed his father's arm. "Isn't that right, Daddy?"

Zal Papa nodded.

"But she can stay in the upstairs apartment," Cyrus said.

"You're not kicking her out?" I said.

"Of course not." Cyrus frowned. "Why would we behave like monsters?"

I held up my palms, looking at them both. "You can do whatever you want. Who's to judge?"

"Noomi!" Zal Papa stopped his weeping to glare at me. "I've had enough of that smart lip."

"You need to grow up, my dear," Cyrus said. "There's no one to indulge you anymore. Jeh's dead, and that's not my fault." He gave me a sideways look. "In fact, if anyone is to blame," he said pointedly, "I'd say it was you and your mother who harassed my brother to death."

I rose from my chair. "My father loved me more than any other person from his life. You can paint it otherwise, but it would be a lie. I don't have to listen to this bullshit."

"Where do you think you're going?" Zal Papa demanded. "Take these papers with you.."

"Destroy them," I said. "I don't care. I'm going out for a drive. To think."

"Fine," Zal Papa said. "But don't do anything stupid, understand? I won't hesitate to kick you out."

When I was little, Zal Papa would throw me in the air and catch me, saying, "Come on, pigeon, flap your wings!" He'd toss me higher, again and again. I'd flap my arms, laughing until I couldn't breathe. "One day," he said, kissing the top of my head, "one day you'll learn to fly, my bird. And then we'll never see you again."

Ignoring the looks of men whose only job, it seemed, was to hang about the blue-lit shopfront of Lakshmi Wines, I paid the cashier for a nip of vodka along with a soda, then hurried, holding the bags close to my chest, back to my car. I honked at the fool who'd double-parked his motorbike behind me. He came jogging up, staring as if I had horns growing out of my hair. I flipped him off and enjoyed how his eyes popped out of his head, before maneuvering around to join the crush of cars, buses, and rickshaws. The market at eight o'clock meant traffic was more convoluted than the plot of an art house film. Three bony cows decided to plonk down in the middle of the street, tucking their hooves under them. Rather than shooing off these sacred creatures, traffic flowed past like a river around a boulder. Begging children weren't granted the same kindness. They had to leap quickly out of the way once the lights changed, or risk losing a limb.

At the traffic signal, a man selling plastic sunglasses rapped on my window. He put on a bright pink pair, offering a sad but funny contrast with his old, lined face. I waved him off. The thought of going back home was becoming unbearable, the longer I waited for the lights to change. Instead of turning right, I drove up jewel-green Seminary Hills, past the deer park bordered by the tracks of the toy train. Heads close to the ground, the deer licked blocks of pink salt, ignoring the calls of children who thrust fistfuls of grass through the fence, hoping to tempt them close enough to pet.

At the corner of the deer park was a red mica road lined with teak trees that led to the Parsi Aramgarh. I drove on, listening to the dirt crunch under my tires, and stopped in the parking lot overlooking an overgrown gully. Why was I here? Jeh had been cremated; I didn't have a grave to visit. The soda fizzled as I poured half of it out on the red dirt. I topped the rest up with vodka. I lit a cigarette and, taking a drag, studied the showy sunset in front of me.

The caretaker, an ancient Parsi who wore white pajamas and a sadra, who could tell by your features what grave you were looking for ("Ah, that's the Wadia nose, they're buried in the south corner by the lantanas"), didn't seem to be around. Keeping the bottle close, I pushed open the clanky wrought-iron gate and began to wander among the gravestones. *Look at me,* I thought, *drunk in a graveyard.*

The cemetery, with its beautiful carved headstones, was of another era. Most of the graves dated back to the British Raj. There were a few children's ones, heartbreakingly small. I saw a simple marble chiseled with the same name as my grandmother: LILY AMBER, AUGUST–OCTOBER 1912, A SUNBEAM GONE TOO SOON. Stray dogs lay around like ghosts. I whistled to a white one with a pink nose. She trotted over, tail wagging, bum wiggling, and allowed me to pet her. The dog ran off to her friends.

You had to wait a year before installing a tombstone, as the ground needed time to settle. I saw a fresh grave with a wooden marker bearing the number 125. That was our house number. 125 Banyan Street. I could pretend this grave belonged to Jeh. I sat by its side.

I drank from my plastic soda bottle. The sky looked like blue carbon paper scattered with glitter. Clouds began to gather. It started to drizzle. I looked up. The rain fell into my eyes, blurring my vision. I got up from the ground, brushed off clumps of soil stuck to my jeans, and began picking my way back through the graves in the dark.

The half-finished vodka was waiting for me on the passenger seat. My friend. I started the car's engine and took sips from it while I found my way home in the rain. I've never liked the taste of alcohol. I associated its smell with my mother. What feels familiar is always comforting, in its own horrific way. The rain looked like it was being poured out of a bucket. In any other town I'd have had an accident, but thankfully this was Kamalpur, and at nine o'clock, the streets were empty. At the front gate, I killed the car's engine, letting it gently roll down the driveway in the hope that no one would find out. Zal Papa would be asleep. Lily Mama might be watching late-night TV. If I could get upstairs without being caught, I'd be fine.

The garage's harsh tube light hurt my eyes. I squinted at my reflection in the car window. Bruises appeared and disappeared, like weeds under the surface of a river. On the ceiling a lizard the color of chapati dough blinked twice. I tossed the vodka bottle into a garbage can.

Climbing up the stairs to my parents' flat took some effort, as if my legs had turned to lead. I reeked of smoke and vodka, of rain and sorrow. I looked forward to taking the small blue pills and falling into a dreamless sleep. The light in my bedroom was on. The door was ajar, making a yellow column in the dark hallway. I stepped inside to find Lily Mama on my bed. Standing over her, looking like a priest in a frilly nightie, was Binny.

"Where were you?" Lily Mama said. "We were worried that you'd had an accident."

"I had... I was..." I cowered at the door. I sighed. "I was at the Aramgarh."

"You smell terrible." Lily Mama scrunched up her face. "I can smell you from across the room."

"Noomi," Binny said, in a voice like a bad soap opera actor, "have you been... drinking?"

"Could we talk tomorrow?" I dumped my handbag on the floor and headed to the bathroom.

"*Now*," Lily Mama said, catching hold of me. "Be honest, have you been drinking?"

The bedroom door creaked opened. Sliding herself around was Asha. "What's going on?" She looked at Lily Mama, then at Binny, then at me. My eyes met hers. Asha seemed to know instantly.

"Asha," Lily Mama roared, pointing at the door. "I'll handle this, please." She was easy to rile up but hard to calm. Binny had been tending to Lily Mama's rage like a steam engine's boiler. Stoking it, throwing in more coal when needed. I hoped Asha would stay. If there were ever a time for my mother to be her stubborn self, this was it.

Asha left, closing the door behind her.

"You are a disgrace to my son's memory," Lily Mama said. "He loved you so much. He had such hopes for you. And you are hell-bent on turning into *her*." She pointed again at the door that Asha closed behind her. "He deserved better than you both."

"Leave me alone, please." I grabbed my head. "Leave me alone, or I swear..."

"I swear, I swear," Lily Mama mimicked. "What do you swear?" She looked like she had more to say, but she stared at the ground. Binny put a hand on her shoulder. Lily Mama looked up. "You should be in a hospital, where they can help you. It breaks my heart to do this,

Noomi. I think you might—not tonight, but soon—do irrevocable harm to yourself."

"What?"

"Noomi, dear," Binny said. "You've been behaving so bizarrely since you landed in Kamalpur. Do you know that Sheila called me last night, absolutely terrified? You were screaming so loud the neighbors came over." Binny began walking toward me, lamplight filtering through her nightie, her carroty legs silhouetted against it. "A few nights under a professional's care couldn't hurt."

"Don't touch me!" I said.

"Enough!" Binny said. "We've had enough of your constant havoc. Look at your poor grandmother. Have you ever seen her cry?" Her grip was strong. "You're going, whether you like it or not."

The bedroom door flew open. Binny, who'd put her hand on the knob, was knocked flat backward. Asha put her body in front of mine. "You're not taking her," she said, her voice low and fierce. "They don't treat us like human beings in those places. Binny, Lily Mama, you need to leave our house at once."

"Asha, I told you already—stay out of this," Lily Mama said, bustling across the room. "It's hard enough already." She took Binny's hand and pulled her up with a grunt.

Asha showed them her cell phone with the number already punched in. "I will call the police."

Something that felt like love—or perhaps it was just gratitude—for my mother alighted on my heart.

"You can't drag the police into a family matter," Binny said. Her plan was quietly backfiring. She'd banked on Asha being complicit, on her lack of any maternal instinct to protect me.

Asha held the door open. "You have a minute to leave this house," she said, her voice like stone.

"Come, Lily Mama," Binny said, taking my distraught grand-mother's arm. "They are beyond all help."

"Noomi," Lily Mama said, crying, "please, I'm begging you. Let me help before it's too late."

"This isn't over," Binny said. "I'm going to tell Veer all about what happened tonight, Noomi."

"Go ahead. Veer is *my* family," I spat. "Mine. He's not going to swallow any lies you tell him."

Asha and I watched Binny and Lily Mama leave.

"Thank you, Mama," I said. "For coming back."

Asha accepted a hug from me but didn't give one back. She trudged down the hall looking tired, so very tired, then turned and said, "Eat something. I'll tell Shanta Bai to warm up your dinner."

Rain sizzled outside my bedroom window. I shucked off my smelly clothes and crawled into bed. My cell phone lit up and started to buzz. I picked it up. A text from Veer.

WAT U UPTO POTATO? LUV YOU. FLIGHT AT 7AM. SEE U TOM.

I tossed the phone on the floor. Tomorrow. Tomorrow hovered over my life like a guillotine. Under the sheets, my bare legs felt cool, smooth. Wishing for some kind of peace, I slipped a hand past the waistband of my underwear. I tried to unravel the coil of my body. But alcohol works like an anaesthetic between your legs too. I gave up, disgusted. *You need to sleep,* said a voice. *A nice, deep sleep. A forever sleep will soothe the pain.* I groped around on my bedside table for the small blue pills that Asha had left behind.

In my dream, I was back at the cemetery parking lot. Jeh and I sat on the waist-high brick wall that separated the lot from a cliff that dropped into a forest gully. Dawn broke operatically, singing arias of pink clouds and golden-orange sunrays. Unafraid that my legs were dangling over what appeared to be an infinite fall, I put my head in the dip of Jeh's shoulder. The smell of him, Old Spice and sweat. It struck me anew how much it hurt to miss him. I took his hand and felt the familiar rough-dry skin of his palm. When Jeh spoke, his voice was exactly his.

"So," Jeh said, smiling his Mona Lisa smile. "Here we are."

"Yes, but where are we?" I said, tears streaming down my face.

"You should know." Jeh pointed to the sky and the gleaming forest below. "You built it."

"What about there?" I pointed toward a place covered by the shadow of a vast, dark cloud.

Jeh smiled. How much I missed that smile. "That," he said, "is an undiscovered country." He wiped the corners of my eyes. "Piglet. Your life wasn't meant to be easy. It'll get better, though. We're so much more than the sum of all the things we've done so far," Jeh said, stroking my hair.

"I want to go back home," I said. "I don't want to die. Please."

Jeh turned to me, his face glowing. "Give me your hand."

The bed I woke up in smelled unfamiliar, cotton sheets washed with industrial soap and left to dry in the sun. A rough woolen blanket was pulled up to my midriff. This wasn't my bed.

"Noomi." Veer's face swam into focus. He held my hand. Behind his head, I saw a room with plain white walls, with bars on the window. A framed poster on the door, of a kitten holding on to a branch, its hind paws dangling in the air, said HANG IN THERE!

"What happened?" I asked. My head hurt powerfully. I tried to bring my hand up to my face but couldn't—it was hooked to an IV slowly dripping liquid. Panic spread in my chest. I breathed fast; dark spots mushroomed in my vision. "Where the fuck am I?"

"It's okay," Veer said stroking my hand. "You'll be fine."

I saw my reflection in his glasses. My hair was a mess. My eyes were small and bloodshot. I looked like a sick, sad child. "Where am I?"

"A hospital room," Veer said, pressing his palm to my face. "Here, drink some water." He brought me a glass from the nightstand. The cold hurt like razor blades going down my throat.

"Why can't I swallow?" I said, sitting up, grabbing my throat with both hands. "It hurts so bad."

"Lucky for us, Shanta Bai came into your room last night," Veer said, putting the glass on the nightstand. "You were snoring in a strange way. When she tried to wake you, your head lolled on your chest. She immediately went and got your mom. Asha searched your bed and found the empty pack of sleeping pills. They shook you awake, made you drink *a lot* of salt water. Then Asha put a finger down your throat and forced you to throw up."

"Is she here? My mother?" I said. Dizziness pounded my head.

"Shh, shh, lie back down," Veer said. "She's staying at Rhea's. I'll call her for you."

Asha's voice sounded as if she were speaking from outer space. I could barely hear her. I said that I took too many pills by accident. She seemed eager to believe me. I said I'd talk to her later.

"That wasn't the truth," I said, handing the phone back to Veer. "I didn't take those pills by accident."

A person trapped in a burning building might jump out the window, preferring a quick end rather than being eaten slowly by the flames. I'd taken the first pill. I dared myself to take another, another, another, until I couldn't lift my hand to my mouth. Then there was nothing except the noise of the rain, like television static.

"Why, Noomi?" Veer lifted his glasses and pinched the bridge of his nose.

The door opened with a sharp knock. A nurse in a white sari and white canvas sneakers walked in to check on my IV. "Mrs. Malhotra isn't allowed more than one visitor at a time," she said. "Doctor's orders." Mrs. Wadia was waiting outside. Could Mr. Malhotra let her have a turn?

"No problem." Veer flashed his corporate-guy smile. "I'll see you soon, potato," he said to me.

"Veer... Binny," I said, grabbing his wrist. "Has she... has she been talking to you?"

"We'll talk about it when you're feeling better," Veer said.

"Please." I pulled him closer. "Tell me what she said."

"Please stay calm," the nurse said, fixing a new bag on my IV. "Or I'll add a sedative to this."

"That won't be necessary," Veer snapped at her. "Stick to your actual job."

The nurse spoiled her neat, pretty features by making a sour face. She finished her task and left.

"Be careful," I said to Veer with a smile. "She might put an air bubble in my drip."

"Don't waste your time worrying about Binny," Veer said. "She tried to fill my head with some nonsense. I told her to fuck off."

"Thank you," I said. "Thank you, Veer. I really mean it. I love you."

I left the hospital three days later. Veer flew back to Bombay with a promise that he'd return for me. Lily Mama tipped the hospital staff a ridiculous amount. That was her love language.

I called Jung. She was sorry I'd felt I had to take those pills and glad that Veer had shut Binny's discord machine down. The next thing I did was to spend one day emptying out Jeh's closet and giving his clothes away. All except for the shirt laid out on the chair. That I saved. Asha came home from Rhea's place and, predictably, flipped out.

"How could you?" she said. "You should've at least asked if I wanted to keep anything!"

I gave her Jeh's shirt, folded, ironed, and wrapped in brown paper. "Here, this is for you."

Asha looked like a dog running after a car that had stopped—she didn't know what to do next.

"Thanks," she said, holding the packet. "Although I wish you hadn't laundered out his smell."

"There's something else I want to give you," I said, handing Asha a file.

"What's this?"

"This was Dad's will. Read it. You might realize something," I said, holding the papers out.

"What?"

"That, in spite of everything, he did love you."

Asha put the shirt under her arm and took the file; her hand dipped slightly from its weight.

"How are you feeling?" she said, looking at me. "I was so scared I was going to lose you too."

"I'll be okay." I nodded.

As promised, Veer flew back to pick me up. We were set to return on Sunday.

The hours before we left, I spent walking around the garden. I stopped by the old wall against which my small hut used to lean. The stone was cool, rough, like Jeh's hands when he held mine. I rested my head on it, stabbed with pity for the little girl who used to hide alone in this place.

They'd put Milo's grave under the pink champa tree. Jeh had swiped the sapling for Lily Mama from a traffic island on M.G. Road. A petty crime; pink champas were rare. I plucked a few flowers and placed them on Milo's grave. I put my hand in the dirt, to feel the earth thrum as it did the quiet work to take back his body.

The car honked in the driveway. They were done loading our suitcases. I stood up, put the rest of the flowers in my bag, and gave the garden a last, long look.

Lily Mama kissed me goodbye. I felt her lips on my cheek and printed that kiss on my heart. Zal Papa asked me when I would come back—*with Veer*—to visit. I lied: "Very soon."

On our way to the airport, I asked if we could stop at the cemetery. I took out the pink champa flowers, crushed and bruised from my bag, and scattered them on grave number 125. I should've brought mogras; those had been Jeh's favorite. I saw a terra-cotta bowl, the kind Lily Mama used for birdbaths. It was filled with mogras, small star-shaped flowers with a big, beautiful scent.

"I'm sorry," I said to the stranger's grave. I turned and walked away, thinking about what Lily Mama had said to me in the hospital. After Veer had left, the door was propped open by a ward boy. Lily Mama had shuffled in. She sat in the chair pulled up to my bedside.

"Did you know that Jeh was born in this same hospital," Lily Mama had said. "Sometimes"—she looked around the room and blinked up at the ceiling—"I wish he was born all over again. So I'd get a chance to do things differently." She unclasped her purse and pulled out a black-and-white picture: Jeh wrapped in a swaddle like a baby elf. "He was early, and so little." She parted her forefinger and thumb. "Zal walked around the hallways with him, saying to nurses or doctors who passed by, 'Meet my new pocket edition son.'"

"Daddy was always his favorite." I smiled. "Was he a good child?"

Lily Mama treated me to her Mona Lisa smile. "Mostly." She laughed. "But he could be very bad. One time, he jumped up onto my sister's dining table and swung on her crystal chandelier with his belt, shouting, 'Me Tarzan!' The bloody thing came crashing—the crystals rolled across the dining room and down a flight of stairs. It sounded like chattering teeth." Lily Mama covered her smile with her hand. "Jeh hid like a cat. I looked in the kitchen, the bathrooms, all four bedrooms. 'I won't get angry,' I said to convince him to come out. And he did, after many hours. He was tiny, you see. He'd hidden under a bed, squeezed between suitcases."

"Did you keep your word?" I asked. "Or did you punish him?"

"Oh yes," Lily Mama said, chuckling. "I thrashed him with his own belt."

"Why couldn't you have lied," I said, feeling sad, "and not told me that?"

Lily Mama winced. It looked, oddly, like the beginnings of a smile. "There are times," she said, her voice breaking softly, "we do terrible things, believing we're acting out of love."

The door opened. The nurse poked her head in. She had a broad middle part; a streak of red sindoor ran through it. "Madam, your driver is here," she said. "Visiting hours are over."

Lily Mama put her hand on mine. Large tears ran down her smooth face. "You will never hurt yourself again. Promise me."

"I'm sorry," I said.

"When they took you to the hospital," Lily Mama said, "your eyes were rolling back in your head. It was frightening. I couldn't sleep. I looked up and shouted, 'Jeh! Noomi needs you!' Thank god your grandfather is half deaf, otherwise he'd have woken up and given himself a heart attack."

"He did come," I said, grabbing her hand as she was about to leave. "We had a talk."

"He was always a good son."

Lily Mama smiled. On her way out the door, she stopped to neaten a pile of my clothes on a chair. A lamp illuminated half her face, while the other half remained in shadows.

PART
FOUR

The doctors' hands moved like shadow puppets behind the pale blue surgical sheet. They cut a smile into my belly. They'd given me an epidural; all I felt of the incision was a tugging below my navel. A strange pulse started beating inside my head. It died out as soon as the baby appeared, mewling like a kitten. I felt them drag her from my half-useless, half-frozen body. I tried to get a glimpse of her on the other side of the cloth partition.

The doctors sewed me together, chatting like they'd run into each other at a buffet. A nurse said, "You're doing great, Mama," into my ear. She took my shrieking baby to wipe away the gray-white goop that covered her like model clay. Veer had been holding my hand; he dropped it and followed. I heard the snick of a phone camera. Veer returned with a picture of a scrunched-up pink face. Our baby looked displeased, groggy, as if we'd suddenly switched on all the lights in her bedroom.

"Six pounds eight ounces," Veer said with a smile.

"What sweet little rosebud lips," I said. "Can I hold her now?"

The nurse brought the baby over in her fuzzy arms, wrapped up warm and dry. My daughter, unamused at being born, was pinch-faced in her blue-and-white blanket, wearing a little hat. The nurse undid the swaddling and put her on my chest. This baby weighed as much as a small ham. I took one tiny hand. I smiled as her jelly fingers curled around mine.

"Thank you for being perfect," I whispered into her shell-shaped ear. "Your name is Maya."

"Noomi, come on, smile for the family," Veer said. He lifted his phone high above our heads for a picture. My face was like a puffy mushroom, my arms full of tubes, holding our daughter. "I said smile! Argh, never mind." He flipped the camera, got in with us, made a victory sign, and took a number of rapid selfies. I managed to smile in at least a few.

Three years had passed since my father died. Veer had made partner at his consulting firm. We moved into a bigger flat in Bandra. I was four months pregnant. If getting away from Kamalpur was possible, then so, perhaps, was another life. One where I could be a good person, even a good mother. I'd held the pregnancy test in both my hands, waiting on our small balcony for Veer to come home from work. He arrived at the usual time, his shirt, crisp when he left in the morning, now wilted from the heat. He held two shopping bags full of new clothes.

"There was a sale on men's formal wear," he said with a shrug at the door. "Partners wear suits."

I turned toward him. I held out the plastic stick with two lines. "I'm pregnant."

"What?" Veer dropped his bags and strode up onto the balcony. He leaned one hand on the metal railing and covered his mouth with the other. "Are you sure?" he said, frowning at me.

"The lines don't lie," I said, slipping the test into his shirt pocket.

"Ew, what the fuck, Noomi?" Veer took it out and held it between his fingertips. "It's got pee on it."

"I know," I said. "I'm the one whose pee it is."

I looked down to the driveway. Boys played cricket. Crows cawed in the trees. The sea, always close, breathed in and out like a sleeping giant.

"So, what do you want to do?" Veer asked, frowning. "Shall I make an appointment with Dr. Mistry?"

One of the boys swung his bat and hit the red cricket ball so hard it flew up into our apartment. Veer caught it. He leaned over the railing.

"Arrey, watch what you're doing!" he yelled. "You could've broken our windows."

"Sorry, sorry, sorry," the boys cried together. "Please, bhaiya, we'll be careful. Give it back, na."

Veer threw the ball at them. He looked at me, his face stamped with a question mark. "So?"

"I want it," I said, staring at the sea. "I feel"—I looked at Veer— "it'll be different this time."

Letting out a groan, Veer folded his arms. "Are you sure?" he said, and nodded at the kids. "They're a lot of work." He squeezed my shoulder. "You're not scared?"

"Terrified," I said, smiling. "But I need..." I hugged my stomach with both hands, searching for the right words. "I have all this, I don't know what to call it." I held up an imaginary bundle. "I guess you could call it love. It's like"—I paused—"like having lots of money but nothing to spend it on." I rested my head on the wall.

Veer was skeptical, but after everything that'd happened, he couldn't say no.

When you're pregnant, people love telling you terrifying stories about being pregnant. Lily Mama called every Sunday to recount the latest birth horror she'd heard about over the week. "You know Silloo Patel, my friend who lives in Civil Lines? Her eldest daughter had to be induced. Then the umbilical cord got wound around the baby's neck, so she had an emergency C-section. Something went wrong, and now the poor girl can't pee or poop."

"Lily Mama," I said, "that's awful, but why do you keep telling me these things?"

"Just so you're prepared, love," Lily Mama said. A pause. "Remember what happened with your mother?"

"I do," I said. "But please stop. You're not helping."

I called Asha with news of Veer's promotion.

"Oh, so lucky," she exclaimed. "Moving to a fancy new flat with your husband, having a baby. I wish I'd had a chance to leave. Maybe my life would've been different then." She paused to let out a sigh. "Instead, I'm stuck here in Kamalpur, getting sicker and sicker every day."

"Mom," I said, sitting down gingerly on the sofa, "the doctor said the new arthritis medicines would help with the pain, but only if you don't drink." I picked up a mug of tea from the table.

"Don't lecture me, Noomi," she snapped. "You've been sober for what, six months? You don't get to be all holier than thou."

"Ma'amji, we are done packing up the bedroom." The young man sent by the moving company came into the living room, wiping the back of his neck with a handkerchief.

"Thank you," I said, and gave him a tip. I wondered if he could make out that I was pregnant. I felt like a smuggler sometimes. I thought of the fetus as a bag of contraband under my clothes.

"You need to sign this," the man said, holding out a paper stuck to a board.

"Mom," I said into the phone, "I've got to go."

"When are you moving?" Asha said.

"Tomorrow."

"Call me from the new place."

"Okay," I said, getting up to look for a pen.

"I miss you."

"That's nice."

"Aren't you going to say you'll miss me?"

"I'll miss you," I said robotically. "Now I've got to go."

"Call me."

"I'll call when it's convenient, Mom," I said. I found a ballpoint pen in the kitchen drawer and signed the paper, holding the phone under my chin. "Thank you," I said to the man.

"What'd you say?" Asha's voice had that edge I remembered from my childhood, the one it took on before she gave me a slap. "Speak up, I can't hear you. Will you call me or not?"

"Yes, okay." I sighed. "Now please, let me go."

"Tch, tch, tch, so lucky," Asha said. "Such a lucky girl." I imagined her slowly shaking her head.

"Bye, Mom," I said, and cut the call.

It was my thirty-first birthday, so Dimple, Aunt Kitty's daughter, invited us for dinner at the Royal Bombay Yacht Club. We were staying in the club's guest rooms for a week while our landlord finished painting our living room. I didn't want to take a chance with fumes during the monsoon.

"Pali Hill, really, Bandra. When there's all of South Bombay to choose from." Dimple took a sip of her drink, leaving red lipstick on the brined rim.

"You'll have to show us around this place, Dimple." Veer gave her a toothy smile. "I've passed it on the way to work a million times, but I've never been inside before. Thanks so much for organizing a guest room on such short notice."

"Yes, thank you," I said.

"Oh, you're welcome." Dimple, whose buff skin was the color of a besan laddu, tousled her blond-streaked hair, wrinkled her nose, and said, "I mean, it's not the Taj."

"It's not," I said, looking about. Portraits of viceroys loomed large and bright in the club's hallways, tut-tutting at the natives, clearing their oil-on-canvas throats. A world-famous artist was once told to tuck his shirt into his trousers before he could enter the dining room. He still donated a lithograph to the club auction. "The Taj wouldn't stop a pregnant woman and ask her to change out of flip-flops into heels."

"Huh." Dimple pouted. "Maybe you should practice being grateful."

"Don't mind her. All hormones." Veer slid his eyes over at his cousin with a grin.

"I can imagine," Dimple sniffed. "Being so puffy mustn't be good for one's mental state."

"At least I have a mind—not just cotton balls between..."

Veer, desperate to change the conversation, cleared his throat and offered to drive Dimple back in his new company car.

"Okay," Dimple said. "But I don't have much faith in your driving skills."

"If you learn to drive in Delhi, you can drive anywhere," Veer said.

I spent the remainder of my last baby-free birthday alone, watching television and picking at leftovers from a Styrofoam box. The only cure for this sort of abandonment was vodka. But now, look at me, pure as Mother Teresa. I wish I had some kind of epiphany to share, that I'd found a guru or a new life philosophy to help me stay off booze. The fact was that I had terrible, horrible morning sickness; the sight of alcohol literally made my stomach turn. It was like having a hangover *all the time*. I learned that sobriety stemmed from being okay with feeling not okay. And also—it was incredibly boring.

I got under the fluffy, clean-smelling comforter embroidered with the club's golden monogram and turned on my laptop. These days, I'd become addicted to the dopamine reward of social media, and googling anything that popped into my head.

A notification bloomed in one corner of my screen. *Sid Sehgal posted new photos.* I clicked on it. There was Sid, traipsing all over fucking Europe with Anushka. And... Ammu and Shivraj? Since when did those four holiday together? Jealousy grew out of my heart like an orchid. I studied their laughing faces, their white teeth. In her photos, Anushka did a duck face, threw up a peace sign, or stuck out her tongue. Her body, slim and sinuous as ever, showed zero evidence of having given birth. Standing under a pretty streetlamp, Ammu laughed with Shiv's arms wrapped around her waist. I saw my mother's bracelet glowing on her wrist.

My phone buzzed with a text. It was Veer.

WATS UP? ALMOST HOME. LOVE YOU.

I typed, *Don't look at your phone while driving, stupid,* and smiled at the next text: a blurry view of the Sea Link, its spindles wreathed with moonlit clouds. I posted it.

Lying in bed at the hospital, pressure cuffs gently massaged my calves, a prophylaxis against blood clots. I had to sleep sitting up so as not to bust open my tender stitches. I dreamed my milk came in, but instead of milk, it was wine. I put my baby to my breast only to find that she was an old woman with a fluffy skull. She suckled toothlessly. Her hands clawed the sides of my breast.

At dawn, I woke up to the squeak of trolley wheels as the nurse brought Maya, in a clear plastic crib, to my bedside. I sat up straighter, wincing with pain, and stretched out my arms, attached to an IV of Motrin. I'd refused the harder drugs on offer, afraid I'd never wean myself off. "Plus, it makes you poop concrete," the nurses said. "The caesarean moms are all very constipated."

"Good to know," I said.

The nurse handed Maya over and showed me how to insert my nipple into her mouth. Maya began to cry, her mouth pink and cavernous like the belly of a whale. After a couple of tries, she latched on. I sighed with relief, but a blood pressure machine on my right showed the numbers going up. A mother for less than forty-eight hours, I already knew I was going to be bad at it. Maya got tired of sucking and fell asleep. My milk hadn't come in yet. The nurse said that the teaspoonful of colostrum I'd made was plenty.

"The more she stimulates your ducts, the faster your milk will show up."

In my head, I'd named the nurse Dianne, after Dianne Wiest. She had that same smizey face.

"When she's asleep, you should use a breast pump so that your supply won't dwindle. It'll hurt at first. Your nipples will crack and bleed a bit. Tell your husband to buy you lanolin ointment."

The nurse wrote "lanolin" in neat Goan Catholic cursive on a note-pad, tore out the page, and gestured toward Veer, snoring like a chain saw on the narrow blue sofa next to my bed.

I threw a pillow at him.

He snorted awake and looked at me. "What?" he said, blinking slowly.

The milk, when it came in, came in like a firehose. Maya would choke and scream like I was trying to murder her. I had to nurse her lying on my back to slow down the flow, holding Maya on my stomach, her mouth plugged to my nipple. We looked like a pair of sea otters. I'd read that otters link their arms while sleeping so that the sea doesn't sweep them apart. Maya drank two ounces at a time. She fell asleep with my nipple still in her mouth. I'd lay her in the crib and pump the milk still aching in my breasts. I dated the bags and stored them next to the ice cream and frozen meat. Wasn't it sort of gross to keep breast milk in the same place as the food? Veer asked. I told him to cook to free up the freezer space. He said he was too busy with work.

"We live in Bandra, potato," he said. "Order whatever it is you're craving."

The thing I craved was Shanta Bai's mutton dhansak. I decided to call my mother. I had to check on Asha anyway; the doctors had put her on steroids for her arthritis. They made her face round, like a full moon. Sometimes we video called, but only if I'd washed my hair and put on makeup, or else I'd spend the whole call listening to how exhausted I looked. Am I doing okay? Should she come visit? I didn't want my mother to visit. I called her at night to make sure that she wasn't drinking. To my relief, she sounded sober. I asked her to put Shanta Bai on.

"Nooma," Shanta Bai said, shouting into the phone. "How are you, my sweet darling girl?"

"I'm fine," I replied, smiling. "You don't have to shout, Shanta Bai. This isn't a trunk call."

"How is Maya baby," she said. "Is she a good, happy child? Or a bad, angry one like you?"

"She is..." I paused, wondering what to say. "She's her own person, I think."

"Make sure you tie a black thread around her ankle to ward off the evil eye."

"Shanta Bai"—I reached for a notepad on the table—"tell me how to make your dhansak."

After I'd written down Shanta Bai's recipe, we chatted. I tried to describe my new life as best as I could. Then Asha took back the phone.

"How is Maya?" she asked. "Is she putting on weight? I hope you're making enough milk."

"Too much milk," I said. "She's doing fine. And I'm fine too, thanks for asking."

"Of course you're fine," Asha snorted. "You're a cockroach. Indestructible."

"Yes, I'm a cockroach," I said. "Cockroach milk is one of the most nutritious substances on earth. It's better than cow's milk."

"Oh, yuck," Asha said.

I imagined her making the face she made when Jeh farted.

"I realized something," I said. "I don't know if you ever breastfed me."

"Sorry?"

"As a baby. Was I breast or formula fed?"

"Formula?" Asha went shrill. "God, no! Only breast milk was good enough for you, Your Highness. You'd scream if I brought a bottle anywhere near you. Exclusively breastfed."

"Did you enjoy it?"

"Enjoy what?"

"Breastfeeding," I said. "Did you enjoy all the oxytocin release and whatnot?"

"No." A pause. "No, I didn't. I wanted to wean you quickly and get back to the kids at the orphanage. They *really* needed me. You had your father. But"—Asha sighed—"you were stubborn, even as a baby. You weaned yourself off when you were ready."

"I've always had my own back," I said, irritated. I looked at the picture on my nightstand: my mother holding me in our garden; my small hand outstretched toward a fat red rose. She is smoking a cigarette, one smooth brown arm supporting my diapered bottom. By the drowsy look in her eyes, I can tell that either it is very hot or Asha would rather be anywhere than with me.

"You're lucky," Asha said. "Maya seems like a sweet, easygoing baby."

"Unlike me, you mean," I said.

"Your words, not mine." She chuckled.

"How are you so sure what she's like?" I said. "You haven't even met her."

"And whose fault is that?"

"Mom, we've been through this," I said. "The apartment isn't ready yet. I don't even have a guest bed." I heard a cry. "Okay, I have to go. Maya woke up. She needs to be fed."

"Next time, at least make it a video call so I can see my sweet baby."

"Okay, bye."

"Noomi?"

"Yes?"

"Say 'I love you, Mom.'"

I cut the call. Maya was making small pre-cry snuffles. Her movements seemed strange and animatronic, like ET's. I smiled. "Hi, Mayoo Jaan." She closed her eyes, frowning like I was an idiot. I picked her up and put her face to my nipple. It still felt bizarre to feed a person I made with my body with food made *from* my body. It felt animalistic. Outside, I had to hide my nursing baby under a hot, itchy blanket. My mother had turned me watchful as a child. Drooping corners of the mouth meant Maya would bring down the house if I couldn't figure out what she needed fast. Eye contact with grunts— poop incoming. Hands flung above the head—contentment. A mouth in an O—wonder? Or gas? A red face and tight fists—anger.

With Maya steadily nursing, I relaxed into my chair. Before Maya was born, my nipples were my number one erogenous zone. Veer knew this. My ballooned, postpartum breasts excited him. The doctors said we should wait twelve weeks or so for my body to heal from the surgery. Veer said, "Why not try some heavy petting? It might make you feel like a teenager again." He seemed unaware that giving birth had turned the valve of my libido to the off position, maybe permanently. I said we should really wait. He sulked and moped. Life was unbearable enough already. I relented.

Veer asked Dimple to take Maya to a mommy-and-me class—that would be enough time, according to him, to get me "in the mood."

"Nothing below the waist," I warned, as Veer crawled toward me on the bed, his erect penis pendulating between his thighs. Ribbons of afternoon light streamed in from the windows. A beam slanted across Veer's face, turning his eyes a honey brown. His abs looked like a candy bar. Veer worked out at the gym five times a week, while my belly sagged like a defeated boxer on the ropes. My breasts were of porn-worthy proportions with none of plastic surgery's gravity-defying perkiness. I lay on my back, hoping it would make my boobs stand up like yurts.

From the state of his penis, it appeared Veer didn't mind my flabby belly. For a brief moment, I was grateful he still desired me. Then gratitude gave way to resentment. Why did he get to keep his abs? I was so annoyed at that thought, I didn't notice Veer taking my left nipple between his lips. He jerked his head away and spat breast milk onto our sheets, staining them a translucent yellow. Thinking it was mealtime, my breasts had begun spontaneously erupting.

"Why are your boobs doing that?" Veer cried out.

"Sorry," I said, getting off the bed. Drops of milk spattered across the floor as I walked to the dining table. I sat down on a silk cushion that felt cold and slippery under my naked bottom, took out my pump, and began filling up bag after bag. My breasts became empty and floppy. Veer draped a light shawl over my goosefleshed shoulders, throwing me a sorry look as he gathered up the bags. He opened the freezer door, a sigh escaping him like air from a tire. Milk bags were stuffed in all the corners, wedged in the crevices between our frozen leftovers.

"Should you see a doctor?" Veer looked at me. "Is this normal?"

"Of course it's normal," I said. "What would I tell them? Help, I'm making too much milk?" I gave him a look. "You know how doctors talk to women who complain about nothing."

"What the hell should I do with all of this milk?" Veer asked, slamming the fridge door.

"I don't fucking know," I said. I covered my breasts with the silk cushion and ran to the bathroom. I needed to shower away my embarrassment. "Make ice cream!"

"Perhaps we should ask family to come help," Veer said a few minutes later from the other side of the bathroom door.

I'd finished shampooing my hair and had turned the water hot, letting it pummel my unhappy shoulders. "Who?" I shouted back, lathering under my armpits. "Who do we call? I cannot deal with your parents right now, Veer."

"Why?" Veer sounded exasperated. "My mom loves babies. She would be amazing."

"Oh please," I yelled, scrubbing hard. "What about the gift they sent?"

"What gift?" Veer asked.

I turned off the shower for a moment. "They sent Maya a doll, Veer. A baby doll."

"So?"

"Isn't it obvious?" I leaned my head against the tiles. "She's literally just been born, and they want to start grooming her for motherhood." I wiggled a finger in my ear. "Sexist!" I turned the water back on.

A week ago, my mother-in-law had called at 5:00 A.M., a reminder to fast for Veer's long life that day. I'd put Maya down after her first feed of the morning. I was exhausted. Rita wanted to "wish me a good fast" and make sure I'd prepared the thali and the sargi meal. I shook Veer awake and handed him the phone, telling him to let his mother know I'd rather throw myself into the Arabian Sea.

"You're acting crazy," Veer said.

"Whatever," I said. "Your parents are not coming." I turned the water back on. "And that's that."

"Okay. How about your mom?" Veer said, tapping what sounded like his wedding ring on the door. "She's been dying to come see Maya. She keeps emailing me, asking for pictures."

"No!" I shouted, turning off the water. My voice echoed off the bathroom tiles. "No. I can't deal with her." I wrapped a towel over my head, wrinkling my nose at the smell of my hair. I'd washed it with an Ayurvedic potion the color and smell of tar that my friend claimed stopped postpartum hair loss. "She can't see me like this."

"Can't see you like what?" Veer said.

"Like..." I said, rubbing my body so hard it turned pink. "Like I don't know what I'm doing. She'll use my struggles with Maya to make me feel like shit. That's how she usually feels good about herself."

"You're being stubborn," Veer said. "Stubborn and selfish."

I came out of the shower tired. Veer was off to the gym. Picking up his keys from the dressing table, Veer said he'd bring Maya into the bedroom. From the pitch of Maya's wailing, I could tell she was hungry. I threw on a dressing gown, took Maya from Veer with a curt nod, and carried her back to bed. Wearily, I felt the milk filling up in response to her howls. Maya gobbled up my nipple, thwacking at my breast with her fists. When that no longer entertained her, she grabbed the end of my towel turban and pulled down. My damp, tar-smelling hair tumbled over us both like a black curtain, ragged as waves.

Veer decided to "surprise" me by buying Asha a ticket. After screaming at him for an hour, I had a headache. When I saw Asha walking out of the airport terminal—rumpled clothes, sallow face, flyaway hair in a Miss Trunchbull topknot—my heart dropped into my shoes. She looked ill. We hugged. I studied my mother's face. I knew it better than my own. A mother is the first mirror in which we see ourselves. If that mirror was broken, you'd see yourself in pieces too, no use to anyone, and take that as the truth.

When she saw Maya snuggled in the baby carrier, Asha's scowl melted into a smile. She lifted Maya out and took a deep whiff of the top of her head. It took me by ambush, how much Asha would dote on Maya. She was an Enid Blyton grandma after all, reading to her, playing with her, feeding her, changing her diaper. On sunny days, she'd carry Maya up to the picture window in our living room, which held a jigsaw-piece view of the Bombay skyline. She whispered stories into her tiny ears. Two weeks with us, and Asha's face became clear and oval. Her dark circles vanished.

A few days before she was supposed to head back home, Asha lost her wallet. She insisted that I drop whatever I was doing to help her look. As the hours passed and we couldn't find it, Asha started to wind herself up. She had this weird tic, a sharp intake of breath like a hiss. The more anxious Asha got, the more it sounded as if there were a snake loose in the apartment.

"Will you calm down?" I said. "Your wallet doesn't have legs, you know, it hasn't walked out the front door." I went to the guest room and threw off the duvet. "It's got to be in your room somewhere."

"I am calm, okay, Noomi?" Asha said, riffling through her handbag. "Where the fuck did I last see it?" She pulled out a ballpoint pen, absentmindedly put it in her mouth, and began to chew on the end. I knew she was dying for a smoke. And a drink, most probably. I was too. "Keep looking."

I got on my hands and knees to look under the bed, irritated that I had to spend Maya's precious naptime hour looking for Asha's stupid wallet, instead of taking a nap myself. My mother was a selfish, joyless, frustrating... Oh, wait, there it was, stuck between the bed slats.

"Found it," I said, standing up. I wiped the dusty wallet with my T-shirt. Something slipped out of it: a photo. A man around my age. He was on a beach. His skin was a dark brown. His teeth were white, a first world white. Next to him stood a tall blond woman, holding a little girl with skin and hair the color of clover honey. They were smiling.

"Do you know who that is?" Asha asked, pointing at the photo.

"No," I said. "Who is it?"

"That's Raju, the baby you picked up from our doorstep." My mother smiled. "A family in Amsterdam adopted him. That's his wife, Annelise, and their daughter, Swati."

"They're beautiful." I smiled and gave back the photograph. "Happy."

"No one cared about my orphanage kids. Not your father, or your grandparents, or you. The work I did, it mattered, Noomi," Asha said with a note of longing in her voice. "You were always clinging to me. I was never enough for you."

"I was never enough *for you*." I threw the wallet at her.

"Those kids would've done anything for a mother like me," Asha said. "But you? All you ever did was act like an ungrateful, selfish girl." She picked up the wallet from the floor. "You traumatized me."

I called Jung. I felt dangerously close to drinking.

"Noomi," she said, "you don't have to be triggered by every single thing your mother says."

"But how?" I said. "Asha's always out to prove that I'm a terrible person. I don't love her, I'm rude, I suffocated her career, her life. Now she says I punish her by trying to keep Maya away."

"Noomi," Jung said, her tone softening, "you're not a bad person because your mother says so. I want you to understand that. Remind yourself that you are good. Be gentle with you."

"She has never, you know," I said, scrubbing tears, "never *once* acknowledged the harm she did. To me. To Dad. But what was done to her comes up in every conversation. Every chance she gets." I paused to stifle another sob. "I've been feeling so lonely since she arrived. I brought Maya into the world so I wouldn't feel alone, but having Asha around cancels it all out."

"Noomi, you have to realise that Asha's mind is shattered," Jung said. "Whatever it reflects will always be distorted. She's a fun house mirror."

If Veer was late or traveling for work, Asha and I would eat dinner in front of the television, in part because we both enjoyed TV, its mindless energy, and in part to avoid having to talk. On the news, lately, there'd been chatter about a cyclone—but not any old cyclone, a once-in-a-hundred-years storm. "Cyclone" sounded like "cyclops," a one-eyed monster of climate change. Viewed from a satellite, the storm looked like a flying pinwheel made of clouds and rain. Or like whipped cream swirling in a huge blue porcelain bowl. We had to postpone my mother's flight home.

Asha and I watched the news while Maya napped in a bassinet next to us, arms flung above her head. The home minister, my father-in-law's boss, updated the reporters gathered around him in a scrum. He pursed his thin lips when they asked about the scale of the disaster, as if the cyclone were an ill-behaved houseguest.

"I like this fellow." Asha smiled, pressing the volume-up button on the remote. "He reminds me of your father. Reliable. Relatable. Means what he says."

I looked at her sideways. Asha never had a good thing to say about Jeh when he was alive. In death, she gushed about him like a schoolgirl. "Dad was useless in an emergency. Remember that time I broke my wrist? He drove us to the wrong hospital. You got out of the car and yelled at him on the street."

Asha gave me a look as angry as a bird's eye chili. She pointed a finger. "Why would you talk about him like that?"

"What the hell, Mom?" I said. "You spent every minute Dad was alive criticizing him. You did your very best to make him miserable. Now that he's no longer around"—I took the remote from her to switch channels—"you've turned him into some kind of a saint." I looked at her.

"You're cruel, Noomi, do you know that?" Asha snatched the remote back.

I was angry but stayed quiet so as not to wake Maya. The news channels couldn't get enough of this "Frankenstorm." TV anchors brought on a kickline of experts with charts, graphs, spaghetti models. Two days from now, they predicted that the cyclone, the first ever severe tropical system of its kind, would turn sharp right and slam the western coastline. In the bassinet, Maya wriggled, threw out her hands, scrunched her face, and revved up to bawl. I scooped her up, making the whooshing noise that baby books said mimicked the womb.

"You'll spoil her with all this picking up." Asha turned the TV volume higher.

"Ugh, my breasts are leaking again," I said, trying to fix my nipple into Maya's tiny lips. "I need to lie flat with her." I plunked down on the sofa and nudged Asha with my hip. "Ma, move to that chair."

"Go to the bedroom," Asha said, flipping to another news channel. "I want to watch TV."

"I'm trying to get Maya to settle down and feed." I snatched the remote from her hand.

"I'm not your peon," Asha snapped. "You can't order me around. Go here, go there."

She stomped off into the kitchen. Pressing Maya to my chest, I muted the TV and willed myself to lie still without getting into a fresh fight. I coaxed Maya to latch on. Breastfeeding turned out to be the worst part. When we found out I was pregnant again, it had made me feel powerful. Maya's cries made me feel the opposite. They brought forth bouts of rage, rushing out like blood clots from a broken nose. Where was Veer when I needed him? On a work trip somewhere in Bumberfuck, North India. He'd wheeled his bags out and then come back through to kiss me. "I'll be home before the show!"

There was a sound of glass breaking. With a hand under Maya's head, I rushed to the kitchen.

"What happened?" I asked. The ceiling lights made moons glow on the black-tile floor. Across the moons was a comet's tail of broken glass: a bottle of expensive lemonade that I'd bought for myself as a treat.

Asha lowered herself to the floor. The inflamed joints of her knees made her wince with pain. She stumbled, toppled over, and was stabbed in the leg by a shard. Blood leaked out of the tear in her cotton pants. I put Maya back in the bassinet. She resumed her wailing. I fetched a dustpan from the closet and began sweeping up the glass.

"Leave it be, Ma," I said. "There are bandages and ointment in the bathroom. Go clean up that cut."

"Can't you get her to stop screaming? It makes me anxious," Asha said, holding her knee.

Whenever we'd speak on the phone, Asha talked only about how she couldn't wait to see Maya, how I was a terrible person to keep her only grandchild from her. I stared at her.

"Don't make that face," Asha said.

"What face?" I said.

"The contempt," Asha said. "You've looked at me that way ever since you opened your eyes."

As a child, I used to get fevers so high that I felt like a teakettle on a stove. My mother and Shanta Bai would stay up, swabbing my shivering little body with damp towels, listening to and ignoring my tortured screams. By the morning, the fever had broken. Sitting up in bed, I pressed a palm to my forehead, which was specked with beads of sweat. Sunshine slid through gaps in the curtains, casting pale slats on my white sheets. Outside the bedroom window, loutish city crows cawed as they weaved through the white bougainvillea. Their racket cast me from my bed and out of my bedroom.

The door of my parents' room had a pneumatic closer, and it shut behind me with a moody hiss. A pashmina of cold air fell on my shoulders. It took a few seconds for my eyes to adjust to the room's hazy darkness. Thick blinds didn't let in a crumb of light. I slipped over to the bed and slid under the blankets between my parents' sleep-musky bodies. I put an arm over my father, pressing my nose against his back. His muslin kurta slipped about under my palm. He stirred, grunted affably. I flung one leg over his side, nudging his flabby belly with my heel.

The AC turned on with a shudder and I sneezed. My right ear began to throb with a dull, regular pulse. My parents had my ears looked at by a number of specialists, who'd scolded them both for smoking. It wasn't healthy for a child to get such frequent ear infections, which could harm my hearing. And yet, overfull ashtrays still decorated rooms like potted plants. On my mother's bedside was a blue Murano one filled with cigarette butts. Smoke clung to the walls, curtains, sheets, and my mother's hair, which looked like black smoke shot across her white pillowcase.

The sneeze woke my mother. She lifted her head a bit off her pillow and frowned. I smiled and reached out a hand to touch her face, thinking she'd be happy to know that I was feeling better. She slapped my hand away and shouted, "Get out! I was up all night with you. Let me sleep!"

"Better go, sweetheart," my father urged, yawning. "Maybe Shanta Bai is up. Go to her room."

Quietly, I slunk out of their bedroom. Having finished with her bath, Shanta Bai was sitting cross-legged on her chatai, rubbing a small pat of butter into her leathery arms. I sat on the floor next to her and placed my head on her lap.

Maya let out another scream. Breast milk dripped from me onto the floor. I wiped the drops off with the towel I'd used to pick up the glass. I glared at Asha. "How should I look at you?"

"Some appreciation would be nice." Asha crossed her arms. "For coming all this way to help."

"Help?" I said, tossing the crunchy glass into the trash can. "This is what you call help?"

I went to the sink and scrubbed my hands in hot water. Maya's screams were so high-pitched it was a miracle the windows didn't shatter. I began anew the torturous process of getting my angry red infant to accept my breast.

"You were more easygoing," Asha said, coming up behind me. "You took to my breast so naturally. To relax you, I had the ayah give you a massage. You should be massaging your baby."

"Stop acting like you were mother of the year, okay? Because you were anything but," I said. Maya latched and finally started sucking hungrily. I slumped my shoulders and let out a sigh. "And baby oil is dangerous for infants. So you almost killed me, per usual."

"If you hate me so much," Asha said, "why did you ask me to come all this way?"

"I didn't," I said. "Veer 'surprised me' by buying you a ticket."

"Oh," she said.

I sat down, put the nursing pillow under my aching arms. "The next thing I know, you're here." I stroked the top of Maya's head. The urge to get drunk hijacked my brain. The Rat Park scientists had said that alcohol mimics the comfort one feels in a parent's arms.

"Did I even tell you that I chose to have a C-section?" I said, shifting Maya to my other breast.

"You wanted the easy way out." Asha shrugged, sipping a cup of cold tea.

I turned my head to stare at her. "What's so easy about having your body cut open? And this," I added, indicating Maya at my breast, "this isn't easy. I wish you were more supportive." Tears pricked my eyes. "I was scared if"—I kissed Maya's head—"if something went wrong during the birth..."

"Oh please," Asha said. "When things don't go your way"—she slammed her mug down on the table—"you find someone to blame. Me. Your husband. The whole bloody world."

"What is wrong with you?" I said. "Why can't you give me what I need for once?"

"I don't know what you need, Noomi," Asha said. "I have nothing." She showed me her empty hands. "You're the one with everything. A husband, a beautiful child. And yet, you can't stop whining. Why won't you stop whining?"

Rage made the edges of my vision go dark. I needed to get out of the apartment, get away, or I'd explode. When Maya fell back asleep, her eyes half closed like new moons, I put her in the bassinet. Without bothering to change out of my pajamas, I grabbed my bag. "I'm going out for a walk," I said over my shoulder.

"But, Noomi, the weather." Asha came trailing after.

"Relax," I said. "Landfall isn't until tomorrow."

Around the corner was a line of rich people huddled under their umbrellas, checking their phones, waiting to grab what remained on the almost bare shelves at the supermarket. Poor people sat inside their blue tarpaulin huts, looking resigned. Folding my arms against the rain, I walked past the shoppers toward a liquor store that, shockingly, had no queue. I glanced at my reflection draped on the colorful bottles in the window, then went inside, paid for a fifth of vodka, and flashed a smile when the storeowner asked me if I was headed to a party.

"Sort of," I said.

The sea usually billowed gently in the winter, like a silk scarf in the breeze. But the storm surge had made it gallop in crested waves up to the tetrapods, spilling across to the road. The wind hissed through the trees, sounding like boiling water, plucking off what remained of their leaves. People around me held up phones, hair whipping across their faces, to film the surge. I ignored them and walked to the railing, unfazed by the dirty water soaking the cuffs of my pajama bottoms. A plastic toy dog bobbed past me with a friendly, gap-toothed smile. I unscrewed the red cap of the vodka and kissed the bottle's mouth.

"Remember, alcohol can be dangerous to a baby," Zal Papa had said when I told him I was pregnant.

"Not baby," I said flatly. "Fetus."

Zal Papa made it a point to call me at least once or twice a week. With the phone wedged between my chin and shoulder, I'd listen as he fed me the latest gossip in Kamalpur—who said what to whom at what party, who was having an affair, who'd built a new house. I breastfed Maya or rocked her to sleep. His calls made me ache for home, but also, I felt relieved to be far away.

The calls would start off as friendly and funny, but then would pivot to amused, offhanded disparagement on Zal Papa's part and slow-boiling rage on mine. Like a bird that can build a nest out of whatever it finds on the ground, Zal Papa could weave a mean word into everything he said.

"The pictures you sent of Maya are sweet. She looks like a good baby. When she's older, I must tell her what a difficult child you were."

"Your cousin Adil has moved into a flat. I must say he is very good at saving money. You, on the other hand, are not so good. I've heard you're spending your husband's money faster than he can earn it."

"I can tell from the way you talk about Maya that you're probably going to ruin her."

I stopped taking his calls. Then suddenly, for the first time, there was no one to tell me who I was, how I should behave. Like roommates who know each other's habits and quirks, I became acquainted with myself: what I liked and didn't like. Instead of the words that had been chosen for me, I finally had the freedom to use words of my own.

Which words would those be? "Lonely" was one. Above the sea, flying in the murky sky, was a Brahminy kite whose shriek brought my eyes to it. The kite was struggling to catch an updraft to glide on. Violent gusts of wind batted it away like an invisible hand. But the kite kept fighting the storm. For a moment, it looked like it would drown in that lead-colored sky. Then it found a way to surf the air and sailed away, disappearing like a remnant from a dream. "I want to come back as a bird." Watching the kite was like being slapped by god. The vodka burned in my mouth. Everything I'd lose by drinking it flew across my mind, like a flock of birds. I closed my eyes, spat the alcohol out, and wiped my mouth with my sleeve. The police began yelling at people to go home. Walking past a pile of trash, I threw the bottle into it, then trudged on toward my apartment.

Maya tried to lift her head off Asha's shoulder and focus her eyes on me, her disgrace of a mother. Asha rocked her back and forth, whispering words: "good," "strong," "clever." Maya seemed to be listening intently. I tiptoed past them to the bedroom and took off my clothes. I stood under the shower for a few minutes, washing away the rain, the vodka, and then reappeared with a towel on my head. Maya put up her fists and kicked out her legs, bawling.

"I tried to feed her a bottle while you were out," Asha said. "But I think she wants the real thing." She handed Maya to me. I pulled out my breast meekly, ashamed at what I'd almost done. "She's stubborn, like her mother." Asha smiled at me. It was an apologetic smile.

I walked about the room, swaying Maya to the rhythm of the whooshing gale outside the window. "What were you saying to her when I walked in?" I asked, turning to Asha. "Good, strong, clever, et cetera."

Asha folded her arms around herself. "You must speak life into children. I used to do that with you too. That's why you've turned out so resilient." She admired me like I was a statue.

For a few minutes, neither of us spoke. I stared out the window, with Maya sleeping in my arms. From her pocket, as if she'd been waiting for the right moment, Asha took out a photo. "Here," she said. "Take a look at this, before you start fighting with me again."

The picture was of me at six years old, sitting with my doll on Asha's lap. She is in a wheelchair. What protrudes from her spindly body is a big, pregnant belly. There are hollows under her eyes. She is holding on to me like I'm a lifesaver thrown from a boat.

"We wanted to name him Adar," she said. "It means 'wealth,' 'respect.' But he came early, and his poor lungs... Anyway, the worst was that they still put me in a ward with other nursing mothers. The nurses would bring each her baby in the morning. My breasts would start to leak and leak, watching them. I begged Jeh to get me out. I begged him. He said I couldn't. Not until the doctor gave the all clear. Meanwhile, your grandparents made sure I knew it was my fault that the baby had died."

"Is this why you didn't want to be around me?" I said, holding up the picture. "Because of him?"

She took my hand. "I'm sorry," she said, pressing it to her cold, wet cheek.

When she woke up to feed later that night, I brought Maya into the bedroom. Sitting cross-legged in bed, I changed her diaper. Then I walked about in circles, jiggling her up and down. It was getting a little chilly. I took Veer's shirt from a pile of clothes and pulled it over us both. There was a commotion in the living room. I heard the front door open, and Veer's voice rang out in the silence. "Hi there! Mom? Noomi? Maya? Where is everyone?"

"Mom is sleeping," I whispered. "We're in here."

Veer walked in, smelling of rain. "I managed to get the last flight out from Delhi," he said.

"That was risky," I said, pulling him in for a kiss. "Must have been a very bumpy flight."

"It was," he said, putting his arm around me, touching Maya's silky, sleeping face. "I didn't want you guys to be by yourselves." He laughed. "This is our very first catastrophe as a family."

The storm clouds broke open, revealing an impassive moon. The rain fell in sheets against the window, turning it into a mirror that threw our blurry reflections back at us.

"Look, Chanda Mama," I said, pointing, calling the moon by a lullaby name. On the street below, trees flailed in the wind. The storm was on its way. Lightning cracked the sky in half. Yet the moon, like a large ship on a choppy sea, remained steady.

Maya stared at the moon. The moon stared back at Maya.

I hugged Veer a little closer. He smiled. "Show's about to begin."

ACKNOWLEDGMENTS

I am grateful, in no particular order and no small amount, to Julia Kardon, Olivia Taylor Smith, Rahul Soni, Kanishka Gupta, Victor LaValle, Susan Bernofsky, Vikram Chandra, Melissa Danaczko, Diksha Basu, Brandon Taylor, Elissa Schappell, Jenessa Abrams, Katrine Ogaard Jensen, Doireann Ní Ghríofa, Marilyn Stasio, Sreekumar Menon, Shaill Jhaveri, Nalini Rajan, the LaValle Dojo, Room Six, Team D'Erasmo, the Baxter crew, my Word for Word mates, Arup Sen, Bhavani Parameswar, Sowmya Ramanathan, Aruni Kashyap, Amy Long, Columbia University School of the Arts, Asian College of Journalism, Bread Loaf Writers' Conference. And finally, I am grateful for my family—especially my partner, Vikram Chachra, and our wonderful daughter—for their love, support, and patience while I wrote this book.